DEDICATED

To Lee Lee as always.

ACKNOWLEDGMENTS

Thanks to my wonderful critique partners.

ISBN 97817751287-6-2

Praise for Dangerous Denial

What readers say:

"Very exciting, suspenseful, and intense! This had me on the edge of my seat the entire time, and I could not put this book down! Very well written. Tons of action, danger, threats, increasing tension, and romance. Amazing and powerful, this had me hooked from start to finish."

"Reggi Allder will hold you on the edge of your seat as you follow her real-to-life characters."

"Excellent book - exciting thriller with a touch of engaging romance! Loved it!"

"A great read! Loved it."

About the author

Reggi Allder writes suspense and contemporary novels. In both genres, as in real life, her characters must overcome difficulties. The males are strong. The women are determined. They make changes in their lives to manage their future and cope with life as each fight to discover a hidden strength and work toward a lifelong goal.

Reggi studied creative writing and screenwriting at the University of California at Los Angeles (UCLA).
She enjoys hearing from readers.
Follow her on Amazon, bookbub.com, allauthor.com, and like her on Facebook.

Books by Reggi Allder
Dangerous Series

Dangerous Web
Dangerous Denial
Dangerous Money
Dangerous Moves
Shattered Rules
Coming Next
Dangerous Sisters

Sierra Creek Series

Her Country Heart
His Country Heart
Our Country Heart
My Country Heart
Historical With Glowing Hearts

Dangerous

Denial

By
Reggi Allder

Chapter 1

"**Damn, late again**," Skye Turner swore under her breath. She loved her job and her boss. But if she didn't manage to be on time from now on, she might soon be looking for a new career.

With her bag, coat, and file folders, she rushed into the modern foyer of the office building in San Francisco's financial district.

She glanced at Mathew, the thirty-something barista at the coffee station in the lobby. Maybe a latte for her boss would mitigate being tardy.

"Hey, Mat, the usual for my boss."

"Coming up." He smiled. "The same for you?"

"Yeah." She shuffled the papers in her arms and adjusted the strap of her shoulder bag. "The traffic was horrible this morning. It's worse every day—you ever have one of those days when everything goes wrong? Oh God, I forgot my wallet."

"No problem. Pay me when you can."

"Thanks. The coffee smells great. I'm so late and Andrew needs these files. I'll be back with the money.

"No worries."

Balancing the tray of coffee and her paperwork, she ran for the elevator. A man bumped her as he rushed past. She stumbled but managed to remain standing. Still, the files and her bag crashed to the floor. "Hey, watch where you're going."

The well-dressed man glanced at her but didn't stop to help her pick anything up.

"Skye, you okay?" Mat shouted.

"I'm good—people are so rude." She rubbed her shoulder. "At least I didn't spill the coffee."

At the elevator to the private penthouse, she punched in a code and entered.

On the twelfth floor, the doors opened to the sleek modern foyer of the penthouse office. White marble floors were clean and a huge stone Buddha greeted her. In front of the statue, she usually took a moment to slow her breathing and contemplate the day, but not this time.

Still holding the tray of coffee, she set her handbag and folders on a desk, then knocked on the door to her boss's office. "I bought coffee."

She entered, careful not to spill the tray of coffee. "Andrew?"

Two men held her boss by his arms, dragging him toward the large shattered window. Cold wind blew into the room and paperwork swirled on the nearby mahogany desk. Startled, the men froze when they saw her.

"Andrew, what's going on?"

"Grab the bitch, no witnesses," the smaller thug yelled.

"Do him first."

"Skye, run!" Andrew bellowed just before he was thrown out of the twelfth-floor window.

***

Three months later.

In the Sonoma wine country surrounded by the golden California hills, Jon Lancaster parked the rented sedan near a rural farmhouse. From the windshield, he glanced at the vines in the open fields, absently wondering what kind of grape grew there.

A hawk, no doubt searching for a rodent for dinner, circled overhead, gliding on the wind currents in the cerulean sky. Evening approached, but in summer, the temperature was as blistering as midday. He wiped the sweat from his forehead, took a deep breath, and immediately regretted it, but the smell of the rich soil, mixed with fertilizer, wasn't what bothered him.

Released from the hospital after a long stay, his healing ribs still ached if he breathed too deeply. Waiting for the pain to subside, he rubbed his left leg encased in a plastic medical boot worn to support a broken ankle and tibia.

He should exit the car and settle into the cottage behind the whitewashed farmhouse. *What's the hurry?* Here to relax and recoup after a violent and tumultuous year, would he enjoy the seclusion, or be bored?

His older brother, Webb, and his wife, along with the rest of the family, had returned to work in Washington D.C. Unable to do his job, Jon decided to stay in the San Francisco Bay Area for the moment.

A lump formed in his throat when he remembered his loss. Three years ago, his wife had been killed. Afterward, he continued to work with the government's Rapid Advance Task Force. Still, he'd been like the walking dead, appearing to function but not capable of feeling anything. Now all the emotions he'd denied rushed into his consciousness and seemed to suck the oxygen from him.

All things considered, maybe peace and quiet weren't a good idea. It gave him too much time to mull over the past. But in his current condition, unfit to do much else, what good was he?

Learn to take it easy. After you mend, you can decide what you want to do next.

With a grunt, he swung his legs out of the car, then limped to the trunk and grabbed his duffle bag.

Skye Turner had rented the front house and held the key to his one-bedroom cottage in the backyard.

Overlooking the yellowing grassland that surrounded the home, sunlight glared off the farmhouse windows. He put on his sunglasses and wishing for the crutches he needed, walked down the stone path toward the front.

A brass knocker, in the shape of a horse's head, was fastened to the oak door. After knocking several times

4

without a response, he beat on the paneled entrance with his fist.

Too damned hot and exhausted, his shoulders slumped. Why didn't people keep their appointments as promised? When she'd answered his phone call, Ms. Turner had been pleasant and had told him she would be waiting with the key when he arrived. Well, so much for keeping her word.

However, he might as well know what kind of a person she was. It would save him exasperation and disappointment later. No need to depend on an unreliable woman.

They had discussed her helping him with the simple household chores until he could manage better on his own. The compensation was generous, thus allowing her to work less outside the home, and permitting her to concentrate on her art and the classes at Sonoma State University.

He'd try knocking one more time. If no one answered, he'd find the cottage and see if he could jimmy a window and crawl in.

It would have been easy before the beating he'd taken a couple of weeks ago. Even so, determination was ninety-five percent of the battle. After all, he had a history of completing assignments, regardless of his condition.

He mopped his forehead with the back of his hand. Was it the heat or his exhaustion wearing down his weakened body? A little shaky, he leaned on the door and took a slow breath. *Shit.* He hated this sense of helplessness.

In twenty minutes, he'd take the pain meds ordered by the doctor.

Harder than necessary, he pounded on the door again. "Ms. Turner, are you in there?"

He turned the handle, surprised when it opened.

"Hey, anyone home?"

Chapter 2

Someone struck Jon when he entered the house. Pain spread through his chest. Fortunately, he saw the baseball bat coming and blocked the full impact of the blow.

"Get out!" A woman held the bat up ready to strike again as her hazel eyes exhibited fear.

"What the hell!" He lunged forward and yanked the weapon from her hand but struggled to keep his balance as agony shot through his leg. "Are you crazy?"

"Leave!"

"Lady, if you don't want people to come in, lock the damn door—I'm Jon Lancaster. I understood you were expecting me."

"I thought it was locked. Give me my bat."

"I'll keep it for now."

She stepped back from him "Show me some ID."

"My family owns this house."

"Driver's license."

Grunting with annoyance, he dug out his wallet and held it up.

As she squinted to read it, he studied her. In tight-fitting but ripped blue jeans, with full breasts pressing against a white t-shirt splattered with various colors, she smelled of oil base paint and floral perfume.

She brushed a strand of long brown hair from her face, leaving a streak of green tint on her high cheekbone. Under different circumstances, she could be a beauty. Though angry, she oozed sex appeal, not that it interested him.

"You're early, Mr. Lancaster."

He wanted to ask if she greeted every person who came before the appointed time by whacking them with a bat but said, "Give me the key to the cottage and I'll leave you alone. Skye Turner?"

"I'll take you." She pushed past him and went out the front door.

He shouldered his bag and followed her down a narrow path toward the back of the property, admiring her tight ass as he did.

Though three years had passed since Miranda's death, guilt slashed him for looking at another woman.

He shook his head and concentrated on managing the loose graveled walkway.

The cottage stood to the right of a graying wooden barn.

"I'm told the bungalow was built first, before the

larger house. As you may know, it's a California adobe with handmade mud and straw bricks, so popular in the eighteen and the nineteen hundreds. I guess there are still a lot of them around this area, or so I understand. I'm new to Sonoma. Anyway, I cleaned it and filled the kitchen with the list of things you wanted."

She bounced up the stairs to the entry, talking as she did. He had stopped listening to her prattle, aware she was nervous and filling the air with chatter to cover her embarrassment about their meeting. The red cheeks gave her feelings away.

With some discomfort, he managed to navigate the steps, entered the large living space, and dropped his duffle bag near the door.

"Well, this is it, living, dining, and kitchen all in one." She waved her hand. "Oh, there's a small bedroom and bath down the hall. As you can see the house is furnished and I bought the stuff you wanted, so I think you're good to go."

From an entry closet, she pulled out bedding, including two standard pillows, and then tossed them onto a brown leather couch. "There's an ancient TV in the bedroom and a radio in the kitchen, if you're into old electronics." She gawked at him.

How old did he look? After the last few weeks, he must appear forty rather than his twenty-eight years.

"I'm off to an art class. If you want something while I'm out, text me. You have my number. Right?"

She didn't wait for an answer and left before he

could ask for it.

He sank onto the couch and groaned. Where had he put the pain meds? *Shit, it's hot in here.* With his last bit of energy, he pulled off his shirt and leaned back.

"Oh." Skye peeked in the front door. Her eyes widened when she saw him. "Uh, I forgot to mention the crutches you ordered are in the bedroom closet—hey, what happened to you? You're bruised everywhere. Were you hit by a truck?"

"Something like that."

"Oh my God, I'm so sorry I slugged you. I hope I didn't hurt you even more. You must be in terrible pain." Moisture filled her eyes. "What can I do?"

"My medication's in the bag, over there." He pointed, her concerned expression surprising him.

"I'll get it."

He did his best to sit up, while she grabbed the pills and went into the kitchen for a glass of water.

"Thanks." He swallowed hard.

"Why don't I make up the bed for you? Afterward, I'll help you to the bedroom."

She didn't wait for him to respond. With her arms full of sheets and blankets, she left the living room.

Damn. He hated needing her assistance.

Minutes later, they walked slowly down the hallway. He sat on the queen bed, the sheet and comforter already turned down.

"I'll grab the pillows and then be on my way."

"Thanks."

When she returned, she handed him the pillows. "Remember, text if you need something. I left my card."

"Yeah."

"I'm out of here. Bye."

She ran from the room and the door slammed behind her.

"A damned whirlwind," he said under his breath and smiled, thinking of the softness of her skin and her sweet perfume when he wrapped his arm around her shoulder to keep his balance as they made their way to the bedroom.

Leaning on the pine headboard, he reached for her card, *Skye Turner Executive Secretary to Andrew Jenkins, The Jenkins Group. Inc.* and her cell number.

A big title for someone so young. She couldn't be more than twenty-five. So, why was an executive secretary from San Francisco living in rural Sonoma? She couldn't have retired at her age. And why greet strangers with a baseball bat?

***

Skye's face burned with embarrassment. Jon Lancaster must think she was crazy.

She sat in her compact and rested her head on the steering wheel. How could she focus in class now?

She drove in the direction of the university, knowing she wouldn't go to class. Maybe she should look for another place to live. Where? She was lucky to find this one and could only afford it because of the agreement to assist Mr. Lancaster.

He had come to the cottage to recover from some terrible accident, judging by his condition. After slugging him with a bat, she'd be lucky if he let her stay the night.

His family owned the property and when Jon Lancaster told them about the irrational person who lived in the front house—she might as well pack now.

The thought of his piercing blue eyes unnerved her. Forced to put her arm around his waist to steady him while they went down the hall, his muscles had tensed and for the first time, she understood the meaning of a rock-hard body. He'd been hurt and appeared to be in pain, but was as well built as any athlete.

The memory of touching him sent an ache to experience the sensation again. Stupid, because he was in no state to do anything but try to recover his health. She exhaled and took a deep breath to slow her heart rate.

Suddenly, she thought of her boss and the reason that brought her to Sonoma. After Andrew died, the police report listed his death as a suicide. Though she swore, in writing, he'd been murdered the authorities didn't believe her.

When the police had asked for a description of the men, she'd gone blank and couldn't say if they appeared to be Caucasian or a minority, tall or short, young or old. Written off as a hysterical woman, today, she still struggled to remember the details. She only recalled one sentence from the killers. *Grab the bitch, no witnesses.*

In the university parking lot, she turned off the car's engine and considered her options. She didn't like the notion of returning to the house and perhaps running into Jon again. Even so, the idea of attending her math class was unpalatable.

The cell phone rang. Half expecting it to be Jon, telling her to move, with some trepidation, she glanced at the number.

Ruth, Andrew Jenkins' wife. *Widow*. She corrected her thought. After his death, rather than believe her, Ruth accepted the police's version of her husband's death. Skye understood. Who wanted to think someone had killed their mate?

She and Ruth were friends, so she grabbed the phone on the third ring. "Hello."

"Skye?"

"Yeah."

"I want to see you—but not here in San Francisco."

"Where, when?"

"Now. I borrowed my neighbor's SUV, so I won't be followed."

"You think someone's watching you?"

"Yeah. I'm about to drive across the Golden Gate Bridge. Meet me at the Vintage Shopping Center in Novato. I'll park in front of the shoe store we like."

"Ruth, it's going to take a while to get there."

"I don't mind. I'll wait. We need to talk—I have

something for you. It's from Andy."

"I'll be there, ASAP."

A chill ran down Skye's spine when the cell went dead in her hand.

At times, Andrew had been anxious, but Ruth had never shown apprehension. The woman had been the lighthearted person in their group. A fifty-something lady with an easy smile and quick wit, Skye couldn't recall her ever expressing fear—until today.

Heading south toward Novato, the heavy traffic slowed. Impatient, Skye honked at the cars, for all the good it did.

Ruth was parked in front of the shoe store, sitting in a fire engine red SUV, not Skye's idea of an inconspicuous vehicle for one trying to hide from people following her, but...

Her friend jumped from the car and rushed to hug her. "Thanks, for coming."

"God, it's good to see you, Ruth." She hugged her friend back.

"I'm sorry for the way I treated you last time—I should've believed you. Can you forgive me?"

"Nothing to forgive." She paused. "Let me buy you a latte."

They walked to a little coffee shop they often frequented when shopping at the open-air mall.

Before lunch and after breakfast, the place was almost empty. They took a seat in the back of the room, near an exit and away from the large window.

Skye ordered two large decaf lattes and a brownie to share. The same thing they always ordered when they came there. Too bad the circumstances were so different today.

"I looked in the shoe store while I waited for you and tried on the cutest heels." Ruth paused. "I'd give anything if I could complain to Andy about having to attend another business cocktail party. I wish…" A tear slid down the woman's cheek.

"Yeah." Skye squeezed her friend's hand, then pushed the chocolate brownie toward Ruth.

"I should've paid more attention to his work. I don't really understand what he did. I mean he kept books for some high-powered companies, but I didn't ask questions. I should've..." Her voice trailed off into silence.

A clerk stocked display shelves with newly wrapped sandwiches and another cleared a table of coffee cups near the window seat. Background music filled the room and Skye hoped it masked their words, in case the clerks wanted to listen.

"Can you think of a reason for men to attack Andy?" Ruth whispered.

"I've racked my brain, but I can't come up with anything." Skye gulped her decaf and coughed. *Too hot.*

"A funny thing happened. Someone called saying they were from Andy's life insurance company, but they asked about you, Skye. They wanted to know if I had your home address or a relative who might be able to tell them where you live." She paused. "Or how to get a hold of you. They have important information for you."

Chapter 3

How long had he been sleeping? Jon rubbed his eyes and opened them to the darkness, then grabbed his smartphone—three in the morning.

Used to living in the city, he glanced out of the bedroom window and expected the locale to be illuminated, but in the rural area of the wine country, without a full moon, the stars gave little light.

With a moan, he struggled to a sitting position and searched for the medication and water Skye had left for him. He should eat something before taking the pills.

The crutches stood in the closet as she said they would. He adjusted them to fit his six-foot one-inch height and managed to make it to the kitchen.

To his surprise, a covered plate of food waited in the fridge, two chicken quesadillas, guacamole, and a side salad. A bowl of corn chips sat on the counter—all looked appetizing. For the first time, he realized he hadn't eaten since early yesterday morning.

After drinking a glass of milk, he swallowed the needed pain meds, dug into the food, and wiped crumbs from his lips with the back of his hand.

Maybe having Skye help him *was* a good idea. Though he'd keep the bat until he could be sure she wasn't crazy and wouldn't club him to death in the middle of the night. He laughed. Ms. Turner had been vetted by his family and found to be free of any criminal past, not even a traffic ticket—just a ditsy woman. Nevertheless, if she became a problem... He came here to rest not be involved in someone else's minor situations.

Not ready to go back to the bedroom where he'd spent most of the day, the couch appeared comfy. He sat and decided to stream the news on his phone. Time to catch up on the events around the globe. Living so far out of the world's action gave him a sense of uselessness.

If he didn't recover without residual complications, would there be a place for him with the government's Rapid Advance Task Force? Or would he be obsolete, a retired soldier at twenty-eight, now worthless to the team?

He grabbed his phone. Moving too fast, his injured leg objected, sending pain to remind him to slow down. *Shit.*

The newsfeed reported another attack in the Middle East and a shooting in a Texas school. This time, only the shooter died. Of course, more gridlock in the halls of the U.S. Congress, nothing new there. He rubbed his stubbled chin and yawned.

With careful movements, he went back into the bedroom and turned off the light. For the next few days, the best thing he could do was to catch as much sleep as possible.

***

A week later, in the yard near the adobe cottage, the sun beat on Jon as he rested in a lounge chair. His bruises had yellowed and were much less tender. Today, he took deep breaths without concern and considered cutting down on the pain meds ordered for him.

Damn the sweltering heat, he should throw on a T-shirt before he got sunburned. Sitting up to grab his shirt, a shadow blocked his sun.

Skye. They hadn't talked much since the day he arrived. Still, her chores had been completed, often anticipating his needs and doing them before he'd asked.

In baby blue shorts and a white cotton blouse, she watered the small flower garden nearby.

"Hi Jon, feeling better?" She smiled, covering her eyes to shade them.

"Yeah." He stared, wondering why she didn't ask the question showing in her expression.

"I—I wondered since you're doing better if you'd like to go for a drive. I'd be going nuts with cabin fever after staying this long in one place. I'll show you around Sonoma." She dropped the hose and ran to turn off the water.

"It's important not to use too much water," she said when she returned. "I'm trying to save the world and all." She grinned. "You know—global warming. If I didn't have to worry about drought, the whole place would be planted with gorgeous flowers and vegetables. You want to go, or not?"

He grinned. She didn't seem to use a filter. Instead, her thoughts poured out in every direction for all to hear.

19

"A ride sounds good. Give me a chance to clean up. Twenty minutes?"

"Okay."

***

What had she been thinking, asking Jon to go with her? Insane, all she had to do was say something aggravating and he could tell her to move.

She gasped. Sometimes her mouth ran faster than her brain. Still, unknown to him, she'd noticed his struggle to do the daily routines she took for granted. For the first few days, he'd barely left his bed. Then, he'd sworn when he'd dropped something and tried to pick it up.

Her first reaction: rush to help, but not wanting to embarrass him, she'd ignored the impulse, pretending she hadn't been aware of his situation. However, the desire to lend him a hand remained.

Her mother often said, "Skye, you can't take care of every hurt or lost puppy you see." Yet, in some weird way, though he had nothing to do with puppies, she was drawn to Jon.

As he crutched toward the cabin, his well-formed shoulders and back muscles flexed. For sure he was no puppy. Hurt or not, this full-grown man conveyed power.

Did a chill or heat just run through her?

In the bedroom, she changed into white cotton pants and a maroon T-shirt, ran a brush through her hair, applied lip gloss, and glanced in the mirror. Why did she care how she looked? This wasn't a date.

All she wanted to do was to be kind to a man who'd been hurt. Okay, maybe pick his brain to find out what to do about her employer's death. The box of paperwork Andrew left for her was still sitting in her bedroom closet. Too upset, she didn't want to check it out—yet.

Could Jon help with her predicament?

When she'd rented the house from his family, they'd explained he would be moving into the adobe cottage for a short time.

His sister-in-law mentioned he was on a leave of absence from his responsibilities because he'd been injured on the job. He was some kind of a United States government investigator. Why hadn't she paid more attention to his job title? Maybe then she'd understand if he could help or not.

Should she trust him with the truth her boss was murdered? The police understood but dismissed the veracity of her account. Would Jon care enough to listen to her description of the event?

True to his word, twenty minutes later, he was waiting near her compact car.

Leaning on one of his crutches, he pointed to his left leg. "With this broken limb, better if you drive."

"Sure." She scanned him. His piercing blue eyes were hidden behind aviator sunglasses. His muscled arms flexed in a short-sleeved polo shirt. The jeans he wore had been cut open on one leg to accommodate the boot supporting the broken bones. "Jon, where do you want to go?"

"You choose." He smiled.

A nice, warm smile, and something she hadn't seen before.

"Bodega Bay?"

He nodded and opened the passenger door.

Midday traffic was light, unlike later in the day when commuters would clog the roads. The air from the coastal waters cooled the interior of the small sedan and the sunlight glistened off the cobalt sea.

"The town is known for beautiful water views and fresh seafood. It's not too far. I love the drive—be awesome to live with a view of the bay."

A sense of well-being began to relax her. "It's a cute little community—four miles inland there's the town of Bodega, famous as a place where part of Alfred Hitchcock's movie *The Birds* was filmed. I'm a film buff and the first time I saw the movie, it scared the blank out of me. I'm still afraid of birds. I mean, I like to look at them if they're not too near. I sure wouldn't want them to land on me." *Shut up. You're talking too much.* "Anyway—what do you think?"

"Okay," he answered.

Okay, to what? Her rambling or going to Bodega Bay? Again, she'd said too much. Appearing to be a man of few words, the rest of the way he rode in silence.

As they neared the village, the smell of fresh fish filled the air, the perfume of the day. Fishermen docked at the wharf in the Bodega Bay community and started to unload their catch. Seagulls circled and squawked, a chorus of discordant music riding on the air currents.

Jon leaned forward and looked out at the panorama. Was he pleased? She wouldn't ask and he probably wouldn't offer an opinion.

"Skye, shall we buy some fish to take back?"

"Uh, yeah." His question surprised her.

"How about I buy you lunch first?"

"Jon, why don't we each pay for our own?"

"Sounds like a plan," he agreed.

She wouldn't be beholden to him, even for a meal. The relationship, if she could call it that, would remain equal. She shook her head. After today, this might be the last time they talked, except to greet each other.

"You pick a restaurant, Skye. There seem to be a few facing the bay and they all look good to me. Do you have a favorite?"

"I often go to the one just down the street. The Wharf."

"Let's do it."

The restaurant's parking lot allowed her to pull into a space near the entrance, so Jon wouldn't need to walk far.

In the casual atmosphere of the large room decorated with fishing nets, a huge fish tank, and green potted plants, they choose a window table overlooking a spectacular view.

A middle-aged waiter, in a white dress shirt and dark slacks, gave them menus and left a basket of sourdough bread and salt-free butter. He took their drink orders of diet coke and a glass of local Cabernet Sauvignon and left the table.

Jon stretched his left leg and stared out of the window. "Great view." He took a sip of the wine. "It's peaceful here."

His expression suggested he didn't always spend time in quiet locations. Was he posted in violent locales? War zones?

"You work for the U.S. government?"

"Yeah. I've lived all over the world. When I can, I prefer being near the ocean. Still, I enjoy the mountains for recreation."

"Do you ski?"

"Used to. Now…" He shrugged. "We'll see. Maybe."

"Oh, I'm sorry. I should have thought—your leg."

"A compound fracture, broken in two places and held together with metal shanks and screws."

"Wow. Amazing what doctors can do." She wanted to ask if it hurt and how it happened. Stupid. Of course, it was painful and if he wanted her to understand what caused the injury, he'd tell her.

For once, she kept her mouth shut. No reason to annoy him when they were getting along.

She sipped her cola and enjoyed the ambiance while he drank his wine in silence before saying, "I'm a film buff too."

"You are? What are your favorites?"

"Thirties black and white classics and action films

of any kind. Speaking of Hitchcock—*39 Steps* is a favorite."

"I love that one." She laughed and soon she shared how she became interested in old movies while going to the university, astonished they had something in common.

He disclosed his mother's love of film and that she'd passed her interest to him. "Somehow, I missed *The Birds*.

"Now you've been here, you will have to watch the film."

"Yep." He grinned.

"I'll drive by the town of Bodega when we go back and you can check out if the famous building in the film is still there."

Her fresh crab salad arrived and his Petrale sole with vegetables and pasta in red sauce was served quickly.

"Amazing fish. It's been a long time since I've enjoyed a meal like this. I wondered…" He stopped.

"What?" She asked before taking another fork of crab.

"Nothing. It's just different from my usual workday." He frowned.

He wasn't telling the whole truth, but she let it go and reminded herself he owed her no explanations. Nevertheless, she recognized the melancholy in his voice. The mood mirrored her own since Andrew died.

The waiter came to make sure they were pleased

with the food and to ask if he might bring them anything else.

Jon engaged him in conversation and soon the man's history in Bodega Bay, where he lived, and how many children he had, including a little girl he'd adopted, was known. All done in a matter of a couple of minutes.

As a guy who didn't often speak, Jon appeared to understand how to obtain information from others without sharing his own narrative. Would he help her talk to friends and clients of Andrew's to find out what had been bothering him before he died?

If new information became available, maybe the police would listen to her.

"Coffee?" Jon interrupted her thoughts.

"Decaf would be nice."

He waved to the waiter. She noted the employee stood at attention when Jon ordered the coffee. What was it about him that demanded respect?

After they left the restaurant, he crutched to the wharf where some of the fishing boats were moored. She wondered if he would be able to get around on the rocking pier and keep his balance.

The breeze picked up and sent the seagulls fighting the wind currents as they tried to hover near the bobbing fishing boats. She pushed her hair from her face, smiled into the sun, and took a deep breath of the salty air.

A gull dove toward her and she screamed, covering

her head. Jon waved the bird away.

"You all right?"

"Yeah." Her heart pounded and she glanced at the other birds circling near the catch being unloaded.

"Guess they don't want to share the fish with us." She tried to make a joke, but it fell flat. "Silly of me to be afraid." Her cheeks burned with embarrassment. "I told you I don't like gulls to come too close."

"Just remember you're bigger than they are." He smiled. "It's okay, Skye," he added. "We all have fears. Some of us are better at hiding them, but they still exist." He squeezed her hand before leaving to look at another available catch of fish for sale.

After checking a couple of trawlers, he paid a fisherman for fresh halibut. She protested, wanting to pay for half of the bill, but he pointed out her contribution would be to cook the fish.

"You're right." She laughed.

On the way to the car, she admired Jon's ability to get around on the moving pier and up several stairs, to the parking lot using crutches, but he groaned when he sat in the passenger's seat. Maybe he wasn't handling the task as easily as it appeared.

At a farmer's market down the road, he insisted on leaving the car and helping inspect the vegetables and Gravenstein apples. This time she paid for the items before he could.

She drove the long way home to allow him to take in as much of Sonoma County as possible.

Later, in the heavy commute traffic on Highway 101, she kept her patience. Though there was the occasional honk of frustration from other drivers, most of the people commuting were used to the rush hour and sat calmly in the congestion.

Considering the wonderful afternoon spent with Jon in Bodega Bay, she enjoyed the slow drive home.

At almost seven in the evening, the temperature remained hot and the daylight was strong. She parked the car in the driveway of the farmhouse she now called home.

"I'll have the fish dinner ready in about forty minutes. Does that work?"

"Sounds good." He left the car heading toward the cottage.

Not since Andrew's death had she thought her life might return to something close to normal. Was she foolish to believe there was a chance?

Chapter 4

The next morning, Skye woke late. Last evening Jon stayed longer than expected. Before he came to the house, she'd found her copy of *The Birds* and after dinner, they talked as friends over the film and a bowl of hot buttered popcorn.

She smiled remembering.

Focus.

If college was to remain an option, she needed to pass the math exam today. Summer school finals came up way too fast. Yet, there was no way she'd fail, not with her future riding on the results.

Working for Andrew was no longer an option. She understood he'd paid her more than the going rate. If she didn't add to her skills, how would she acquire a job and make an adequate amount to support herself in the expensive Bay Area?

With her backpack in hand, she rushed out of the front door.

***

Jon enjoyed last night's dinner with Skye more than he wanted to admit. Not his type, she was so different from his murdered wife. Miranda had been very British. She'd spoken the Queen's English and rarely lost her cool. At least not in front of anyone but him. And beautiful, well, his image of her might be colored by the passing of time, but her look—flawless.

If he compared Skye with Miranda's perfection. Skye Turner would lose, no contest. But he couldn't deny her openness and lack of pretension attracted him. She laughed, screamed, and probably cried without restraint. Her willingness to help him came without complaint and she even appeared to enjoy doing it.

His earlier years were spent near gorgeous women with goals of upward social mobility and membership in the correct associations in order to meet the "right" kind of people.

Of course, Miranda had been different. He'd realized it as soon as he met her. And after experiencing her perfection, what was the point in asking for something less?

Only his career mattered now. Rest, recoup, and go back on the job. He forced his body to relax in the leather club chair near the window and glanced out, squinting to see Skye enter her old compact and drive away.

An arrow of pain shot through his left leg and the vision in his right eye was blurry again. He covered it with his hand to block the bright light coming from the living room window.

Hell.

Perspiration slid down his face. He wiped it away and took a slow breath. Forbearance remained out of reach for him. Nothing he wanted to cultivate, but his injuries were forcing him to consider the idea if boredom didn't kill him first. He laughed.

Find a mission. There had to be something a young, strong, but limping, half-blind man could do while waiting for his injuries to heal. Better find it soon, or...or what? He shrugged.

He must have dozed off because he was startled when someone knocked on the door.

"Yeah?" he yelled.

They knocked again.

"Hold on."

Stiff after sitting in one position too long, he hobbled to the front door and yanked it open, ready to growl at someone for annoying him.

Skye stepped back from him. "I'm sorry. I didn't mean to bother you. It's not important. I..."

"Don't do that."

"What?"

"You came for a reason. Come in and tell me."

She looked scared. Was he so fierce?

"Well, I..."

He moved to let her enter the room. "You caught me. Want a cola? There's one in the fridge."

"Okay."

With one crutch under his arm, he swiftly walked to the kitchen.

She sat at the counter and he joined her.

"You manage with one now." She pointed to the crutch resting next to him and smiled.

A nice smile, sincere.

"Part of the time. I've been practicing. Frees up one hand for me to grab whatever I need."

"Cool."

He set a can of soda on the counter. "So, what's the question?"

"You used to be an investigator for the government, right?"

"Sort of."

"And you're not working now?"

"No."

"I wondered if you—well, this might sound weird, but if you'd like to work for me? I mean I wouldn't be able to pay much…"

"Don't downgrade your request before a person has a chance to answer or you'll never hear a yes."

"Oh." She gulped her drink and almost chocked, then coughed.

"Hey, calm down, Skye."

With the back of her hand, she wiped her chin. "I'm nervous. This means so much to me. I—"

"Tell me what you want."

"It's kind of a long story."

"Then get comfortable. Sit on the sofa. I've got all day."

He grabbed a cola from the fridge and carried the can to the side table next to the club chair. She left her drink on the counter and sat on the sofa with her jean-clad legs curled under her. She tugged on her tank top but didn't say anything.

"Where do you want to start?"

"With the death of my boss, Andrew Jenkins."

"The story was in the paper not long ago. I read about his suicide."

"No."

"What?"

"He was killed."

"Hey," he said leaning toward her. "if that's true, you need to take the information to the police."

"I have. They don't believe me."

He sat back again. "How do you know he didn't commit suicide?"

"Because I was there."

"Whoa. You better explain."

She started and barely stopped to take a breath until she finished her story. "…then I ran." She swallowed a sob and looked at him with a pleading expression.

Her emotions were real, no doubting them. Skye believed she'd seen a murder. However, if the police didn't think she told the facts, why should he?

"Do you think I'm telling the truth?"

"What reason would someone have to take out your

33

boss and make it look like a suicide?" he countered.

"I don't know. He was a nice guy. I've racked my brain, but I…"

"Okay. Calm down."

"I'm sorry. I—if you don't help." She shook her head, her eyes filling with tears.

"Listen. Could you…" He stopped. Did he want to get involved with this woman in what might become a messy situation? He scratched his head and glanced at her again. She sat quietly, hands in her lap, waiting as if she were in the principal's office expecting to find out her punishment for some undisclosed offense. "Could you talk to a family member or a friend?"

"Not about this. Anyway, my best friend took a teaching job overseas, and Ruth, my boss's wife, is moving back to Minnesota to be with *her* family. So..."

"No family?"

"A brother I rarely see. He's ten years older. We don't have much in common." She paused. "I love my mom, but I can't share this with her. My father still thinks I'm fourteen. When we're together, he spends the time lecturing me on how to behave and to sit up straight." She shrugged.

A faint smile crossed her lips but quickly disappeared. "Daddy means well. I know he cares, but I've heard the same speech since I *was* a teen. Mom nods at the right moments to support his rants. Afterward, she serves a rich dessert, you know chocolate cake or frosted sugar cookies. For her, food solves everything." She paused. "Don't get me wrong. My parents are wonderful people, but this is more than they can handle."

"How old *are* you?"

"I'll be twenty-five in August."

"Oh, an old woman."

"You can laugh, but since my boss died, some days I feel like I'm a hundred."

He was inclined to give her a comforting hug. *No.* If they were going to work together, they needed the wall of the employee-employer relationship between them.

"Did you return to the office after Mr. Jenkins' death? Search it?"

"No." She shivered.

"Are you willing to go?"

For a time, there was no response. He thought she hadn't heard him, when she said, "Uh, maybe."

"Did the police make the place off-limits?"

"Why would they? They've decided there's no reason."

"Can you open the office?"

"Yeah, with the security code."

"And as far as you understand, no one has gone in since your boss died?"

She sighed, stood, stretched and adjusted her tank top. "I don't have any idea. Ruth never said anyone did. We're the only ones with the code, except for the cleaners." She hesitated. "I think Ruth asked them to stop. Oh, and the broken glass was replaced."

"Okay, here's the deal. I'm willing to look into the death and the business Jenkins was involved in. After a quick check, if I don't find anything suspicious, you let his death go as a suicide and move on."

"Are you telling me I can't trust my own eyes?"

"I'm saying, we'll find out. It was a traumatic day. A man you cared about died. The mind can play tricks on a person to allow them to cope."

She frowned and sat down. "What do you want? How much of a payment?"

"I don't need your money, only your cooperation. I'm not busy. I can give you a week or so."

"Thanks. Thank you so much." She sighed again.

"Ready to go to his office?"

"Now?"

"Why not?"

Chapter 5

Skye controlled her shaking hands, hoping Jon wasn't paying attention as she punched in the code to Andrew Jenkins' penthouse. The elevator door opened, but she didn't move. "Jon, I can't."

"I'm with you. No one's going to hurt you."

"Yeah, but this is too soon. So close to Andrew's…" She couldn't finish the sentence.

He held the elevator door. "Go ahead. I'll be right behind you."

They rode to the top floor without speaking.

When the doors to Andrew's penthouse opened, she froze. Images of the morning he died, played in her mind.

Jon squeezed her hand. "Skye, you're stronger than you think?"

"Am I?" Ignoring her wish to return to the lobby, she let him coax her into the entryway.

They paused in front of the statue of Buddha and

she asked for wisdom and enlightenment, a habit of hers.

Moving closer to her desk, the smell of stale coffee wafted in the air. She waved her hand to push away the stale odor, stifling a gag. "The cleaners obviously haven't worked here since Andy's death."

"Where's his office?"

"What?" She had trouble concentrating. *Focus.*

"His office?"

"Over here." She hesitated with her hand on the door handle of Andrew's domain.

"Skye, I've got this. Don't go in unless you're ready." Jon entered and shut the door behind him.

She paced in front of the office. *It's wrong to let him go it alone.* With a deep breath, she moved inside and leaned against the wall.

As if evil continued to lurk, an eerie sensation filled the room's atmosphere. She scanned the area, and a shiver shook her. Where was Jon?

"Jon," she screeched.

"Hey, I'm here." He stood up from behind the large cherry wood desk. "I was checking the window and saw something…"

"I thought…"

"Skye, nothing in here can harm you."

"Only my memories," she countered.

With tweezers, he slipped something into a small envelope and she noticed he had put on single-use gloves like doctors used.

"Did you find something?"

"Yeah, some blood splatter."

"Oh God," she gasped. "Andrew's?"

"That's what we're going to find out. If you can discover Jenkins' blood type, we'll understand if this is from him, or maybe there *was* another person in the office as you reported."

"Two men, big guys, they grabbed him."

"Did the men call each other by name?"

"No. Uh, sorry, Jon, I can't stay in here. I'll wait for you in the conference room next door."

***

What was Jon doing? *He's taking so long.*

Skye resisted the need to pace and sat in a chair at the long conference table where she had often taken copious notes during the many meetings her boss once led. The minutia-filled records of the gatherings might be called boring but never dangerous. Certainly, nothing in those engagements would've triggered his murder.

Again, she wondered if there was information in his background that provoked his demise. Should she mention the idea to Jon?

When quizzed, Ruth had withheld something about a reason for people hurting Andy. The fact the woman had been indignant, seemed to indicate she covered up the truth. However, as his wife, maybe it was to be expected.

When she asked Ruth for Andrew's blood type,

Skye would broach the topic again, hoping for a motive for his slaying. Wives often protected their partners against loss of reputation, but months after his death, it wasn't necessary.

Though they weren't related, in the last years, the Jenkins often said, she was family and like the daughter they'd never been blessed to have, so why wouldn't Ruth trust her?

She rubbed her forehead to stop the ache throbbing behind her eyes. Her muddled thoughts went in circles. Until new information could be added to the mix, no point in thinking about Andrew's death.

Jon entered and sat heavily in a chair next to her. In obvious pain, he rubbed his left leg and breathed deeply. "I've done what I can in Jenkins' office. You okay?"

"Yeah—I can't stop the idea if I'd arrived on time the morning he died, I might have stopped his murder."

A stunned expression crossed Jon's face. "Skye, if what you told me is true, if you'd been on time, you'd be dead too."

"Oh, God!"

"Making the decision to stop for coffee before work, saved your life."

Shocked, she didn't speak.

"Come on, let's get out of here and buy some lunch. I can't take painkillers on an empty stomach." He stood and grabbed his crutch.

Trembling, she got up. "I'm afraid."

"Yeah." He held her in his arms and she clung to him.

"Is it going to be all right, Jon?" She wanted reassurance, but he didn't answer. Nonetheless, he held her a little tighter and she inhaled the aroma of soap and shaving cream.

"We need to go, Skye."

On the way to the elevator, they decided to check with the security guard on duty to find out if the security video for the morning her boss died was available.

"Hey, Pete," she said to the guard sitting at the desk in the lobby. She'd met him the day she started working there.

"Hey, Skye, you haven't been around."

"No."

"Sad about your boss. You all right?"

She stared at the uniformed man she had gotten to know over the last few years. "I'm fine. How are your wife and kids?"

"They're good. One kid is in summer school. The other is training for the soccer team." He grinned. "What do you need?"

"This may sound strange, but I'd like to look at the video from the day Mr. Jenkins died. I mean if it's still available."

Pete rubbed a huge hand over his chin and his forehead wrinkled in a frown. "Might, we keep things for six months, but I should ask the big owners first."

"We're only going to be in town today. If you would expedite things..." Jon added.

"A friend?" Pete said to Skye, interrupting Jon.

"A good friend. Even with his broken leg, he came here when I asked him."

The security guard nodded. "Well, I guess that rates something." He rubbed his stubbled chin again. "Give me half an hour. I'll see what I can find."

"Thanks, Pete. You're a pal." She mentioned the date of Mr. Jenkins' death.

"Okay, grab a snack and come back in thirty or forty minutes. I should be able to retrieve the video."

"Will do. Thanks again."

Outside on the busy street, she pointed down the street. "Jon, there's a coffee shop about a block away. Is that too far to walk?"

"Let's go."

When they entered the diner, too early for dinner and too late for lunch, the place was doing little business. They found a table near the window and ordered.

To her surprise, he ordered milk with a grilled cheese sandwich. She ordered decaf. Nervous, there was no way she could eat.

When the drinks were brought to the table, he took a pill and gulped down the milk. "These pain meds are wreaking havoc with my stomach. Milk is supposed to help."

"Sorry."

"Not your fault."

Later, he took a bite of the cheese sandwich and swallowed, "Do you have a list of the people scheduled to call on your boss the day he died?"

"Yeah. In my calendar at the farmhouse. Why?"

"I want to check into the people and find out how each is connected to him. Might be good to look at the whole week's schedule. Did any of them carry a grudge? He could have cheated someone or been in debt."

"No. I've always thought of Andrew as an honorable man."

Jon finished his sandwich and ordered another glass of milk. "Tell me what you remember about the men in the penthouse. Had they visited before? Any scars or accents?"

"No, to everything." She closed her eyes and tried to remember the men. "White men, one, forty? The other one, in his twenties—I guess."

"What did they wear?"

She sipped her coffee before saying, "Now you mention it, the older man wore the most fantastic suit. It would cost a fortune. I mean, the fabric, silk, or the finest wool, and the cut was nothing you can buy in a regular department store. It had to be tailor-made. My dad wears designer suits to work, good quality, nice, but they can't compare with the one I saw that day."

She finished the decaf. "The younger man wore what looked like a uniform. A shirt like the delivery drivers wear, brown with an emblem over the pocket and on the sleeve. I'm surprised I remember this. After it happened, my mind was blank, nothing, nada. For weeks, I tried to recall details and couldn't. I…"

"Slow down, take a breath."

"Yeah. Okay."

"You're probably remembering because you saw the office again," Jon pushed away the empty plate. "What did the emblem look like? Can you draw the design?" He stopped rubbing his knee, handed her a pen, and a paper napkin.

"The logo's a pretty simple design." She held the pen poised over the napkin and drew a square with a circle and the capital initials DME in the circle. The letters were done in silver. I don't know what font was used and I have no idea what the letters stand for."

"After we check with Pete for the video, let's find out."

Chapter 6

The man sat on a bus stop bench across from the building housing Jenkins' Penthouse. He grunted. For three months he'd spied on the place—an effing waste of time.

No complaints though, he was paid well for lounging on his ass. He adjusted his ball cap and glanced at the couple heading toward the building. A short but damn good-looking brunette, and a tall man walking with a crutch and wearing a medical boot on one leg. They slowly made their way up the street.

He yanked out his cell snapped a photo of the couple and checked the close-up of the woman from the Jenkins Inc. website. Funny no one had taken down the site but good for his needs. Easy to identify her from the picture taken for publicity, no doubt. *Yep, Skye Turner.*

Damn, his boss was right. *People are creatures of habit. They eventually come back to their nest, so to speak.*

The woman returned to the scene of the crime. The police didn't believe her story, but she understood the truth. That made her dangerous. The police might deny the crime. Still, if she was able to convince even one of them that they'd made a mistake, all the work plotting Jenkins' appearance of self-destruction would be for nothing.

She had to be stopped, but not before he understood how much she knew and who she had been talking to.

After the couple went into the office building, he stood, stretched, and then managed to cross between the vehicles on the busy thoroughfare.

Wait, watch, report, he leaned against the stone wall of the edifice and pretended to use his smartphone.

The sun broke through the fog as it often did this time of day in San Francisco and he unzipped his black hoodie. At least he didn't need to wear the damned ugly brown work shirt used three months ago.

When the girl and the guy came out, he'd follow.

***

In a small office, Pete cued the video and told them they would find him in the lobby at his desk.

After the security guard left, Skye turned from the screen. "Jon, you better take a look. I don't think I can stand to see Andrew's killers again."

"It's hard. I understand." He hesitated. "I'll run through the video, but when I ask, you'll need to tell me if I've found the right guys. Take a seat and relax while I do this."

A few minutes later, she checked on Jon. He ran the visuals as if he did it routinely, like an old hand operating the machinery. She sat back in the chair and swiveled from the monitor. What did he do for the government?

"Lots of suits entered the building. Several

46

businesses are in this office block, insurance, accounting, law offices?"

She glanced at him. "Yeah, pretty much."

"So far, no uniformed delivery drivers, but they may use the back entry of the building. I wonder if there's a loading dock at the rear of this place." Jon spoke, but his eyes never left the images on the monitor. "Wait. Skye take a look."

A blurred photo of a man in a brown shirt hovered on the paused screen.

"I don't know." Her voice cracked. She closed her eyes to prevent the memory of the morning her boss died.

"Look again."

Ignoring her fear, she considered the guy's features. "It could be him. He's the right age. I wish everything wasn't out of focus."

"Can you make out the logo on his sleeve?

"The shape is right, but I don't ... this is too much."

"Hey, calm down. We're making progress."

"Yeah, you're right." She sniffed and swallowed hard.

"Maybe I can ask a friend to clean up the image." He took a screenshot. "Of course, even if the emblem is correct it doesn't prove this is the guy. The truth is there might have been many deliveries that day."

"I just remembered something. Drivers have to sign in. I wonder if Pete has a record of that day," she said. "I'll go ask him."

"Good idea, but we should finish here first."

"Okay." She reluctantly sat down again.

Several males were possible choices for the suited man who was in Andrew's office. Since she entered the penthouse today, she'd hoped she would recognize the men if she saw them again, but with so many faces to choose from she was at a loss.

After taking several shots of various men, checking with Pete, and making a copy of the sign-in page of the date in question, they headed back to the car.

Commute traffic had started and the vehicles moved slowly in the downtown traffic, not to mention the bottleneck at the Golden Gate Bridge.

"Why don't we take the Vista Point exit and wait until the rush hour is over? Otherwise, we will sit in gridlock for over an hour or more.

They parked facing the panoramic view of San Francisco.

"It was warm today and the fog will be coming in through the gate." Skye gazed at the scene she never tired of. "Just being near this outlook, I relax. Soon the mist will blanket the bay and the warm day will be forgotten."

"You love it."

"The Bay Area's my home. I've lived here all my life. I can't think of going anywhere else."

In silence, she forced any idea of what to do next from her mind. Already on overload, any decision made today would only be reconsidered tomorrow.

"Where are you from, Jon?"

"Here and there. I was born in the United Kingdom to an American mother and a British father." He paused. "When I was a teen, my father died and later my mother married a U.S. citizen. So, we moved to the East Coast." He gazed out of the windshield as if recalling those days.

"I'm so sorry to hear about your dad. Do you miss

the U.K.?"

He shrugged. "I go back often, for work and to visit. I travel a lot. It must be good to have a steady home."

Did she hear the longing in his voice?

The lights twinkled one by one brightening the city and the bridge, a welcome to anyone who entered.

They stayed so long that the wind blew thick mist to hide the well-lit glow of the skyline as if to say the time had come to leave and return to the reality of her chaotic life.

She wanted to shout. *Not yet*. Instead, she started the engine of her compact and drove onto Highway 101, through the tunnel heading north toward Sonoma, and her temporary home.

A car pulled out at the same time and followed her through the tunnel.

***

The man stood at the edge of the vineyard and stared toward the blue sky. His face burned from the heat of the sun. He smiled. For too many years, to squeeze out an honest living, he'd endured living in the cold of the far north.

With the back of his hand, he wiped his brow and strode toward the heavily fruited vines. This was his land. No one would be able to demand a share or tell him how to manage the farm.

Soon, the new crop would be harvested and the renowned boutique wine would start its journey to completeness.

The labels had already been designed for this year's

wine, black with embossed gold letters. Subtle, unique, and classy, just like the person he had never been, no matter how expensive his tailor-made suits were. A pig dressed in fancy clothes was still a hog.

He realized the gentleman farmer he appeared to be was a lie. Nevertheless, he enjoyed the respect of the wine-growing community.

To create an illusion of kindness, he never missed a chance to donate to a local cause, be it a public school project or something to safeguard the environment. He understood there might be a time when he wanted the goodwill of the local citizens.

With a careful hand, he touched the Chardonnay grapes on the vine. Not long now and the promise they displayed would come to completion. A patient man, he could wait.

The job he hated kept the money flowing and tied him to the profession that disgusted him, but allowed him to hold on to this precious plot of land.

Still, if someone tried to cross him, they might as well forget his good manners and educational refinements, because they'd find the mean streets of the inner city were branded on him.

He popped a grape into his mouth and grimaced, bittersweet like his life. He spit it out and crushed it with his boot into the rich soil. The sun still had work to do and so did he.

The last decade he'd spent cultivating both his property and his demeanor. Even so, to own the land outright, he would cope with one last kill before he dropped the moniker of "hit man."

After all, Skye Turner had seen him and it sealed her fate.

Chapter 7

The ride from San Francisco was pleasant until Skye slammed on the brakes to avoid a stalled car blocking their lane on the freeway. Though the seat belt held Jon, his head jerked forward and back again. He experienced no pain, but in his right eye, he saw flashes of light. The second incident of the strange vision in his eye since the beating he'd sustained while on assignment. Last time it cleared up after a few minutes, but today it was lasting longer.

At the Sonoma ranch house, he stumbled over the rough surface of the path to the cottage and struggled to stay upright. He leaned on his crutch and glanced back at Skye as she turned toward the house. She probably wondered what caused him to leave so abruptly after spending the day with her. The expression on her pretty face suggested her feelings were hurt by his abrupt departure.

Jon blinked several times, but his right eye didn't

clear and his vision remained blurry. He feared something serious had happened, so, he moved as fast as possible to reach the adobe residence.

It was better to be in the cottage if his sight got worse. Not to mention, he didn't need or want to explain to Skye and receive her sympathy. He would deal with this on his own, as he had with all problems for more than two years since the loss of his wife, Miranda.

In the cottage, without turning on a light, he made his way to the bedroom. Should he call the doctor? He grunted. The office would be closed at this time of the night. At least there was no pain, and tomorrow his sight might clear as it had once before.

Ignoring his growling stomach, he slumped on the bed, closed his eyes, and slept.

A woman stroked his forehead and whispered in his ear, telling him everything would be all right, not to worry. He roused with a start. Only a dream, but instead of his wife, Skye reassured him with a gentle caress. As a widower, he'd never thought or dreamed of any woman but Miranda. Why Skye? Why now?

He glanced at the clock on the bedside table—two am. *Go back to sleep.*

***

Jon glanced out of the window and saw Skye drive away from the farmhouse. Earlier, she'd texted, letting him know she would be in classes most of the day and suggested they eat dinner together. Afterward, they could go through the box her boss left. Maybe Andrew Jenkins' paperwork hinted at his problems. Unlikely, but at this point, they didn't have much else to go on.

And what could Skye offer? Though she'd done her best to appear relaxed yesterday, he'd worked with many witnesses and recognized her tension. He recalled her expression while she stared at the monitor. Terrified, she'd stood motionless, her eyes wide with disappointment when she hadn't been able to recognize any of the men.

Munching on the last piece of toast from breakfast, he booted the computer and opened the photo program. After a gulp of his now cold coffee, he downloaded the screenshots taken in San Francisco. If his photo program wasn't sophisticated adequate to improve the closeups, they'd be sent to a friend who was an expert at manipulating difficult pics.

Relieved his eyesight was back to normal, he worked on the first picture. A guy in a delivery uniform appeared on the screen. At first, he concentrated on the man's face and saved the changes, then cropped the photo to a closeup of the emblem on the guy's shirt. The letters, DME came into view.

Bingo.

DME, Delivery Made Easy, their website proclaimed, discreet, secure, and confidential delivery. No job was too small or too big, and transactions were worldwide. They had a San Francisco headquarters as well as offices in other cities in North America,

Europe, and Asia. Thousands of reviews praised the company for exemplary service.

Why would a man work for a thriving business and toss Jenkins from his twelve-story window? The whole idea seemed implausible. However, Skye was insistent and steadfast in the retelling of the event. With fear palpable, she swore she'd told the truth. He didn't have a reason to disbelieve her or for that matter, believe her.

Attractive or not, Skye was a stranger. Therefore, he'd checked her out. He'd searched her finances and found a woman careful to live within a budget, with no expensive clothes or jewelry purchased. She hadn't used her credit card to take trips to exotic sites or gone over the card's limit. The local police and the FBI had no record of her. Skye appeared to be a secretary taking university classes and staying within the tight confines of a secretary's pay, nothing more. Somehow, the realization pleased him.

Webb Craig, his brother and the leader of the United States Rapid Advance Task Force, had helped him obtain the FBI information on Skye Turner.

However, he still waited for material on Andrew Jenkins and his wife Ruth. Which didn't bode well for them. If it was taking this long, there might be something on the couple.

After spending hours on the computer, his eyes became blurry. He shut down the monitor. He'd mention the problem to his doctor at his appointment.

He blinked a couple of times to clear his vision. *Good.* He grabbed the keys to his rental car and headed toward San Francisco and DME's main office.

The Delivery Made Easy building sat in the warehouse district near the bay. Rather than the chrome and glass of a modern office, the headquarters had gray cement floors and walls. Cold, the large open room had a desk near the front door, but he could view uniformed people working and boxes and bags lining the nearby walls. Loud voices of the employees, as they shouted to each other, filled the space.

"How can I help you?" a stout, gray-haired woman in a company uniform asked, adjusting the pencil behind her right ear.

"I'm trying to locate a guy and I understand he works here."

"We don't give out personal info on our employees. If you want to leave an address or phone number where you can be reached I… She stopped talking and stared at him, an unspoken question on her dry lips. Finally, she asked, "What happened?"

"A damned car accident," he said. "You should see my car."

"Really? I lost my van to a drunk driver last month. You ought to see what the insurance company gave me for a car in good working condition." She sniffed. "Damned near nothing."

"Hey, it's a crime. Right? We pay and pay and when we need the insurance company to cough up money, they give us squat. You busing it now?"

"Yeah." She sighed. "Even with the bus lanes, it still takes longer to get home. Now, after I leave the bus, I walk almost a mile to reach my place."

"Frustrating." He let the photo of the man, he wanted to identify, slip onto the desk.

"Hey, that's Grady Enders. He's not here today. Oh." She covered her mouth and fear spread across her ashen face. "I shouldn't…"

"I didn't get it from you. In fact, I was never here." He winked and grinned.

She smiled sheepishly.

"Have a nice day, miss."

As quickly as possible, he limped out of the building and went to his car in time to stop a traffic cop from writing a parking ticket.

For once, the information he wanted had come sooner than he'd expected. Too bad she couldn't tell him more about the man. The receptionist probably wouldn't have said anything if she hadn't had a car accident too. Life's coincidences were strange and this time they worked for him.

***

In the university cafeteria, Skye threw her cotton shirt onto the back of a chair, adjusted her tank top, and sat across from her friend, Libby. "Whew, I didn't expect it to be so hot today."

Libby looked up from her milkshake. "Climate change," she said as a drip of chocolate ice cream ran down her chin and she wiped it off with a paper napkin. "There's the guy again."

"Who?"

"The tall, handsome, and menacing one staring at you."

"Short dark hair and wearing a blue plaid shirt?"

"Yep. Take a look."

"No reason. He's been wherever I am all day." Still, she turned. "I don't see him."

"He left as soon as I pointed him out. Do you know him?"

"No, but he keeps showing up. It's creeping me out."

"He's not bad looking if you like the type."

"I don't." She scanned the room again to be sure he was gone. "A week ago, he showed up in one of my classes, then he was in all of them. Now, he's everywhere I go."

Her friend pushed her empty glass away and leaned forward. "Scary. You should report him."

Skye rubbed her eyes. "What would I say? This guy is staring at me?" She gulped her iced tea. "I'm just jumpy." She paused. "Hey, I shouldn't have said anything. Since my boss died, I'm... Never mind, it's not important."

"No worries. He didn't look like the bad guys in movies. He's kind of clean-cut, almost a like government official. Could be he wants to date you."

"Maybe," Skye agreed, not really believing it.

"Dating's not my thing right now. You remember last year when I went out with Todd. Man, what a mistake."

"That reminds me, I saw Todd the other day. He asked about you. I didn't say much, only you were fine. He kind of suggested he wanted to date you again."

"Wow. It'll be a cold day in…" She shook her head remembering the man who said he loved her, then behind her back, went out with a friend of hers. *I mean, he didn't think I'd find out?*

"Todd's a jerk." Libby offered.

"Yeah, and I was a fool. Well, that's not going to happen again."

"I should've kept my mouth shut."

"I'm glad you didn't, Libby. It makes me realize I'm over him." She smiled. "Besides, I'm finished with men for a while. I've more important things to think about."

"Okay." Libby's expression said she didn't believe her. "Don't wait too long. If a good guy comes along, grab him."

She laughed. "Thanks, Lib, but I need to take care of myself first."

"Always a good plan, but don't say I didn't warn you." Her friend glanced at her phone. "Getting late. I don't want to miss my flight back to So Cal. What are you doing for the rest of the summer?"

"Not much. I have a job helping a guy who was in an accident and his family gave me low rent and a great house to live in for a year."

"Nice." Libby grabbed her backpack. "Got to go. Stay in touch."

"Will do. Bye."

With Libby out of the area until late August, she had a sense of loneliness with nowhere to turn for a friend. Why did an image of Jon flash in her mind? Her cheeks burned remembering how he felt when she helped him to the bedroom of the cottage. More than that, she liked his concern and his willingness to help her even though he struggled to recover from his injuries.

The cafeteria was clearing out when she grabbed her bag and left for the parking lot, all the while checking to look for the man who had been following her.

As fast as possible, she drove from the university parking lot, fearing the stranger had followed her.

On the way home, she stopped at her favorite Chinese restaurant to pick up takeout.

Tonight, Jon promised to help look through the things Andrew bequeathed to her. The box he gave her was of medium size and not especially heavy. *Paperwork?* Not, when he could've put anything paper on a thumb drive. So what?

She paid for the order, went back to the car, and searched her bag. A chill ran down her spine. Stupid, but she had the feeling the guy followed her.

Chapter 8

In the country kitchen of the Sonoma farmhouse, Jon ate the last of his vegetable chop suey and steamed rice, then finished his Oolong tea.

Skye ignored her food and continued to ramble on about her garden, the lack of rain, and a friend who left for Los Angeles today. He had no idea who Libby was. Still, the woman appeared to be important to Skye. He leaned forward in the wooden chair and enjoyed her company, but how long should he let her avoid the reason they were together?

She offered him more tea and a fortune cookie.

"Thanks." He took the one nearest him and cracked it open. *The future is best when faced without fear.* This might be for Skye or him. He tossed the fortune onto his plate. "Are you ready to look at the stuff from your boss?"

She startled and a sad expression replaced her happy countenance. He shouldn't have been so direct.

This wasn't work or an interrogation of a suspect.

She stood cleared the table of the leftover rice and went to the refrigerator. With the door open, she stared into the interior but didn't place the food on a shelf.

"Skye, you all right?"

"Uh, yeah." She slammed the fridge door. "It's so hard to think Andy's—gone." She sniffed, poured more tea into his cup, and refilled hers. "Bring it into the living room and I'll get the box."

He sat in an easy chair near the low coffee table and straightened his booted leg.

She set a worn, corrugated box on the table. Someone had written "miscellaneous stuff" on the box with a black Sharpie. Nothing suggested there might be important items or information inside. It looked ready for the dumpster. With a sigh, plopped onto the couch. "I can't do this."

"Hey, I could go through this on my own."

She touched the box and appeared to consider the idea, but shook her head. "You'll need me to answer your questions—so no." She glanced at him with moisture-filled eyes. "I'll manage."

"All right. Let's do it. Breathe. It's going to be okay." He reached for her hand. "Relax. Nothing in here can harm you."

"I know, I know. I just—go ahead."

He slid the package closer and opened the lid. As he had thought, the first items in the box appeared to be personal. Old photographs of her boss and her, at work and play. Andrew looked to be a jovial guy, at least in front of the camera.

She took the picture from him and examined it. "I didn't realize someone took this. I'd forgotten about that day. Andy, Ruth and I had so much fun. Oh my God, I look so young."

"You're cute. How old were you?"

"Twenty. Almost six years ago. I'd just joined his company."

Jon took the rest of the photos and piled them in front of her. "You want to look through those and let me know if you see anyone you recognize, besides Jenkins and his wife, including the men in his office on the last day?"

Still staring at the earlier picture, she nodded.

"What did your boss do for a living?"

"He originally worked in the loan department of an international bank but started his firm about the time I came to work for him. Guess he used his expertise to help private parties and corporations secure funding for their acquisitions."

She set down a photo and took a sip of tea. "I should have been more aware of his business. To be honest, I answered the phones, made appointments, and typed his letters. I did my work, cashed my checks, and went home."

"And he paid you well?"

She stared at him with a timid expression. "That's the funny thing. Maybe too well. Six years ago, with little experience, he suggested I be paid the wage of a more seasoned worker. I grabbed it and never looked back, but today…"

"You wonder why he offered a twenty-year-old such a good deal."

"Yeah."

"Good question." Unable to answer, he shrugged. He went back to digging in the box, wading through the minutia of Andrew's life, hoping for a clue to his death.

Skye continued down memory lane, apparently enjoying the bittersweet history. Did she hope to solve his death or was she afraid the man could be a person she didn't understand?

"Here's something with your name on it." He handed her a large blue envelope. Looks like a birthday card.

"OMG. My birthday is next week. He'd bought a card for me." She clutched it to her heart. "Excuse me." She ran from the room.

"Take your time." He pocketed a couple of jump drives to check later when he returned to the cottage.

The middle of the box was filled with crumpled newspaper. He removed some of it and found a glass frame with a picture of a middle-aged man and woman with their arms around a younger Skye, everyone smiling. Andrew and his wife?

One word was written on the frame, family. His throat tightened and the pang of his loss jolted him. The vision of the ripped portrait of his family, found on the floor of his home, after the death of his wife and son, threatened to overwhelm him. He pushed back the collection. He hadn't been able to help his people, but he might assist Skye.

He placed the framed photo aside, not wanting to stir her emotions further. After they finished tonight's mission, he'd give it to her.

The wrinkled newspaper fell to the floor. As he reached for it, he was surprised to find it was written in Russian. "What the hell?" he said under his breath.

Jenkins wasn't a Russian name. Still, Jon couldn't be sure of the man's heritage. Given that, why would a guy put a foreign paper in a package for Skye?

Though Jon spoke Norwegian, it was of no use here. Smoothing out the foreign edition, he wished Webb was nearby. His brother had a commanding knowledge of Russian.

As far as he could tell, it was not the front page, but more likely a back section of the paper, perhaps a calendar page with events for the week. The date: the week Andrew Jenkins died.

"Sorry," Skye said when she returned, her eyes red from crying.

"You okay?"

"Fine. I was surprised by the card being addressed in Andrew's hand."

"What did he say? If you don't mind my asking."

"I didn't open the card. I'm saving it for my birthday. I recognized his writing on the front of the envelope. What's all this paper?" She asked.

"A Russian newspaper used for packing. Did Jenkins ever mention someone in his family came from there?"

"I don't think so." She sat down in a chair close to his. "Andy never said anything."

"I'll take the paper with me and find out if there are any articles of interest to us."

"Okay, but I can't think how."

"Skye, there isn't much else in the box except three business magazines." He paused. "We can read through them later and check for marked pages."

"What's this?" She reached into the box and pulled out a canvas bag.

"Be careful with that." He took it from her.

"What?"

He slowly opened the fabric. "A gun, a Glock 43, nine-millimeter, perfect for a woman's hand and easy to conceal, and a box of ammunition. Is this yours?"

"Are you crazy? I've never seen it before. What would I do with a handgun?"

Another question he had no answer to. "Why don't I take charge of it for now."

"I don't want it."

She handed him the bag and something fell onto the table. She grabbed for the note. "Skye, if I'm not able to protect you, this gun will," she read out loud. "Enclosed is a prepaid card to use at a shooting range of your choice. The funds should take care of the cost of learning to use the gun. I'm sorry you're involved in my mess. I'll explain soon. I promise."

When her hand began to shake, he took the letter and continued to read. "Everything you need to protect you is in this box. Watch your back and forgive me."

"I don't understand what my boss is trying to say. He never explained. Not a word."

"Maybe he was killed before he told you."

"Oh, God."

She looked so distressed, he wanted to comfort her. But how? What could he say? "Skye, I'll keep the firearm, the newspaper, and magazines. If I find any useful info. I'll...."

"Don't leave. Not yet. I don't want to be alone."

His leg ached and he wanted to sit in bed with his foot up on a pillow, instead, he sat down again.

"Thanks. I..." her voice dwindled into silence.

Instead of leaning forward, he sat back in the chair, making sure he didn't enter her personal space and intimidate her. He smiled. "Hot today." The weather was a safe topic. "A great day for the beach," he added.

"It was sweltering at school. The beach would have been perfect."

"Is school over? No more finals?"

"Yeah. Honestly, after my boss died, I didn't think I would finish."

"But you got through."

"Yeah—I did." She appeared to relax as her shoulders lowered and her smile warmed him.

"Jon, how come you know so much about the pistol Andrew left for me? You barely opened the bag before recognizing the model, the manufacturer."

"On-the-job training. Do you mind if I put up my foot?" He pointed to the scarred wooden coffee table.

"Go ahead."

He lifted his injured limb to the table and sighed. "Thanks, that's better."

"I don't want to push you, Jon, but soldiers don't

use small handguns. So, where do you work?"

He saw fear in her eyes. Did she think he would shoot her with the weapon? Maybe she wanted to take the gun back.

"I studied small arms, specializing in ones easy to conceal."

"FBI? No, you can't work for them because I went to school with a girl whose father worked for them. We had him come to school for 'show and tell' and he spoke about his job at the FBI."

There she went again, talking too much and answering her own question. He couldn't suppress a smile. In her earnest desire to dig out information, she stepped all over her chance to allow him to say what she wanted to understand.

When she took a breath, he jumped in, "You're right. I'm not employed by the FBI."

"Okay. Well then?"

"I haven't been clear about my job. I'm on leave. But even if I was still working, I wouldn't be able to give you details about what I do."

"You mean, like special ops? Jon, don't look so startled. I've seen those movies."

He laughed out loud, then stopped when she looked hurt. "I'm not laughing at you. But I've watched those films too." He grinned. "I'm no hero. Don't you go thinking I can save the world or The President of the United States."

"But Jon, you were hurt on the job." A statement, not a question.

"Yeah," he admitted, but wasn't about to go into the top-secret territory of his past assignment.

"You're not going to tell me what you do."

"Can't."

"I get it. I work for you, not the other way around, so, none of my business."

"Hey, Skye, that's not what I meant."

She stood. "Remember to take the newspapers and the gun with you."

He was being dismissed. "Thanks for the Chinese food." He paused and searched her guarded expression. "Skye, I…"

"Good night."

Chapter 9

Skye knocked on Jon's cottage door, waited for a moment, and knocked again. He'd better answer quickly or his breakfast would be cold. In the hope this would make up for her behavior last night, she'd made hotcakes with locally milled flour and an omelet from free-range eggs.

She cringed. Was she becoming her mother, thinking food cleared up every argument or disagreement? She decided to leave, but the door flew open. Jon stood in the entry wearing only pajama bottoms, his scarred bare chest well-muscled. An urge to run her hand over the scars and onto the tanned skin caused her fingers to tingle and her lips parted.

"You look like you've been up all night." *Damn.* When was she going to think before she spoke? What he did was none of her business.

"I have." To her relief, he smiled. "Mr. Jenkins gave you a lot of interesting reading to keep me awake. What's that?"

"Uh." She glanced away from his chest and at the

tray she held. "An apology breakfast, I acted like a jerk last night." Her face heated, what a fool to think this was a good move.

He rubbed his chin and stifled a yawn. "Don't stand there." He moved out of the doorway and she entered, careful not to brush against him as she did.

"Can't say anyone has served me my morning meal." He grinned. "Thanks."

"Jon, this is a mistake."

"Hey, relax. Show me what you brought." She watched his pecs, then his abs as they flexed. Half-dressed, he appeared to be demonstrating some of what he had to offer. She tried not to stare.

He limped to the kitchen counter and sat on a stool.

"Jon, I brought hotcakes and a cheese omelet. Oh, butter and maple syrup. I'll make coffee, then be on my way."

"What's your hurry? Sit down and join me."

"You sure? I don't want to step on your privacy."

"Do I look like I want you to leave?"

Whoa, no way she'd answer. Was it hot in the room or just her?

"Go ahead, Jon. Eat. I'll make the coffee." She ground the dark roast Italian beans, making it impossible for the conversation to continue, at least for a while.

Over coffee and a second helping of pancakes, he talked about some of the information he found in the business magazines her boss left. "Jenkins marked several articles. The odd thing is, they were marked in two different colors, red and blue. If I were relating them to governments, red would stand for Russia and blue for the U.S. Still, he might have used the nearest pen available."

He gulped the last of his coffee and she refilled the mug without asking if he wanted more. Somehow, she sensed he would.

"Thanks. You're not having any?"

She slid onto a seat next to him. "I had two cups earlier this morning. That's my limit if I want to sleep tonight." She'd been awake last night wishing she could take back her words when he left the farmhouse.

"This is the best breakfast I've had. You like to cook?"

She found herself telling him about her desire to grow vegetables, spices, and own a small company selling them, even cultivating grapes. Her idea of a good time was to find a new recipe to try. He must think her boring.

"Sounds like you want low stress."

"I do. Andy's death shook me, and made me question everything I wanted and what I believed. Until it happened, I thought life included striving for prestige and climbing the business ladder. Afterward, it didn't seem important anymore." She took his empty plate and placed it on the tray.

When he didn't speak, she added, "Not only that, I thought the police could be counted on to protect and serve. But when they wouldn't listen to me… No one is investigating his death. It's as if no one cares."

"We do."

She looked at him, staring into his clear blue eyes. "We?"

"Yeah. I can't promise we'll figure out what happened to him, but I'm willing to try."

"I'm sorry. I was nasty last night."

"Come on, I'll show you what I found in the articles." He moved to the couch and picked up a magazine. "You can let me know if the info means anything to you concerning your boss and his work."

"All right." She sat next to him.

"By the way, I left a message for my brother asking for help with the translation of the Russian newspaper."

"So, if you still want my help, this is how I see it. We visit the men Jenkins worked for."

"Okay."

Someone may want to tell us about their concerns or provide helpful information."

"Makes sense." She leaned closer.

"Last night I opened the jump drives Andrew left for you. I found the names of the people and businesses he worked for over the last three years. I'm guessing you were there then."

"Yeah."

"He would have included older files too if he wanted you to know about them, but he didn't."

"Okay."

"Skye, look at the screen and tell me if any of these people are familiar."

She scrolled down the list, noting the names and business she'd worked on. "I remember a few, but most of these are files Andrew handled on his own." She hesitated. "Once I opened one of them and he went ballistic. I was to never read anything without his permission. If I did, he'd let me go."

"Did he often lose his temper?"

"No. It shocked me." She sniffed and tried not to get too emotional remembering the day.

"What had he been examining?"

"I'm not sure." She paused. "I wish I knew what I did to set him off."

"Try not to worry about it."

She rubbed her eyes, got up, and found a soda in the fridge. "Want one?"

"I'm good." He glanced at her. "I've made a list of companies in the Bay Area he dealt with. I'll research them. Let's find out if they have any links to each other."

She nodded and gulped cola. "I thought I might go to Ruth Jenkins' place this afternoon. The last time I saw her, she held something back. Maybe she'll be willing to share more before she leaves town."

"I'll shower and go with you."

"Thanks, but I think she's more likely to talk to me if I'm alone. Anyhow, you've given me so much of your time already."

"Okay, but be careful. If your boss was murdered, you might be on the killer's radar too. He hesitated. "You were in the office and I don't like that fact."

Chapter 10

In San Francisco, Skye trembled remembering Jon's words about being careful. Was he overreacting? She glanced in the rearview mirror before taking the Nineteenth Avenue off-ramp from the Golden Gate Bridge and turned west onto a side street.

A for sale sign and a dumpster sat in front of the Jenkins' house. Men were bringing out boxes from the building and tossing them into the bin.

When she'd called and asked to meet with her, Ruth seemed reluctant. After she mentioned it might be a long while before they would see each other again, she finally agreed.

The front door stood open, so Skye entered the home, surprised to find chaos in the usually quiet and immaculate house. Rolled-up carpets exposed dusty parquet floors and most of the furniture in the living room had been removed. Crumpled newspaper lay in the hall. She noted the dining room table and chairs were missing too.

Poor Ruth, this house was her pride and joy. Andrew had wanted to move up to a larger showier home, but Ruth loved the house and the neighborhood. Now, she was forced to let it go and under such terrible circumstances.

"Ruth. Ruth are you here?"

"In the kitchen."

She followed the hall to the room and found her friend staring out to the backyard where they'd shared many good times over barbequed dinners. Back then, Andy called himself the chief cook and bottle washer but had been proud of his ability to handle steaks or meatless burgers.

"I'm glad you called, Skye." Ruth hugged her. "I needed to see a friendly face. I thought... Well, it doesn't matter now. Things are a mess in the house. Let's go out in the back where it's peaceful and we can talk."

***

Jon hurt but wanted to back off the pain medication, to have a clear head. He showered, shaved, and limped to the bedroom.

Exhausted, he sat heavily on the bed and wondered why he'd stayed up all night reading Jenkins' paperwork. He contemplated how much longer his recovery would take. A patient man, he was close to losing his cool. Resting on his ass had never been a good fit for him. An eager mind and a strong body require information and exercise.

Forced to admit he wasn't as strong since the recent beating, he grunted. Before the attack, nothing daunted him. Stakeouts lasted for days, but he never complained because he understood the mission. He'd tracked criminals in rough terrain, without a worry. Now, with no assignment, and no one to trail, boredom dogged him. Unless he recovered his full physical prowess, there might never be another post.

On the contrary, he would be searching for an alternative career. Trying to consider job options, he drew a blank. He rubbed his forehead and blinked to bring his eyes into focus, his vision an additional problem to deal with.

Too much ruminating. It was exactly why he wanted a task to keep him busy and the reason he took the opportunity to help Skye. A half-truth, he wanted to assist her to assuage his guilt for not protecting his wife and child. Whether Skye saw a murder or not, in time, the truth would reveal itself.

Next week, would be soon enough to speak to his doctor about his unsettled vision. No need to think about it now. *Compartmentalize.* The leaders of the Rapid Advance Team trained every member to keep each part of their lives separate. A man must not allow situations in one area of his existence to interfere with the job.

If asked to leave the team, what profession would he pursue?

Enough.

As the physical therapist instructed, he worked through the discomfort and rotated his broken ankle. Finally, he stopped and let the pain subside. Disregarding the angry scar running on the outside of his left ankle to halfway up to his knee, he put on the protective boot.

After a hundred and fifty sit-ups and using upper body weights, he grabbed the list of men who hired Jenkins, time for some action.

***

Rather than the usual hand-tailored suit, Salvatore Romano dressed as a field worker in his own vineyard. He dusted his hands and surveyed the area. Though his fields were drier than he wanted, the local weather report promised the California drought was over.

He, like many of the farmers in Sonoma, expected a dry summer, but it should come after a rainy winter and spring. Time to irrigate the fields and run up the cost of managing his grapes.

The other day when he watched the girl, he related to her devotion to the land. Neighbors spoke of her dream to own a vineyard much as his aspiration had been. Of course, when he completed this last contract...

Maybe he was getting old, too ancient for his current directive. Beautiful, but too voluptuous for today's fashion, she was right for him, not that it would matter. He had taken out all sorts of people with never a thought if they deserved to die. A man like him did his job and moved on. Why did Skye haunt him?

He wiped his forehead and replaced the ballcap he often wore when working on his vines. Perhaps his appraisal of the woman might be a sign he needed to retire. Thinking of the prey as a human was a dangerous habit as it might cause a nanosecond of delay at the moment of the kill. There was time to change the dynamics of the whole situation and allow all his planning to be for naught.

***

"I made turkey sandwiches for us and iced coffee."

Ruth smiled as she sat at the patio table where they'd shared many meals.

"Great." Skye joined her. "Your hydrangeas are beautiful. They're so big this year." She tried to return her friend's smile and pretend everything was normal.

"Hey, lady, do you want the armoire packed or are you selling it in your garage sale?" a workman yelled.

"What?" Her friend jumped up, spilling her tea, and tried to clean the mess before it rolled off the table.

Skye used her paper napkin to soak up the liquid. "Go talk to him. I'll take care of this."

So much for a quiet afternoon making believe all was normal. Andy died, murdered. Ruth would soon return to the Midwest, a place where she hadn't lived for thirty years, leaving dear friends and neighbors. It was so sad and unfair.

Skye leaned back in the chair and closed her eyes,

letting the sun warm her cold body. Soon, the fog would enter the Golden Gate, better catch the rays of the sun while she was able.

Later, she and her friend rushed through lunch and started to pack the kitchen dishware and utensils, careful with the older rare glass the woman collected.

Ruth dropped an antique vase and it shattered on the tile floor. "My grandmother gave this to me," she sobbed and bent to pick up the shards of glass.

"Watch out. You'll cut yourself." Skye helped clear the broken glass.

Not one to show her emotions, her friend sniffed, then stopped. "Things are so up in the air. Right now, I don't seem to be able to find my equilibrium. One minute I'm crying and the next…" She shrugged. "I don't understand what's come over me."

Skye hugged her. "I'll help however I can. Just tell me what you need."

"I lied to you." Ruth sat in one of the two kitchen chairs left in the room and covered her face. "You're a good friend and I didn't tell you the truth." She glanced up at Skye, regret etching her features. "Things changed about three years ago after Andy linked up with men who promised to make him a millionaire. I mean, we didn't need that much money. yet, he began to work longer hours and was too busy for friends or family. He stayed away so long, I began to think he was having an affair."

"Not Andy."

"No, not the old Andrew. But I didn't recognize him anymore. The man I married disappeared and a hardened version showed up." Ruth gazed down and took a slow breath.

"And he didn't mention the names of the men?"

"No—so often during these last couple of years I've wanted to ask if you noticed his transformation."

"Oh, Ruth, I did, but everything happened gradually. I denied it. More and more he lost his temper at work and yelled at me for the smallest thing. I blamed myself for not being a better person, and being extra careful. At one point I thought of quitting, but..."

"Skye, we should have talked to each other. He was troubled and he faced the situation alone. Maybe if we understood... we might have..."

They sat in the silent room. The workers were gone and the air in the kitchen turned cool. At last, Ruth said, "I think he got in way above his head and couldn't fathom how to get out. Because it wasn't like him to be mean. I think he was scared."

"Of what?"

"I wish I could tell you. He didn't confide in me, but I overheard a conversation one night. He was afraid."

Her friend hesitated. "I tell you this in confidence. Andy would never kill himself. A religious man, he believed suicide went against the will of God. He would go to hell. No, he would never take his own life."

"He didn't talk about religion."

"Come into the bedroom." Ruth stood and walked toward the hall.

She sat on the bed, her shoulders slumped and her head down. "Skye, we went to mass every Sunday, wouldn't consider missing communion. In the thirty years we were together, I can count the times he missed church on one hand. Now, he can't be buried in our grave site, can't rest in consecrated ground."

"I'm so sorry."

"The other day, I went back to the police and tried to explain, but they'd closed his case and weren't interested in opening it again."

Skye sat on the carpeted floor and racked her brain for something comforting to say.

"When I was packing, I found this."

Skye glanced at a small piece of paper with figures written in Andy's hand. "Numbers, letters? What does it mean, Ruth?"

"I can't tell you, except to say he hid it in my grandmother's locket. He realized I'd never sell or give away the necklace. When I opened it to see his photo inside, I discovered this instead."

"And you think he put the note in the heart to help you understand the importance of it?"

"Yeah."

She handed a scrap of paper back, but Ruth refused it.

"I want you to keep that. Maybe you'll make some

sense of the message. I don't have a clue."

"Okay. I'll do my best." Skye slipped the message in her pants pocket. "Jon, the renter in the cottage, is helping me investigate. He has experience with these things. Hopefully, he'll have an idea where to start."

Ruth wiped her eyes. "With evidence he didn't kill himself, maybe the police will reopen the case, and Andy can rest in peace."

Before she left her friend's home, Shye hugged her again. She wanted to say something positive but unable to think what, she said, "Take care and call me if there is anything I can do."

On the street outside of her friend's house, Skye's eyes seemed to deceive her. If she didn't know better, she'd swear the man across the lane looking in her direction was the same guy from the university. *Impossible.* There was no way he could find her in San Francisco. She hadn't decided to go visit her friend until a few minutes before she left for the city. No. Her eyes played tricks on her.

Chapter 11

Skye. Why did she enter Jon's thoughts again? Her gentle laugh, her smile. The way she talked, moved.

Even though she was stressed, she still charmed him. He'd never met a woman with the ability to find joy in small tasks and be unaware of her magnetism. She fascinated him. A possible reason he wanted to help?

The real question: had sufficient time elapsed for him to consider dating another woman? After Miranda's murder, would there ever be an occasion to think of a new woman without guilt?

Lost in thought, he glanced up and swerved the car to take the Novato exit.

In an industrial park, the tech company Mr. Jenkins had worked for sat alone surrounded by an expansive parking lot filled with foreign-made cars and expensive bicycles. Jon pulled his compact rental car into a spot near the entrance and reached for his crutches.

Yesterday, when he called, the CEO, Tom Samford, agreed to meet him. The quick acquiesce surprised him. *Curious.*

Still, a person holding a grudge might look for a chance to bad mouth the dead without worry of consequences. He'd seen it happen a few times.

He entered the building and announced his presence to the receptionist. She scanned him head to foot, stopping at his injured leg and ankle. To her credit, she didn't ask what happened. Instead, she offered to bring him herbal tea or fresh coffee while he waited.

"I'm good," he said, then made his way to a mesh metal chair and stretched out his wounded limb.

T-shirt and jean-clad twenty-somethings appeared to populate the building. They skateboarded from computer stations and down a hall.

A Labrador retriever waged its tail, nudging his hand, begging for attention.

Jon smiled and rubbed the lab's ears. "Hey, boy. What a good dog." A memory of his plan for a wife, two kids, and a dog, the American dream, flashed.

"Mr. Samford will see you now." The receptionist interrupted his thoughts.

Tom Samford met him in the hall and extended his beefy hand. A big man in a Hawaiian shirt, he looked more like a middle-aged truck driver than a successful software developer.

"So, you want to talk about Andy."

"If you can take a minute, Tom."

"Wouldn't be here otherwise. Come to my office."

It appeared to be more a cubicle with glass walls than a CEO's office. A simple metal desk and two chairs filled the small space. Samford entered first and pointed to a seat.

"Did the kids who work here offer you coffee?"

"Yeah, thanks." Jon maneuvered to a chair.

"Good. Tech types aren't great with social norms." He grinned. "Their brains are more interested in solving problems."

Jon nodded his understanding. "Looks like you have a bustling concern here."

"We do okay." Tom's expression belied his statement.

"What kind of work did Mr. Jenkins do for you?"

"In the early days of the start-up, he kept the books." Tom leaned back in his chair and put his sandaled feet on the desk.

So much for social norms. Jon glanced over the size fourteen feet and asked, "Any complaints?"

"Not so many." He paused, got up, and on a nearby shelf, poured coffee from a carafe into a mug with the words "You're the guy!" printed on it.

"Want some?"

"Thanks, Tom, but I'm good."

The CEO took a swig of coffee and swallowed. "Damn." He coughed "Hot." He returned to his desk chair.

"You were saying?"

Samford stared at him. "As the company grew and the money came in faster than I could count. I began to wonder why the profits weren't as big as expected. I turned to Jenkins for advice on investments." Tom sat forward and took a careful sip of the hot coffee.

Jon controlled his impatience and waited for him to continue. The yellow Lab wandered in and curled up beside the desk. Absently, the CEO reached down to pet his head. The dog waged his tail.

"About three years ago," Tom continued, "my ventures seemed disappointing. When I checked with Andrew, the books appeared convoluted—I found the investments wallowing in LLCs, so many I couldn't track them and Jenkins' notes were impossible to comprehend. One LLC led to another, not to mention offshore accounts. You sure I can't interest you in a cup?" He refilled his mug.

"I'm fine."

Samford set down his coffee and scratched his head. "You appreciate, I like money as much as the next guy." He paused. "But it's not my motivation."

"Okay, Tom," Jon said, his voice noncommittal. "You let Jenkins go because?"

The CEO rubbed his chin, his expression hardening. "I don't want to accuse a dead man."

"Hey, I'm not here to cause trouble. I'm working for someone close to Mr. Jenkins. They're trying to understand his sudden death."

"How is Ruth? I meant to contact her, but what

could I say?" He shrugged.

"She's as well as can be expected under the circumstance." Let him think he worked for Mrs. Jenkins, no reason to correct the notion.

"Sad. She's a nice lady."

"But you let him go."

"The company decided to change accountants."

"Must have had a reason."

"When we couldn't find the projected profits, I hired forensic auditors. Andrew was stealing from the company."

"That simple?"

"Yup."

"You didn't bring charges against him?"

"Hey, we were a new company. The last thing I wanted was an exposé in social media and newspapers about embezzlement and a public police report to scare off new clients."

"How did Jenkins take the news?"

Tom bristled. "Your time's up. Nothing more I can tell you. I'm depending on you to keep this under wraps."

"I give you my word. Can you think of a reason someone might want to kill him?"

"No—not unless he stole from the wrong person. Some might not be as forgiving as I am." Tom Samford walked out of the office and the dog followed.

***

In San Francisco, Skye drove from the curb and

glanced in the rearview mirror. The man who had gaped at her was gone. She sighed. Her imagination would be the undoing of her. She hadn't thought he had traced her to Ruth's home. Still, she shivered as the killer's words echoed in her ears. *Grab the bitch. No witnesses.*

Chapter 12

Jon squinted. Perhaps the glare of the bright California sun was causing his eyestrain because they were blurry again. He slowed the car. Thankful he was at the adobe. He drove into the driveway.

The elderly woman who lived on the neighboring property waved. He'd met Mei Wang when his family bought the farmhouse many years earlier.

She, like him, was an avid baseball fan. As a college student, he'd often watched ball games in her living room on her huge flat-screen TV.

For over a hundred years, the Wangs owned acreage in Sonoma. They sold off their fields a little at a time because the other relatives now lived in San Francisco and Santa Rosa. Only a few acres surrounding the home remained.

It was hard to guess Mei's age. After spending most of her life working in the sun, her skin appeared lined and leather-like. Still spry and slender, today she didn't smile at him. She jogged to his car as he parked and motioned for him to roll down the window. "Come into my home."

Not a request. But still, he smiled. "I'll be right there, Mei."

She nodded and returned to her house.

The last time she'd issued an order, it concerned her desire that they agree not to use weed killer on the unwanted plants peeking out of the blacktop driveway as the breeze might bring the poison to her property and affect her organic garden.

He balanced on his uninjured foot and reached into the car for the single crutch he still needed.

On Mei's porch, he raised his hand to knock, when she opened the door. "Jonny," she said pulling him through the front door. "Go sit down. I have something to tell you."

He sat on her sofa and stared at the four-panel Asian jade and black lacquer screen that sat across the room. Why was she upset?

"Are you okay, Mei?" He couldn't recall her being so agitated.

"I am, but something's wrong at your place."

"The farmhouse?"

"Yes."

"Ice tea, Jonny?"

"Thanks," He accepted her offer because it would be rude not to, though he wished she'd make her point.

Soon, she returned with a tray holding two tall

frosted glasses of iced tea and a plate of almond cookies.

She handed him a glass and said, "Take a couple of cookies if you like."

When he did, she sat in an antique brocade chair and faced him.

He swallowed a sip of the cool liquid. "Mm, no one makes tea like you, Mei."

"You're a good kid, Jonny." Her eyes twinkled. "People call me the neighborhood snoop, but I've lived here all my life. I consider it important to keep an eye on the area."

"Okay."

"Since you came back, I've noticed a young man hanging around by your place. At first, I thought he might be looking for an address. Maybe thinking of buying real estate." She walked to the front window and pulled back the curtain. Appearing to be satisfied, she returned to her chair. "But the man returned twice. He stands under the big oak tree across the street."

She picked up a cookie and then set it down. "I don't sleep much these days. When you're old, sleep becomes harder to find. Anyway, at dawn, he came again. This time he went onto your property."

"Had he done it before?"

"I don't think so."

He set down the glass, losing his appetite for anything but the information. "What did he do?"

"Well, the strange thing is he got down on his back

and looked under Skye's sedan. He stayed for a couple of minutes."

"Did he do the same with my rental car?"

"No, just walked around it and took off. I thought about calling the police, but he didn't take anything. I understand you and your brother, Webb, work for the U.S. government. And your father works for The President, so I wasn't sure if you wanted the locals involved. Did I do good?"

"Yeah, Mei, you did. Thank you."

"Is everything all right?"

"Probably a thug looking to steal a car. Be sure to keep yours locked. Still, I'll check this out. Can you describe him?"

"Young, like you. A tall Caucasian man, wearing jeans and a hoodie. I couldn't see his hair, but he was strong, and well built. Blue eyes, I think. Not as blue as yours but…"

"Your sight is pretty good?"

"I'm farsighted. Can't see a thing up close. It's hard to read small print. Yet, show me a sign way down the road and I can tell you what it says."

He nodded his understanding. "Did you see what kind of vehicle he drove?"

"No. I don't think he had one."

"Guess he could've parked on another road and walked across the fields," he said more to himself than to Mei. "You'll tell me if he comes back."

"Of course."

Careful not to disturb any of his neighbor's knickknacks, he made his way to the door and hugged her before maneuvering down the front steps. He glanced back at the house. She stood at the window looking out.

After Mei's information, he couldn't help wondering where the hell Skye was.

Chapter 13

Skye drove toward the Golden Gate Bridge, wishing she hadn't waited until dark to go back to the farmhouse. She used to enjoy driving at night. Now, the darkness seemed ominous. Maybe if she hadn't seen the stranger observing her when she went to her car...

Nothing in the rearview mirror suggested a reason to worry, but her back crawled. She sensed someone was following her, and she couldn't forget the expression of the man she'd seen when she left her friend's house.

The car in front of her stopped. She stomped on the brake pedal, honked the horn, and swore out loud. It wasn't like her to overreact to traffic. *Calm down.*

Andrew's death was taking a toll on her and it was troubling that Ruth thought she would solve the mystery of his murder.

She forced her mind to focus on driving. As the traffic moved again, she noticed the red light of her gas gauge flash. Empty? Impossible. She'd checked it before she left Sonoma. How could the small compact use so much fuel on a trip to the city? There should have been more than ample fuel for a round trip.

Before taking the on ramp to the bridge, the car sputtered and she steered the sedan to the curb. In a "no parking" zone, she turned on the emergency flashers and exited the car. *Shit.*

At a loss for where to find a gas station, she searched for her cell phone. Not in her bag or her jacket pocket, she checked the floor and looked between the seats. Nothing. Damn, she'd left it at Ruth's house.

The flow of traffic was moving quickly now, with no chance of flagging down a driver to ask for help. There had to be gas available within walking distance.

A shiny black pickup truck pulled up behind her sedan and a man got out. "Need help?"

"I…" She stared into the face of the man who had been on the street in front of Ruth's home. Afraid, she shivered.

As he came closer, she realized he *was* the guy who'd followed her at school. She glanced around the area. They were alone. *Be cool.*

"Skye, I thought I saw you come out of the house across the street from my grandmother's place." He smiled. "File it under small world—car trouble?"

"Why are you following me?" she demanded.

"Hey, I might say you were following me." He grinned. "I mean what are you doing near my granny's home? And why did you track me at the university?"

"Don't be ridiculous. I don't know you, mister."

"Exactly." He laughed. "Want help or not?"

What if he told the truth and the meeting was a coincidence? "I…" But he used her name? She didn't have a clue who he was.

"I can't wait all day," he prompted her. Though his voice sounded kind, his eyes narrowed. In the shadow of the street light, a sinister glow covered him. "Skye, I can't leave you here by yourself."

"No worries." She cleared her throat. "I called my road service. The tow truck will be here in a minute." Always a bad liar, did she sound believable?

"Good. I'll wait with you." He scanned her. "You must be cold. Why don't you sit in my truck and I'll turn on the heat?"

With a backward step, she shook her head.

"Don't be so nervous. I don't bite."

When he reached for her hand, she recoiled from him, but he grabbed her arm. "I'm trying to help. What's your problem?"

***

In Sonoma, if Jon didn't have a broken bone he'd be pacing. Skye had promised to be back in time to eat with him. Mei told him a stranger had fiddled with Skye's sedan and now she didn't show up for dinner. Apprehension gnawed at him. Should he dial her cell again? *No point.* He'd already left a couple of messages.

Again, he stared out of the front window to the empty driveway. How long would a visit with Mrs. Jenkins take?

Why did he care?

Skye was a grown woman with no obligation to give him her schedule or her change of plans. Still, with the murder of her boss and the threat to her, his gut told him to be concerned.

In the kitchen, he grabbed a beer and a piece of leftover cheese and mushroom pizza. A ball game was on tonight. Maybe he should watch and take his mind off the current situation. Instead, he checked his email and answered questions from his boss, concerning the last mission.

Helping Skye was a temporary gig. Recovering from his injuries and moving back to Washington D.C. and his day job at The Rapid Advance Task Force remained his main focus.

Soon, a decision about the future would be made, stay with the force, the only job he'd had since leaving university, or move on. Perhaps he might find employment and do something important without putting his family at risk. Family, where did that come from? He had no wife or child, not anymore.

He groaned and turned on the game but closed his eyes.

He must have dozed because he was startled when the sound of a car woke him. He grabbed his crutch and hobbled to the front window. In the light of the driveway, Skye's compact pulled up and stopped. She shut off the engine, but instead of leaving the sedan, she rested her head on the steering wheel.

Why didn't she exit and go into the house? Troubled, he threw open the door to the cottage and moved quickly toward the car.

He opened the driver's side door but couldn't see her face until she gazed up at him, fear radiating in her eyes.

"Skye, what happened?" He reached for her hand. She seized him as if unable to move out of the auto without help.

"Are you hurt?" As he scanned her, a strange yearning shot through him.

"I'm okay." To his surprise, she rushed into his arms. Trembling, she didn't speak, so he held her until she moved from him, leaving him cold and missing her warmth.

"Sorry, Jon, I…"

"Will you tell me what went wrong—Skye?"

With a blank expression on her face, she said, "I didn't think I'd make it home again."

Stunned by her reply, he didn't respond. She was obviously in shock, so he changed tactics. "Have you had dinner?"

"What?"

"Food—did you eat anything tonight?"

"No." She collected her bag and locked the compact sedan, but she continued to shiver.

"Come to the cottage." He took her hand again and she went without complaint.

When she sat at the counter, he said, "I can warm

leftover pizza or offer a frozen dinner."

"Jon, I'm sorry we were supposed to have dinner together. I promised to cook. I'm not doing my job...

"Hey, don't worry. Only, let me in on what occurred tonight." He set a beer bottle and a glass in front of her. "Relax."

She glanced at the bottle and then at him. "I don't usually drink beer." She paused. "But this evening, I won't say no."

"Pizza or a frozen dinner?"

"I don't think I can keep anything down."

"It's important to eat something. You're safe here."

"Thank you, and pizza is fine."

She took a sip from the bottle and smiled for the first time and he had the uncharacteristic desire to kiss her. Moving closer, their eyes met. When he leaned forward, her lips parted. He could almost imagine the softness of her mouth on his.

The ding of the microwave, letting them know the pizza was hot, brought him back to reality.

"Food's ready," Skye said in a husky voice, her gaze never leaving his face.

She carried her plate and the bottle to the couch. He sat next to her but was careful they didn't touch.

Talkative, more often than not, tonight Skye ate in silence. Though impatient to find out the details of her troubles, he made small talk and let her eat. After drinking half the bottle of beer, she appeared to relax. She even smiled at a couple of his inane jokes.

"Whenever you're ready," he prompted her.

The details from the night's event chilled him. He wanted to reprimand her for not advising him of the man who had been following her. Yet stressing her further would serve no good purpose other than releasing his own emotion regarding her safety. If anything happened to her…

"How did you get away?"

"A black and white patrol car pulled in front of my parked compact and a uniformed officer got out. He asked who owned the vehicle. I said I did and he told me to move it.

She took a gulp from the bottle. "I explained the gas tank was empty and asked where to find a filling station. Out of the corner of my eye, I noticed the truck drive off."

"Did you get the license plate?"

"No. I understand that's the right thing to do, but…." She paused and stared out of the window. "I was so flustered—I'm sorry."

"The make or the model of the pickup?"

She shook her head. "You're grilling me like you're the police, not a friend."

He cringed. "I don't mean to." She was right, but assuming this stranger happened to be linked to the men who killed her boss, didn't she realize how close she came to dying tonight? Once a female was taken into an auto against her will, chances were small they'd ever be seen again—alive.

He should warn her. As anxious and exhausted as she appeared to be, would she listen and retain his advice?

She stifled a yawn.

"You must be exhausted. I'll walk you to the house."

"It's okay."

"I want to." He hesitated. "You'll check the locks on your doors and windows."

"Yeah."

"On her porch, he waited while she entered and resisted saying "lock up."

He let his back relax when he heard the click of the deadbolt.

He'd wanted her to spend the night in the cottage with him, imagined her sleeping in his arms. To be sure, he would've struggled to keep his hands off her. However, staying with him could open a new set of complications having nothing to do with Mr. Jenkins.

***

Good, Ms. Turner had separate quarters. Wounded, and on a crutch, the man with her still moved like someone who could handle himself in a fight. Even so, no matter how tough, he couldn't win against a bullet.

The guy, in the hoodie, smiled. When the time came to remove Skye Turner, her living alone would make his life easier. He returned to the field across from the farmhouse and settled in for the night.

Chapter 14

At the kitchen counter in the farmhouse, Skye poured a mug of morning coffee and added cream and sugar.

She wasn't going to be able to think straight without sleep, but precious slumber was becoming more difficult to find. Sighing, she rubbed her eyes and didn't bother to suppress a huge yawn.

Last night, the thought of Jon kept her awake. There had been kindness in his gaze but also wariness. Even with injuries, he was a formidable man, exuding strength. His expression told her he wanted to kiss her as much as she'd desired it.

Maybe, whatever happened to him in the past prevented him.

Let it go. Jon's your landlord. He's off-limits.

If not careful, he would ask her to move. With the high cost of rent, she needed this house.

She grabbed a piece of bread, tossed it into the

toaster and poured another cup of coffee.

After the death of her boss, she'd felt frustrated without answers to why he was murdered.

She stared at the scrap of paper Ruth had given her. How would it help her understand the reason he died? She repeated the numbers out loud as if doing so would make sense of the message. But no matter how often she read the digits, they meant nothing to her.

On the back of the note, she found several letters. She shrugged, not useful. The best possible idea might be to give the thing to the police in San Francisco and let them handle the problem. But they'd displayed no interest in Andrew's death.

Jon—maybe he would understand. A professional, he had no interest in knowing her on a personal level. Their business could be clean with no emotions to slow their progress. She'd better control her impassioned response to him and take what help he offered. If she didn't, she might be working on her own trying to discover what happened to Andrew.

After a shower, she spent the rest of the morning cooking and preparing "make ahead" meals for Jon. He wouldn't have to eat leftover pizzas or store-bought frozen dinners unless he wanted to.

She knocked on the cottage door and entered when Jon didn't answer. The living room was neat but the couch held pillows and a blanket. Maybe he'd stayed there last night. Was he having trouble sleeping too? She walked to the kitchen, careful not to make noise in case he slept in the bedroom and hadn't heard her knock.

She put a meal in the refrigerator for tonight and the rest of the dinners in the freezer.

After checking the shelves for the things he needed to have for a well-stocked kitchen, she made mental notes of the missing items.

She sighed, tempted to check the bedroom to find out if he was in bed. *Crazy. What are you thinking?* She turned to leave.

The sun beat down on the front yard of the adobe. She covered her eyes and scanned the driveway. Someone moved near her car. Jon. What was he doing? He balanced on one foot as he looked under the hood. A white cotton T-shirt stretched over his powerful back and his muscles flexed as it did.

Whoa. A desire to touch him went through her. *No. Remember he's your landlord.*

"Jon."

"Hand me the crutch." He stood up and smiled.

He made his way to the side of the car and with a grunt, lowered himself to the ground allowing the crutch to fall. She watched as he lay down and worked his way under the vehicle. On her knees, she observed him as he used his cell phone's light to shine on the underbelly of the auto.

Her inquisitive nature begged to ask him what he hoped to find. But she ignored her instincts and waited.

He scooted out from under the compact and sat up,

then managed to stand, holding his injured ankle out of harm's way. "Come to my place and I'll tell you what I found."

***

Salvatore donned his usual disguise—work boots, jeans, and a chambray shirt. He adjusted the short blond wig covering his black hair and applied blue contacts.

He blinked hard. No matter how much he paid for the lens, they were uncomfortable. Still, he wouldn't need to wear them for long.

When he moved, the rough cotton material in the new jeans rubbed against his skin.

Shit. He already missed his silk shirts and suits.

After a glance in his master bedroom mirror, he left the room.

"Hey, kid," Salvatore said to a young guy standing in the parking lot as he pulled up to a taco stand, near the university in Rohnert Park. "Hop in. I'll buy you lunch."

After ordering and receiving food from the drive-thru, he parked the old turquoise truck far from the other vehicles.

The kid was working on his second burrito by then and sour cream squeezed from the corners of his mouth. He had a napkin but wiped off the cream with the cuff of his plaid shirt.

Still chewing, he said, "I've been watching the girl's place like you said."

"What did you find?"

"It's hard to move near the house without being seen. There's a snoopy old lady next door. The bitch is always home and never seemed to sleep. I see her staring from her windows." He finished the last burrito and grabbed his soda.

"What about the tracker?"

"It's on the girl's car." He belched. "I'm planning to go into the farmhouse soon."

"Don't wait too long. I need to know if Skye Turner has Jenkins' documents. If you find his business records, you'd potentially be on easy street, if and when you deliver."

"Yeah?" He crunched the paper wrappers and the bag into a little ball. "A guy hangs around her too. He's big and might be a problem, but right now, he's on crutches." He threw the bag out of the window to a nearby trashcan. "I thought he was her man, but they don't sleep together. He's in the adobe and she's in the farmhouse."

"Go in and search the house and discover where Skye has stored Jenkins' files. The wife doesn't have what I need." Salvatore sipped the cola he bought, not wanting to eat fast food. He coughed but forced the drink down his throat.

When he returned to his vineyard, a glass of cabernet would be waiting.

"Kid, find the computer she took from the penthouse." He tossed a couple of flash drives to him.

"Download everything."

"What about the girl? You want her?"

Salvatore ran his hand across his stubble-covered chin. "Deliver the flash drives and I'll keep you apprised." He started the engine.

"Hey, how will I reach you when I have what you want?"

"I'll call you."

"I need some cash."

"Here's a down payment." He peeled fifteen hundred-dollar bills from a wad of money he carried to impress guys like the kid sitting next to him. Petty cash, he spent more for a pair of shoes. The real money was hidden in offshore bank accounts.

"Next week, I'll have more. Only hurry up and recover what I want. I'm on a timeline."

"Okay." The young man shoved the bills in his pants pocket, jumped from the truck, and walked away without turning to look back.

***

"You smell good," Skye said as Jon brushed by her and entered the adobe cottage.

He stopped and scanned her. "Do you always say whatever pops into your head?"

"I..." Her cheeks burned with embarrassment. "I try not to, but sometimes words leave my mouth before my brain can monitor them." She grinned. "Jon, it's true, you do."

"Do what?"

"Smell good, all soap and shaving cream…"

Their eyes caught and held. She squirmed under his glare.

"You have a beautiful mouth, among other assets." He smiled.

This conversation was going in a direction she never considered possible. She cleared her throat. "What are you planning to show me?"

His right eyebrow raised. "Show you?" He stepped closer. "There is a lot I could show you." It was his turn to grin.

She backed away from him. "Jon, I didn't… What I said came out wrong. I meant did you discover anything wrong with my car?"

"Yeah." His demeanor became serious

.

Chapter 15

"Jon, this is surreal." Skye stared at the small piece of equipment he had placed in her right hand. "This allows people to track the movements of my car?"

"Yeah, if they have the right gear."

She slumped to the couch, sitting on the cushion next to his. "Haven't I been through enough? First Andy's death, now this."

Silence invaded the room. What was Jon thinking? His stern expression caused her to hesitate before she asked, "Whoever they are, what are they trying to accomplish by following me?" She leaned forward and picked up the tracker.

"You have something or know something about Jenkins. These people won't give up until they get what they want."

"They're crazy?" She shook her head. "I was a secretary and all-around office gopher for Andy. I can't produce anything useful for anyone, not even Ruth." In a fit of exasperation, she threw the tracking device across the room and paced.

"Hey, you okay?"

"Yeah. I just…"

"I understand this is frightening. You must feel caught in a web with no way out. Maybe it'll help if I tell you what I've learned."

She stopped pacing. "I hope so."

"Sit down again. Here." He patted the spot next to him, opened his tablet and displayed a house in San Francisco. "Is this Ruth's place?"

She squinted at the screen. "Looks like it."

"Okay. Good. On the property assessor's website, I discovered the names of the people who own the homes on Ruth's block."

"But I don't know the name of man who followed me."

"Still, if he went into a home across the street from Mrs. Jenkins' house, I should be able to at least start with her name." With a grimace, he paused and adjusted his booted leg. "Yesterday, I checked with Ruth and she sent me a file with camera footage from her front stoop."

"Can't be. I've gone to her house for years and never realized the place had a camera on the front porch."

"Most people don't. Cameras are easy to hide because they're smaller than they used to be." He nodded toward the monitor. "So, Skye, I'll show you the photos from Ruth's place. If you recognize him shout out—ready?"

"I guess."

In a quiet neighborhood, much of the video contained streets with neither cars nor people going by the house. Finally, a small auto drove onto the lane and stopped in front of Ruth's house.

"It's me," Skye shouted and watched the feed of her park and walk up to the front porch.

"Good. We're on the right track."

"Jon, keep going," she said, never taking her eyes off the screen. A few minutes later she yelled, "There. Stop! That's him."

"You sure?"

"He's the guy I saw at college and the one who tried to pull me into his truck."

Jon's eyes narrowed. "Did he hurt you?"

"No." She rubbed her wrist, remembering how the stranger grabbed her with his huge hands. She now realized a bruise had formed.

"This is the guy?"

She trembled. "Yeah."

For several hours, Jon scrutinized websites, searching for the owners of the homes on Ruth's street and any information concerning them.

At the same time, Skye searched for data on the companies Andrew Jenkins worked with. For most of the years spent working for Andy, she'd never considered what the corporations he represented did to earn their money. In the beginning, it didn't seem to matter. Now she wished she'd paid more attention.

She stretched her back muscles and twisted to release the strain of looking down at the screen for so long.

"Here's the name of the homeowner who lives near Ruth. I can cross reference the surname with the students at the University of Sonoma—" He paused. "But he might not have come from that particular house."

"You shouldn't have to do this—my life isn't my own anymore."

"Hey, Skye, calm down. You need to start from where you are today, not at the place you wish you were. The sooner we figure this out, the faster you can do what you want."

"It's hard."

"Damned hard."

"Are you always a pragmatist?" she asked unable to keep annoyance from her voice.

He glanced at her with a similar irritated expression on his too handsome face. "Not always, but I try. In my line of work, if you let your emotions control you, you'll lose." He hesitated. "Is anybody else going to find justice for Mr. Jenkins?" He waited for an answer, his expectant countenance deepening.

"No. No one else appears to care."

"You ready to do it?"

She blinked in shock. She'd been thinking about this situation as a victim, running scared and desperate. Jon entered the fray as a hunter and assumed he'd find his prey and bring him in. "What did you say, Jon?"

"Want to win for Jenkins?"

"Damned right."

"Okay." He went back to his tablet.

Later, he stifled a grunt and moved his leg to a new position. "I should make coffee. It can be a late night if we want to resolve this today," he added.

"Rest. I'll do it. Do you need your pain meds?"

"Thanks." He closed his eyes and leaned back against the pillows on the sofa.

"Jon, you need sleep. We can do this afterward."

"Sleep is hard to find these days."

Another pragmatic statement free of emotion, she stopped herself from asking why he didn't sleep. It wasn't her business. She'd better remember his history was off-limits. Still…

When the French Press was pushed down, the aroma of Italian coffee floated in the room. While the grounds had steeped, she'd made turkey and mozzarella cheese sandwiches and added a dollop of homemade cranberry sauce. Now she set a bowl of blue organic corn chips on the counter and poured mugs of coffee. Remembering he drank milk when he took the pain pills, a tall glass of the stuff waited for him.

He hobbled to the island without the crutch. They ate and discussed the information each had found as if they were at a business meeting.

"I pulled a few strings and was able to cross-reference names of the Sonoma students and the names of the people living on the same street as Mrs. Jenkins."

"That's fast, Jon."

"Helps to network." He swallowed a pain pill and the last of the milk. "Here are the names that correspond." He handed his phone to her. "Unfortunately, two of them of them are very common names Smith and Wong."

"He isn't Asian." She stared at the phone. "Smith?" She shrugged. "Wouldn't be my guess, but I don't have a reason to say no."

"Of course, we'll assume he told you the truth and he is related to the older woman. If not, this is a lost cause and we'll go at it another way. What did you find out about the companies Jenkins worked for?"

"I didn't."

"Hey, Skye, don't look so disappointed. This is a hunt. You don't get the guy the first time out."

"It's only I had my whole summer planned, sun, surf, gardening and instead…"

"Why don't we take a break? I'm sure your garden would welcome your attention." His expression softened. "Leave a list of the companies and I'll see what I can discover."

"Thanks. I'm on overload."

***

At the front window, he watched Skye's graceful movements as she went down the path toward the farmhouse. She made a fast escape from the task of today, but danger surrounded her. The tracker he'd found on her vehicle informed him of the need to keep her close, because someone, wanted to be able to find her. And then…?

He remembered his wife died because he had stayed at work instead of heeding the signs that were available back then. Sure, they'd been small and easy to dismiss, not to mention, he'd been told, by the powers that be, there was no danger to her. However, the result remained the same, he was a childless widower at the young age of twenty-eight. *What if Skye*… Despite the summer heat, he shivered

.

Chapter 16

Jon cursed and uttered an oath that no one else would die on his watch, not as long as he lived to stop it.

Still at the window, he saw Mei working in her front garden. Skye stopped to talk to her. They smiled at each other appearing to enjoy the company.

Relieved, he returned to his tablet and continued to search for information—anything helpful to Skye.

He didn't realize so much time had gone by until the lights in the farmhouse went on. He knew the floor plan sufficiently to realize Skye was in her bedroom.

Maybe she could find relief from her troubles in sleep. He imagined her in bed, a smile on her face as she dreamed of better days.

When he'd offered to help, he'd believed she might be dramatizing her situation. But with a tracker on her vehicle and a man watching her home, she may have underestimated the problem.

But why shadow a secretary for Jenkins?

Strange, in his research he discovered she had been named as co-owner in several LLCs belonging to Jenkins. A couple of the companies incorporated in Delaware and others where the locations were not listed. He continued to rummage through the files she'd given him. What did the companies do, make? And what was Skye's connection to them? Too much of the story remained to be unearthed.

Too damned many questions.

He poured over the pages and pages of legalese. Not his expertise and written in such a way as to make it difficult for the layman to understand. He groaned. He needed an attorney or a forensic auditor—maybe both.

The strain of hours staring at the computer monitor had taken a toll. He rubbed his eyes. His vision blurred again and his back hurt He needed a massage. *Skye. Don't go there.*

His stomach growled. He hobbled to the kitchen, took one of her homemade dinners and put it in the oven.

While the food heated, he texted a member of the Rapid Advance Task Force, hoping Juan would give him the name of the good forensic accountant who might point him in the right direction relating to Jenkins' LLCs. Why were there so many and why was Skye named in the companies? He wanted to question her. If it wasn't so late, he would ask her now.

An aroma of Italian spices reminded him of the lasagna in the oven. With a mitt, he grabbed the casserole before it burned and poured a glass of milk.

After dinner, he took the crutch and circled the property, making sure no one was surveying the place. Mei described the man observing the farmhouse as young, tall and wearing a hooded sweatshirt. What did he want?

Everything appeared quiet, but on the way back to the adobe, he tested the locks on Skye's doors and windows, at least on the first floor. He examined Mei's house as well. Satisfied, he returned to the cottage and hoped for a few hours of uninterrupted sleep.

After a quick shower, he pulled the protective boot on his left leg and stretched out on the bed, a pillow under his head. In the dark, thoughts of past mistakes haunted him. What should he do to stop the guilt battering him? *Nothing.* Action now would not change an hour of the history he was forced to relive every night.

He shut out the images of his toddler son smiling, his hands in the air asking to be picked up by his daddy. His family was deceased, end of story.

The silence of the night hung heavy in the bedroom, stifling, suppressing the oxygen in the room. Perspiration beaded on his body as he struggled to breathe.

He didn't know how long it took for sleep to claim him.

The cell phone roused him. "Yeah."

"Jon."

"Speak up. I can't hear you."

"It's Skye, someone's in the house."

"Is he still there?"

"In the living room."

"Get out. Go out the window, but be quiet."

The phone went dead.

Shit.

He yanked on a pair of shorts and ran for the front door. Limping quickly to the farmhouse, he entered.

In the dark living room, a shadowy figure struck him. He struggled to remain standing as he returned a blow. The man grunted, and then pushed forward, kicking Jon's injured leg as he did, sending him crashing to the floor.

By the time he hobbled to the front door, the stranger was running into the field across the road. No way to catch him with his big head start. Not with his broken bones.

Skye! Dear God, let her be okay.

"Where are you, Skye? Answer me."

He flicked on the lights and went down the hallway shouting her name. He shoved open the entry to the bedroom and called for her.

"Jon." She ran to him. "I've never been so happy to see anyone in my life." She hugged him. "I couldn't open the window. It's painted closed. I..."

"It's okay. He's gone." As he held to his bare chest,

her heart beat fast through the thin cotton nightdress she wore. "Everything is fine." *Not true, but…*

"Hold me." She trembled, her staccato breath sending whips of air against his bare skin.

"I got you. You're safe." His breathing and heartbeat synchronized with hers as he ran his hand down her back. "Hush, Skye. Hush."

"Don't leave. Not yet." She glanced at him as her eyes widened in a plea.

When her lips parted, he kissed her, gently. Her lips were soft and welcoming.

She signed, leaned closer and ran her fingers through his hair. "Jon."

Her heart reverberated in his upper body causing a response in his lower extremities. The need to kiss her again swelled. He released her before things got out of control. "Did he hurt you, Skye?" he said in a husky voice.

"No. I don't think he realized I was home. But if he had come into the bedroom…" She blinked and her cheeks reddened when she looked at him. "Jon, I'm embarrassed. I didn't mean to act like—like that."

"I kissed you, Skye." What had come over him? *Better change the subject.* "Let's go find out if the guy took anything."

"Okay. First, I'll put something else on"

He scanned the short nightgown she wore, examining her full breasts and tightened nipples pressing against the pink fabric. He cleared his throat.

"I'll be in the living room."

Jon locked the front door of the farmhouse and secured the chain on the door. Tomorrow he'd put in a stronger latch. The house had not been hardened as there had never been a reason to expect an attack at the family's vacation home.

He settled in a club chair facing the front entrance and ignored the ache in his knee, probably caused when he was knocked to the hardwood floor as the intruder fled.

Damn. He wished he'd been able to get a good look at the man. With the unexpected attack in the darkened room, the best he'd been able to do was to strike back.

As soon as the stores opened in the morning, he'd add a camera system to the list of items to buy for the home. He hoped it wasn't too little too late.

He understood if the trespasser didn't find what he wanted tonight, he would return.

An image of Skye in the short pink nightgown trembling with fear caused rage toward the burglar. He glanced at his bare chest and shorts. His state of undress might make her uncomfortable. He should go find a shirt and pants. But leaving her alone even for a few minutes made him nervous. Maybe she would go with…

"Hi." Skye entered barefooted the room, wearing jeans and a white shirt, her dark hair pulled into a ponytail. With her face clear of makeup, she appeared to be a young student right out of high school. His need to protect her flared.

"Jon, the prowler's gone—right?"

"Yeah. Skye. I locked the door. Don't worry. Come in and find out if he took anything."

She glanced around the living space. "I don't know where to start." She wandered around the edge of the room touching the empty bookshelves and avoiding the fallen tomes. "So many books—I don't... He knocked down my easel. Now the art is ruined. Damn him! Whoever he is. The laptop!" She ran toward the desk and picked it up from the area rug.

"Don't shut it down. The intruder might have been looking at the files. Be interesting to identify the ones he inspected." Jon hobbled to the desk chair and sat down. "If we're careful, we may be able to see what files interested him."

"This is Andy's computer. I found it in the box Ruth gave me. I don't know why she would pass it to me."

He touched the screen and it opened to a folder marked LLC's U.S. and foreign.

"Well, I'll be... What next?"

Chapter 17

Jon opened a file and scrolled through the information on Jenkins' laptop. Skye leaned near him to observe the monitor.

Finally, she pulled up a dining chair and sat next to him. Concentrating on the screen, for some time they didn't speak.

"Skye, did you see these contracts?" he asked without turning away from the laptop.

"No."

"Odd, because you appear to have signed some of them."

"What?"

He flipped to the last page of one of the documents and next to Andrew Jenkins' signature, he discovered hers.

She startled and began to shake. "I don't remember signing. I…" She covered her mouth and for a moment he thought she might be sick.

"Okay. It's okay. We can deal with this tomorrow. Go get some sleep."

"You aren't going leave, are you?"

He saw it again—fear in her expression.

"Jon?"

"I'll be here."

"Where will you sleep?"

"Hey, Skye, don't worry about me. Rest. I got this."

After she went to the bedroom, he turned off the lights, leaving the room lit only by the computer screen. At the window, he peeked through the curtains and scanned the neighborhood.

Did the thief work alone or had others come with him? Jon could manage one, but a group? *Damn.* He hadn't brought his gun with him—not that he wanted to start a gunfight. Still, men often backed down when facing the possibility of taking a bullet.

At three thirty in the morning, he texted his brother, Webb Craig, the leader of the U.S. Rapid Advance Taskforce, headquartered in Washington D.C., and left a message asking if he had the name of a forensic specialist who was familiar with LLCs, both foreign and domestic.

Six thirty, Eastern Standard Time, his brother would be up and getting ready for work.

Webb texted, "Hey, Bro, what are you doing up in the middle of the night? Call me."

When he did, Webb listened to the situation without interrupting him.

"Jon, you know Juan is the man for your job, but he is on assignment in Venezuela. We don't expect him to return for some time."

"Too bad."

"Maybe I can help. Emma and I will be in San Francisco tomorrow evening. Emmy is checking out a couple of houses for Kate and The President. I'll be free while she works."

"Sounds good. Thanks, Webb."

"No big deal. I'll text when we land."

He ended the call, relieved someone would understand his situation and what he needed.

Was Skye asleep? He stood, careful to test his knee before walking to the bedroom and opening the door to catch a glimpse of her.

The aroma of floral perfume and the gentle purr of her breathing greeted him. The ray of light from the small lamp on a side table gave the necessary illumination for him to notice a frown marred her beauty. She might be reliving the panic she'd experienced tonight. But at least she was sleeping.

He backed out of the bedroom and moved the club chair closer to her door. The upholstered seat was surprisingly comfortable. He sighed and closed his eyes. He shouldn't doze, but he could relax.

A neighbor's dog barked. He sat up, suddenly alert.

At dawn, he breathed easy. It would be simpler to spot someone watching the house during the day. A glance out of the window told him if the home was being watched, it wasn't from the large tree across the road.

He looked toward Mei's place and it appeared to be quiet. He rubbed the tension from his neck and ignored the need for coffee until, back in the chair, he almost dozed off.

In the clean and neat kitchen, he found a bag of locally brewed coffee beans.

While he waited for the coffee, he buttered toast and grabbed an apple. How long should he let Skye sleep? Did he dare go to the cottage and dress for the day before returning? With the mug in his hand, he returned to the club chair and waited.

***

At dawn, Salvatore Romano walked the vineyard he loved more than any person in his life. The grapes were smaller than usual for this time of year. Drought, the dreaded word haunted him. More water was needed and that meant an increased budget for irrigation. He scratched his head. The kid was in communication with information from Jenkins' computer files.

Last night the kid reported his success at retrieving files and filling the jump drive Salvatore had given him with folders and files.

Finally, the boy had done something right, deserving the money he'd promised him.

Romano smiled. If he was correct, the funds Andrew Jenkins placed offshore would be his again. He should never have trusted the liar in the first place, but he bought the idea his money would be safer in the Cayman Islands, untouchable by the U.S. courts and any judgments or taxes against them.

On the day he went to Andrew's office to retrieve currency for his accounts on the island, Jenkins smugly told him he had no idea what he was talking about. There were no accounts.

The bookkeeper had the nerve to say he'd never received money from him. The papers had been ready, but Salvatore had never delivered the promised funds.

The kid worked Jenkins over, but Andrew was tougher than expected, refusing to change his story. Jenkins insisted he never got the capital.

Romano squeezed the bunch of grapes he held in his hand so hard the juice splattered on his crisp white shirt.

Shit.

He needed to control his temper. He was in this current situation because he lost his cool with the Jenkins. If he hadn't thrown Andrew out of the window of a twelfth-floor window... If what he believed about Skye Turner proved to be true, he wanted her alive, at least for now.

He brushed off his shirt and reminded himself when he had Skye in his hands, not to make the same mistake he made with her boss. He'd need her in good condition to sign off on the overseas accounts, then...

***

Skye stretched and smiled. She'd been dreaming of

Jon's kiss. Mm, she wanted more. But reality forced her to remember what had happened last night and panic slashed her. Had Jon left her alone?

Chapter 18

Skye almost screamed with relief when she saw Jon in the kitchen pouring coffee into a mug.

"Morning, sleepy." He smiled.

"Do you have the time?" She yawned and pushed her hair back.

"Ten am. I'm glad you got some shut-eye."

"I thought you'd left." She tried but failed to keep the panic out of her voice.

"I said I'd be here." He paused. "Drink some coffee. You'll feel better."

She flushed when he scanned her, stopping for a second at her breasts.

She should have changed into her street clothes. But she'd been sure he'd left her to fend on her own. With a quick yank, she adjusted her short, thin, nightgown.

"Drink." He grinned. "Lots of cream and a little sugar. Right?"

"Yeah." Her cheeks heated like the coffee she held

as he continued to stare.

"Jon, you're embarrassing me."

"Sorry. But you're so beautiful in the morning." He turned away, grabbed his mug, and refilled it.

"I should shower and dress. OMG, you're still in shorts. You did spend the night here."

"I didn't want to leave you by yourself. In case… Sit at the table and I'll make you breakfast. Later, you can get ready for the day."

"I…"

"Did you eat dinner last night?'

"Well, I…"

"That's what I thought. You've been cooking for me. I owe you. One or two eggs?"

"One. Thanks."

"Scrambled is my best, but I can try over easy if you want."

"Scrambled is fine. I'll make the toast."

The summer heat came through the kitchen window and warmed her as did the hot coffee. For the first time in twenty-four hours, she relaxed.

"You were right, Jon. I was hungry."

"Why don't you dress? Afterward, we'll go to the cottage and regroup."

"Okay." For the first time, she scanned him, flexed abs, scared but muscled chest, and broad shoulders. The bruises she'd seen on his hard body, days earlier, were only shadows on his now-tanned torso. The Sonoma sunshine had done a good job.

His intense blue eyes gazed at her as a slow grin spread across his face. An electrifying flash of longing went to her lower extremities and her breathing quickened. "I'll get ready."

She ran from the kitchen and into the bedroom before the need to kiss him caused her to do something she'd regret later.

What must he think of her? Did she really want to know? She had to see him again, embarrassed or not. He was her only hope of solving Andrew's death.

In the shower, she closed her eyes and let the spray cool her. *Remember he's your landlord and you need his help. Don't make a fool of yourself by coming on to him and forcing him to turn you down.*

***

In the Adobe building, forty-five minutes later, they split up the paper files and started reading them.

"We might want to visit some of these men and find out what Jenkins did for them and their businesses."

"Bookkeeping."

"Skye, it appears he was more involved. At least, with some of them."

"I didn't have any idea. Let me show you something. I almost tossed the thing out. But now…" She jogged to the entry table, near the front door of the adobe, where she'd set her bag. "It's here in my wallet. Does it mean anything?" She handed him the scrap of paper. "Ruth found the note hidden in her grandmother's locket and believes her husband put it there, hoping she would eventually notice."

He examined it. "Bank account?"

She shrugged and sat on the sofa next to him. "I hoped you would know."

He frowned and counted the numbers. "I'm no expert, but it looks like a bank code, nine digits, a zero, a three-digit, and a five-digit branch/transit code." He paused. "An account number with twelve characters."

"Whoa. Ruth wouldn't have given it to me if she understood. But which bank?"

"There's no IBAN number. Probably not a European bank. BIC number?" He counted the digits. "Eleven. RB," he said, "an identifier code."

"I don't understand what you're saying. Can the numbers tell you where the bank's located?"

"Skye, I'd guess this is a Cayman Island account number. I think your boss opened a deposit account."

"You're kidding? Never mind. You don't kid."

He smiled. "Andrew didn't mention this to you?"

"No way—not to me."

She paced the room, then glanced out of the window to the empty yard, wishing she could lay in the sun and ignore all that had happened since her boss died. *Was killed,* she corrected the thought.

"Mr. Jenkins wouldn't tell me about his personal bank account." She faced Jon. "I was only his secretary."

"You signed the account."

"How do you know?"

He held up the paper file he had been reading. "This mentions you as a signatory on the account."

"Weird! If anyone should be on the accounts with Andrew, it's Ruth." Skye rubbed her forehead and tried to find a reason for her boss doing it. "I don't have any idea why he would put my name on the bank account."

"You were his *private* secretary..." His voice trailed into silence.

"What are you suggesting? She stopped and let his words sink in. "How dare you!" She glared at him as anger grew within her.

Chapter 19

"Jon, I thought you understood—how can you think Andrew and I would—would… He's married and Ruth's my friend." Her throat tightened and tears threatened to flow. *No.* She wouldn't let them.

She scooped up the files near her and ran from the cottage, slamming the door behind her.

Emotions spilled out, sandbagging her with unwanted feelings. Jon believed she and Andy had an affair and the bank account was her payoff.

Damn. Would everyone view the account as a payoff for services rendered? Ruth? What would she think?

Skye opened the front door to the farmhouse and realized she needed to find another place to live. No way she'd stay when he thought of her as a … She wouldn't use the word.

Her cheeks burned and anger flared. Frustrated, without a way to improve her situation, she slumped on the couch and put her head in her hands. Could things be any worse?

***

That went well—like hell. Jon grunted. He should've kept his mouth shut. It wasn't like him to speak without careful thought about how the words would impact the other person. *Shit.* What caused him to overreact around Skye?

A better question—what now? Did he go and reason with her? Maybe better to continue to dig in the files and later talk to Webb. His older brother knew more about soothing a woman's ire.

Meanwhile, he might as well discover what else waited in the files Skye had left in the cottage.

A reason for opening the accounts with her name on them would help his current situation.

A cryptic note, in what appeared to be Andrew Jenkins' handwriting, was the only clue he'd found concerning the offshore bank accounts. Addressed to Skye, the note made no sense to him. Perhaps she could decipher the message.

Jenkins' irritating games were making things harder for Skye. Andrew should've explained in person why her name appeared on the financial records. She worked in his office, after all.

Did the man believe he'd live, so had no motive to tell her anything until he needed another signature?

Jon rubbed his eyes and stretched. His back ached after being hunched over the documents. As far as he surmised, Jenkins dealt with shady characters who needed LLCs to shelter their illicit funds.

He blinked and shook his head as his vision blurred making it impossible to focus. *Not again.* He squeezed his eyes closed. *I don't have time for this shit.*

Eye strain. He leaned against the back of the sofa. A five-minute break, that's all he needed.

An hour later, he woke up, yawned and scanned the room, relieved to see everything back in focus.

Skye needed his help whether she wanted it or not. Okay, he'd made a mistake earlier, a stupid one, insinuating she had an affair with her boss.

He glanced at his phone, almost time for dinner, but food was the last thing on his mind.

He grabbed the note from her boss and left the adobe.

At the farmhouse, he knocked. "Skye, it's Jon. Open up."

"Go away."

He swallowed an angry retort and took a deep breath. "Hey, I understand you're upset. But I don't want to yell at you through the door and we need to talk."

"I have nothing to say to you. I'll be out of the house by tomorrow morning. Your key will be in the mailbox."

He knocked again. "Skye, can a guy apologize?"

She opened the entrance and he scooted in before she changed her mind.

"I don't want you to think I don't respect you, Skye." He moved quickly into the living room, hoping she would follow. He shifted a box off the couch before he sat down. "You were serious about leaving?"

"I don't stay where I'm not wanted. Respected, to use your words."

He ran his hands through his hair. "We've both been under a strain. With my recovery and the death of your boss—I didn't mean to give you the wrong impression. I don't think badly of you." He hesitated trying to gauge her response to him. "Can we forget this afternoon and start fresh?"

Because her expression suggested she wouldn't agree, he frowned. "Skye?"

"It's hot today. Want a cold drink?"

Skye's question came of out the blue. An odd response to his request to start over. Still, maybe it was her way of moving past the incident, a peace offering.

"Sounds good."

"Soda or iced tea?"

"Whatever's cold."

As she left for the kitchen, he noted the graceful way she glided around the boxes and other items spread out as if she were packing the things important to her. Maybe not as sophisticated as Miranda, nonetheless, Skye was a beauty in her own right.

With her integrity insulted, her temper flared. Strange, but he admired her for having the guts to leave when offended. Still, he wouldn't let her go unprotected. Not on his watch.

She returned with two tall glasses of iced tea on a tray with a sugar bowl and two spoons. "Why don't we sit on the covered patio in the back?"

He followed her to the backyard facing the open fields of the large property.

After setting the tray on the wooden picnic table, she sat on a bench. "You're maneuvering with only the boot. No crutch." A small turn of her lips, might not be called a smile, but at least she didn't frown at him.

"Yeah, hope to retire the crutch." He lowered himself to a chair across the table from her, pleased they agreed to have a polite, if not a warm, relationship.

It startled him when he realized her feelings were important to him. He worried not only about her safety but what she thought of him.

"Sugar?" she asked.

"No. I'm good."

"I love it here on the land." She added a level teaspoon of sugar to her cold liquid. "You and your family have so much acreage available to be planted. I bet the soil is rich."

"I guess." He wiped his forehead with the back of his hand and scanned the area. "I understand Sonoma is blessed with remarkable dirt." He sipped the tea, something he didn't often drink, relieved to have a conversation about anything but the quarrel he'd started.

They talked easily about what to plant and which grapes could be best for the area. It was obvious she needed to chat about anything but what was happening in her life now.

She'd done her research concerning owning a plot to establish her own vineyard. He smiled and listened with surprising interest. Was the topic so intriguing or was it her?

Later, they shared stories of their first sip of wine. He found himself telling tales of his early university days and the fun he and his buddies had had discovering various wines, then paying the price with headaches the next day.

She laughed. Something he wanted her to do more often, her chuckle a sweet song flowing on the slight breeze.

"My parents don't drink. I found out about alcohol on my own." She tasted the tea, appearing to enjoy it as if it were a vintage glass of wine. "In college, my roommate loved the grape and was knowledgeable about California wines. I listened, learned and we tried many examples."

"Is that why you want to grow them?"

"Yeah, I think so. My mother is a master gardener. I grew up with dirt on my hands, planting and digging holes for seeds. Gardening equals home to me." She grinned, her eyes sparkling.

Seeing her joy, he wanted to hug Skye and make sure no one would hurt her and prevent the dream from coming true. Instead, he sat in relaxed silence listening to her dreams and then the peace and quiet.

Too soon, disturbing truths fought to the surface of his mind. He wanted to unravel what caused her boss to be murdered and Skye to be attacked.

A note in his pocket, that had been hidden in the deep recesses of a file folder, and signed by her boss, must be deciphered. Skye was the only person capable of doing so. What if she refused to explain? Would it destroy the truce they'd agreed to and leave her vulnerable to another assault from the man who broke into her house?

Chapter 20

After a potluck dinner in the farmhouse kitchen, Skye took the dishes from the table and placed them in the sink. "Jon, what did you find in the files I gave you? I mean besides the Cayman Island bank accounts?" she asked hoping to sound casual, though even she heard the tension resonating in her voice.

She hated to bring up the issue after a comfortable afternoon and evening together, but the information needed to be out in the open if they were going to work together.

The last few hours, Jon had been kind and on his best behavior. She appreciated his attempt at easing the atmosphere between them. Nevertheless, his blue eyes telegraphed he had something to tell her.

"Skye, I wasn't planning to mention it tonight, but…" He shrugged and unfolded a piece of computer paper taken from his pocket. "This was in an envelope with your name… I couldn't figure it out— not in relation to the bank accounts."

She took the note and leaned back in the chair. "Andy's handwriting." She read and reread the message. "I don't know."

After scanning it again, she stared at him. "This

talks about an incident that took place on the day we moved into the penthouse, several years ago. He had such dreams and was so confident his company would flourish." She wiped away tears with the back of her hand. "Sometimes I can't believe he's gone." She took a deep breath. "Why write this down and save it?"

"I thought you might understand," Jon said quietly.

"I… Maybe he kept it because he had such high hopes—then."

The summer sky darkened and she reached for the switch for the overhead light and the farmhouse brightened.

"The message must be useful or why would Jenkins put it in the file with the banking information?" He paused. "Most accountants are anal. They pay attention to details. My guess is he had something he needed to tell you but didn't want others to understand. This is a clue." He pointed to the paper lying on the table. "If we work together, we can find out what he was trying to say." He hesitated. "Skye, my concern is someone wants what you have—what you know."

"But I..."

"It's been my experience bad men are not patient. I'm not pressuring you, but if you're holding anything back…"

"I'm not."

"The man who attacked you will return or someone like him."

"You're scaring me." The idea of staying alone in the house sent a shiver down her spine. Would the guy who broke into the house come again tonight?

"Why would Andy do this to me? I don't want the money. If I could interpret the…, don't you believe I want to get this over, so I can have some sanity in my life?" she hesitated. "Jon, what am I going to do?" She gazed into his intense eyes.

He moved quickly toward her and wrapped his strong arms around her and though he didn't answer, his warmth reassured her.

"Sometimes when people sleep on a problem, the puzzle becomes clear in the morning. Let's go to the cottage. I'll feel better if you stay with me.

In the bedroom, as she gathered her clothes for the overnight with Jon, she realized the truth—she loved him. His kindness, generosity, and concern for her when he owned her nothing, won her respect and affection. Today, when he apologized, he had her love.

She had fought the urge to love him and struggled against her emotions. He wasn't interested in her and had never shown a real attraction to her, only the kindness he would probably display to any stranger in trouble.

It had been only three years since his wife's death. A relationship with another woman probably wouldn't hold an interest for him, especially a female in danger.

She'd told herself not to fall into the trap of loving a man who wouldn't reciprocate it. She signed. When did a heart ever listen?

***

Skye yawned as she fastened the seat belt on the driver's side of her subcompact. Jon buckled his and tried his best to straighten his wounded leg, appearing to be unable to find a comfortable position in the small auto.

He must be exhausted after spending the night on the couch in the cottage, a pistol nearby in case an intruder decided to enter.

She had offered to sleep in the living room and leave the bed to him, but he explained he was the first line of defense.

The day warmed the interior of the old vehicle and she lamented the fact the air conditioner no longer worked. Nevertheless, she set the fan on high, a breeze was better than stagnant air. She pulled on the sunglasses she kept in the side panel of the door and then started the engine.

"Jon, are you sure we should bother the clients Andy had?" She checked and adjusted the rearview mirror. "I mean one man owns a vineyard. Why would he hurt my boss?"

"Maybe he wouldn't but could be he's heard rumors concerning Jenkins and how he did business. Local business executives might be buzzing about info concerning your boss."

"Well... I guess. I think it's doubtful, but I've always wanted to check out the winery. The place is quite exclusive. You know, it's a member's only to go in."

Skye headed north on Highway 101, the hot sun shining on the dry earth, yellowing the unplanted landscape. The usual fog from the ocean had not appeared this morning, signaling a scorching day.

Perspiration beaded on her forehead and she wished she'd dressed in less formal attire instead of her business suit. Jon appeared cool in his dark slacks and white dress shirt open at the collar.

She wanted respect from the prominent men they were going to visit. Even in casual California, she probably wouldn't be welcome if she dressed in her usual summer outfit of shorts and a tank top.

A few miles later, she took the turn off to the right and drove along a country lane.

She'd met the first man on the list. An older gentleman, Mr. Jay Randall. He'd apparently retired to his vast estate in Sonoma County.

"Skye, good to see you again." The gray-haired man smiled from the front door of his sprawling rancher. "We are by the pool."

They followed him to the back of the property and discovered a commanding view of the valley and the rolling hills.

A little girl of about seven, dressed in a pink swimsuit, yelled, "Papa look." She jumped into the swimming pool and came up smiling. "Did you watch me? Papa, did you?"

The man grinned. Yes, Mia. The best jump today."

A woman in a gray maid's uniform came out carrying a large white towel. "Come inside, Mia. It is time for lunch and these people are here to talk to your grandpapa. You can visit with him later."

The child ran to Randall and gave him a quick hug, leaving a water stain on his blue silk shirt. He laughed. "Enjoy your meal, little one." He brushed the drops of pool water from his clothes and signaled for them to sit at the umbrella-covered patio table. "My granddaughter."

Skye smiled. "Adorable."

"Thank you. She's my pride and joy."

Mr. Randall motioned to another servant and one brought a tray of fruit juice and iced tea and the other served a plate of tea biscuits.

"Sit," he said as if used to being in charge.

"Lancaster, nice of you to come." He glanced at Jon's booted leg but didn't mention it. "Is the family back in the area?"

"Only me."

"I thought maybe they were staying at the hotel and spa."

"Not this time."

"You two know each other?" Skye asked in disbelief.

"We've met on a few social occasions," Mr. Randall replied.

"Oh." She slumped in a chair and stared at the pair as they chatted. Jon might have mentioned he was acquainted with Jay Randall.

She accepted a glass of orange juice and wondered if she should join the conversation with a question about Andrew or begin with small talk.

"As for Mr. Jenkins, please accept my condolences, Skye." The businessman interrupted her thoughts. "Not much I can say about him." He hesitated. "I certainly didn't expect him to die in such a difficult manner."

"No." She took a sip of juice and looked away so he wouldn't see her emotion.

"Jay, I was hoping you might enlighten us concerning his contacts," Jon said.

Randall rubbed his chin. "I'll share what I can because of who your people are."

Skye caught Jon's eye. "People?" she mouthed. "Who?"

He ignored her.

"There was something rotten going on with Jenkins and the people he dealt with. Sorry, Skye," Randall glanced at her, then continued, "no reflection on you, my dear. Still, your boss was into some nasty enterprises."

"Are you sure?"

"Yes, I'm afraid so."

He turned toward Jon. "The shady deals and the men involved, caused me to reconsider my use of his company."

"Men?"

"Reputed mafia types. Some of them recently in the news."

"I…" Skye stopped in the middle of the sentence unsure what to say.

"He used you, Skye, as he did many others." Randall patted her hand.

"Jay, if you could supply names, that would be helpful."

"Papa read a book to me." Mia poked her head out of the back door.

"Jay, you're busy." Jon smiled for the first time. "Thanks for seeing us on short notice." He handed a card to the gentleman and glanced at her.

"Yes, uh, thank you," she said but had a hard time putting sincerity into her voice.

"I'll email the names. Give my best to your father and The President."

"Will do." Jon stood.

The President? The President of the United States? She stared at Jon.

He took her hand and walked toward the car

Chapter 21

Skye entered her compact and put the key in the ignition. "Who *are* your people?" she asked when Jon was in the passenger seat. "Mr. Randall said to say hello to your dad and the president." About to start the engine, she paused. "He doesn't mean the U.S. President, does he?"

"Yeah."

Her mouth dropped open as she gaped at him. "What's your father's name?"

"My step-dad is Harold Lancaster, The Chief of Staff at the White House."

"And you never mentioned… How could you? I felt stupid. I was the only one who didn't realize."

"Skye, keep your voice down. If you knew, it wouldn't have changed anything." He slammed the passenger side door closed. "Why do you care?"

"I don't. Jon, it doesn't matter to me. It's only I… Forget it. You don't owe me an explanation or any information about your family." She started the engine and drove down the drive. "I'll take us back to the farmhouse."

"Why?" he asked, his voice harsh.

"I thought…"

"We made plans to speak to the owner of The Wine Cave. The place isn't far from here. I used what little influence I have to secure an interview at the private member's club."

"Oh."

"Do you want to go?"

"I guess—yeah."

"First, let's finish this—what do you want to know about my family?"

Her cheeks heated. "It's none of my business, but have you met President Nielsen?"

"Yeah. As a matter of fact, his wife Kate used to be my boss and my brother worked for her too."

"You call the First Lady, Kate?" she gasped.

"She prefers it to Kathryn."

"Well, I'll be…" With a quick turn onto Highway 101, she drove toward Healdsburg. "Wait, I met your brother. His last name is Craig, Webb Craig. Right?"

"Yeah."

"A half-brother?"

"No."

"But…" She glanced at him and then at the road.

"It's a long story, Skye."

She'd said it was none of her business. Still, curiosity gnawed at her. She bit her lip and continued the drive.

Later she asked, "You're familiar with The Wine Cave?"

"I've been there. It has a great rep, at least with those interested in domestic wine."

"The label's way out of my budget. Jon, if we could taste…"

"Don't get your hopes up. After I ask questions, I

doubt the owner will want to share his vintage yield." He hesitated. "We may not be welcome for very long."

His expression said he wasn't kidding. What had he told her? He didn't joke, never kidded.

"Oh, too bad," she whispered. "I would've liked to taste… maybe we should let him show us around and sample the wine before we ask—"

When he grunted, she added, "Never mind." They were on a fact-finding mission not at the winery as guests.

The winery's main building was a commanding two-story, stone edifice which included a turret capped with a metal roof and a flag waving at the top.

"Wow, magnificent." Skye pulled up to the front entrance and a young man wearing white slacks, dress shirt and a red vest with the logo emblazoned on the pocket, opened her door.

"Welcome," he said with a smile. He accepted the key to her subcompact and parked the car next to a yellow Lamborghini.

The cool temperature of the lobby was a welcome relief from the heat of the day. An ambience of rustic luxury pervaded the atmosphere of the stone, open-beamed entrance. She paused to admire the huge crystal chandelier hanging from the rafters.

"Whoa." She nodded to Jon, but he appeared unimpressed.

People, sitting in overstuffed chairs, spoke in hushed tones as if they were in a library.

A blonde from the front desk greeted Jon. "Mr. Lancaster, you are expected. Please follow me." If the woman noticed the surgical boot, she didn't let on.

Skye trailed behind them until Jon slowed and

offered his arm.

"Have you been here before?" the blonde asked her, but she scanned Jon, admiration showing in her smile.

"No, and I can't wait to go to your tasting room."

Jon glared at Skye. He'd already said there would be no wine. She smiled at him.

As they passed the dining room, she saw the student who had followed her to San Francisco, the guy who'd tried to force her into his truck. Dressed as a waiter, he carried an order to a table near the window, then looked in her direction as if he'd felt her staring.

She stopped and their eyes met. His narrowed and fear raged in her. "Jon—Jon."

Still talking with the blonde, he paused midsentence. "What is it, Skye?"

"I recognize the waiter. I met him in San Francisco when I went to Ruth's house. He's the guy standing near the window." Did Jon remember what happened to her in the city when the guy tried to pull her into his truck?

"He's a temporary hire, a student at the university. We often use them during the summer months and on holidays. Shall we continue? Mr. Romano is waiting." The blonde turned her back on the dining room and moved down a hallway.

When they caught up, she said, "As you may know, the caves have been here since the early nineteen hundreds. Though this building was designed to look like a stone chateau, it was not completed until the mid-sixties. The volcanic rock was taken from the nearby hills on the property."

She smiled at Jon. "Each cave keeps the precious wine at a constant temperature, no matter how hot it is outside. Of course, the heat and sun make it possible to grow the marvelous crop of grapes." She stopped in front of large paneled doors. "If you will wait here, I will announce you."

"Skye, are you sure it's the man who attacked you in San Francisco?" Jon said as soon as the woman disappeared behind the double doors.

"Yeah."

"I don't like coincidences." He rubbed his chin. "Stay close to me until we get out of here. I…"

"Mr. Romano will see you now."

Skye had the impression she'd entered a grand reception room of a king. The emperor sitting at an enormous gilt-bronze-trimmed desk. He didn't get up, instead signaled they might sit in his presence.

"Mr. Lancaster," Romano said. "Nice of you to be interested in our little enterprise."

He turned his head to slowly scan her. His blond hair and blue eyes appeared out of place with his olive skin tone, but then he might spend a lot of time in the California sun.

"Ms. Turner." His lips curved upward, but the smile didn't reach his eyes. How did he know her name?

He was friendly. Still, she shivered, something about the man creeped her out and she had the impression she'd seen him before. Where?

He stood. Dressed in tan slacks a white golf shirt, and brown loafers. He walked toward Jon and extended his hand. "What brings you here on this beautiful day?" Before Jon could answer, he continued, "So, your family is finally interested in having a membership with us. I hoped they would. I could show you around now. Your mother and father visited last year."

"Today, I'm not representing my parents. We came to speak to you about Andrew Jenkins. I understand you were a client of his, Mr. Romano." Jon replied.

"Call me Salvatore." He paused and after some consideration said, "Yes, for a short time Mr. Jenkins did work for me." Romano retreated to his desk and sat with his sandaled feet on the desk. "My condolences for his death, Ms. Turner. A sad situation all around."

"Thank you." Skye looked away from Salvatore. He used the right words, but they didn't ring true.

"Were you pleased with his work?" Jon asked.

The air-conditioning swirled the papers on the desk and Skye fixed her attention on them as tension built in the room.

"As I said, he only worked for me for a brief while."

"Was he paid."

"Of course, are you suggesting I owe him money, Mr. Lancaster?"

"On the contrary. I'm wondering if he has funds of yours, Sal."

Skye noticed Salvatore bristled, but he grinned. "You take the license with my name."

"And does he owe you anything?"

"You realize that is none of your business. The man is dead. Let him rest in peace."

"That may not be possible."

Romano stood his full height and glared. "I have other more pressing business. My secretary will show you out." On cue, the door opened, and a huge, muscle-bound man entered. "Rodney, please walk my guests to the exit."

"Secretary?" Jon grinned.

"But Mr. Romano…" Skye was unable to finish the

sentence because he disappeared behind a pocket door near his desk. They were alone except for the bouncer sent to make sure they were ushered out of the building.

Chapter 22

"**Hell!**" Salvatore cleared his desk with a swipe of his arm. The items crashed to the oak floor of the office, but he didn't care. The kid should have discovered the name of the cripple living on the property with Skye Turner and should have told him the man was Jon Lancaster. But no, he'd been caught flat-footed with the son of President Nielsen's chief of staff quizzing him in front of the bitch who should be dead.

He threw a crystal wine glass across the room and it smashed against the far wall. Then he buzzed the outer office, "I want the kid on my secure line, now. No excuses!"

How much did Lancaster and Turner understand? And if he, Salvatore Romano, messed with her, would Lancaster care, or was it a coincidence he lived on the same property?

He took another wine goblet from the cabinet and filled it with his private reserve Cabernet Sauvignon. Might as well enjoy the wine now. If he didn't retrieve the funds stolen by Jenkins, he could kiss the eatery and the vineyards goodbye. When the Russian oligarch called in his marker, the estate would no longer be his.

He savored the aroma of the wine and calmed down. He might offer Ms. Turner a reward for the return of his funds. An idea worth considering, but why should she give up assets for compensation when she already possessed everything? Only a sucker would, and she was no fool.

This appeared to be especially true considering she had hooked up with an influential man and his family with links to the most powerful politician in the world.

He slammed his fist on the desk and slumped to his chair. The itch to kill Skye churned in his gut along with the cabernet, but executions must be done in cold blood and only after the needed information belonged to him.

Mistrust flashed in her eyes when she had scanned him. Skye must understand who he was—maybe not. He tore off his blond wig and rubbed his scalp as his dark hair fell into place. What if the disguise had worked better than expected? Could he meet her again without the worry of being discovered as Jenkins' killer?

Her expression gave him no reason to think she realized he was the man in Andrew's penthouse on the day her boss was tossed out of the window. Rage had overtaken good sense, and with Andrew's death, Salvatore had lost control of his funds.

Skye Turner's beauty might have been the reason Andrew gave her the necessary information to retrieve the stolen assets. She was ripe for the picking, sweet, succulent, and most likely untouched. Innocent? Maybe. Still, he would attest to the fact that looks were often deceiving. No matter—the only thing he needed from Ms. Turner was the information on his accounts.

Even so, he licked his lips.

Ruth, Andrew's wife, a dried prune of a woman, had appeared to be clueless as to her husband's plans.

Anger toward Jenkins seethed. At one point, the money manager guaranteed he would double his investment in no time.

It wasn't like Salvatore to trust anyone, but they'd come from similar dirt-poor backgrounds. Starting with nothing, they'd built flourishing businesses. They both had done things they weren't proud of to get there. Andrew, the nearest thing to a friend, was given a membership to the club to seal their arrangement.

He understood and wanted to help Salvatore retire from the violence defining his life and be able to cultivate his grapes in peace. *Bullshit!*

How could he have been taken by the con? He, Salvatore Romano, who'd run some of the best scams in the business?

He considered opening another bottle of wine. *No.* He needed a clear head.

This behavior would solve nothing. He shook his head, dialed the kitchen and ordered a steak dinner with a green salad to be served in his private chambers. After today, he wouldn't touch the nectar of the grape until he controlled his money once more.

Where was the kid? He should have called by now. He stood, swayed, and sat again. *Too much alcohol.*

The kid had failed to carry out his assignment. What was the saying? If you want a job done right—do it yourself.

***

As Skye and Jon walked down the hallway, Rodney, the bouncer, stayed close behind them to make sure they didn't dally.

The waiter from the dining room came to the hall when he saw Skye. "Hey." He joined them forcing her to slow up to answer him.

"Hi." She glanced at him and then at Jon. He nodded to let her know he didn't mind if she engaged the waiter in conversation. Might as well obtain what info they could from the server.

"Haven't seen you since the day in the city—I only meant to help you, Skye."

"Okay."

"Yeah? Great. I'll call you. We can go out."

Someone from the restaurant called him and he waved them off but said, "Got to go back to work. See you later."

"Keep going." Rodney prodded them.

Out in the parking lot, the sun beat down on Jon and he shaded his eyes from the bright light.

"The car's been moved to the back lot," Rodney said anticipating his question.

Jon guessed the little auto didn't give the correct impression to the people who had paid big money for a membership at The Wine Cave.

Surprised how spread out the lots were, Jon wished he brought a crutch with him. The thug, who must be following orders to make sure they left the property, stayed with them.

Parked in a lot behind a grove of stately oaks and near the kitchen trash bins, the subcompact still managed to sit in the full sun. With the broken air-conditioner, the ride home was going to be damned blistering.

When they reached the compact, Rodney grabbed

Skye's arm. "I have a message for you. Don't come back—get it? You're not welcome here."

She cried out and tried to yank her arm from his grip.

Chapter 23

Jon tapped Rodney on the shoulder. "Let Skye go."

The thug turned and slugged him in the gut causing him to struggle to keep his balance and sending him slamming against the car.

He returned a punch to the guy's gut followed by an uppercut to the jaw.

Skye screamed, but she was freed from the bouncer's hold.

"Rodney, take a message to your boss. Stay the hell away from Ms. Turner."

The bouncer glared. "You'll pay big time for this, Lancaster." He wiped the blood from his split lip but didn't come closer.

"Skye, in the car—now."

When he heard the door open and close and the engine start, without taking his eyes off the thug, he limped to the passenger's side of the car and jumped in. "Drive."

She was trembling but did what he said. "Jon, are you hurt?"

"I'm fine." His vision blurred and his left eye went almost black. He shook his head. "Go before he brings in reinforcements."

"Oh, Dear God. Jon, you don't think they would come after us?"

"Just drive."

***

She maneuvered the subcompact along the lane and out to the highway. Heading south she pushed the speed faster than she'd driven before. The engine strained, but she kept the gas pedal down.

Jon's fierce expression and reaction to Rodney had shocked her. Though injured, Jon took on the aggressor, a much bigger man, and won. What became of the mild-mannered guy who lived in the cottage behind her house?

She realized Rodney wouldn't forget the incident and that worried her for Jon's sake. Because of her problems, he had a target on his back now.

"What just happened, Jon? Why did he follow us to the car and hit you?"

"Good question." He took a slow breath and grimaced.

"You are hurt. I'm taking you to a hospital."

"No. I appreciate your concern—I'm okay." He leaned back in the seat and smiled at her. "It's not my first fight." He paused. "It could be Rodney took his job more seriously than needed or…"

"Hard to think Mr. Romano would order him."

"Maybe. But Salvatore is a weird bird, and he's hiding something."

"You're hurting."

"Stop worrying."

She hesitated before saying, "You were amazing." Despite the situation, she grinned. "Did you see his startled expression when you hit him?"

He chuckled. "It was rewarding to watch his face change."

"He deserved to be slugged, the bully." She rubbed her arm, then quickly grasped the steering wheel with both hands again. "Thanks for helping me."

"It's okay."

"Jon, this isn't your problem and I wonder if you'd have promised to help if you had realized what I was caught up in. I mean, I sure wouldn't. But..."

"I have the name of the waiter." Jon changed the subject.

"How?"

"His name tag."

"OMG, I should have read it. I was nervous, I didn't think." She should ask for the name but so stressed, at this point, she didn't want the information.

She checked the rearview mirror and slowed the car when she didn't find anyone following them.

He sat up and adjusted his seat belt. "My brother will be in Sonoma tomorrow. I'll ask him to run the guy's name and find out what's up with him."

"Webb can? He has options we don't."

The traffic increased as they reached the outskirts of Sonoma. Dinner time and tourists drove into town to dine in the many multi-star restaurants known for locally grown produce and free-range chicken, not to mention the world-renowned wine.

She sneaked a peak at Jon and he appeared to sleep.

"I'm awake," He smiled. "But I've learned to manage my energy and save it until it's needed."

"I wish I could do that." She drove through the main part of the small municipality and headed toward the farmhouse.

"Skye, stop at a taco house and I'll buy. We can take it home. My treat." Jon opened his eyes. "You like tacos? Right?"

"Yeah, but I'm so upset, I don't want to eat."

"Another secret to being able to do my job, eat when you can and keep up your stamina."

"You've got it down."

"I try—Chicken or beef?"

She pulled into the shopping center and parked in front the Madre y Padre Restaurante. "Chicken."

He ordered Chicken tacos, salsa, sour cream, and chips.

***

In the cottage, Jon smiled. "Sit next to me on the sofa." He scooted over to give her space.

They ate in silence. Then he said, "Glad to see you eat something."

"They're yummy."

Their eyes met. She glanced away and stared at her feet, trying to ignore the sudden craving his gaze sent pulsing through her. Did she dare continue to sit this close and manage to keep her need to touch him under control?

When his intense eyes, scanned her, she lost focus and struggled to think rationally.

Was he aware of his effect on her? More importantly, what would he do about it?

"Skye."

Just his use of her name sent desire coursing through her again. What should she say? Was longing pounding in him too? "Yeah, Jon."

If she kissed him, would he ask her to leave?

Chapter 24

Jon reached for her hand. "Skye, you're cold." He put his arm around her and she leaned against his taut body.

For a moment they didn't speak, only the quickness of their breathing heard in the room.

"I was so afraid at Romano's today."

"I wouldn't have let you go. If I'd realized…" He stroked her cheek with the back of his hand.

"I wanted to be there."

"We're on the right track. Salvatore sending Rodney after us proves it."

"I guess we hit a nerve when we were in his office." She reached for his hand. "It's swollen. You're hurt."

"Rodney has a hard head." He laughed.

"It's not funny." She sat up. "You were protecting me."

"I didn't do anything." He coaxed her to sit back again.

"Yeah, you did." She held his injured hand to her lips and kissed his open palm. "I owe you."

"You don't owe me anything." He caressed her cheek again and gently placed a kiss there, sending a shiver of longing through her once more. She gazed into his intense eyes. Her mouth opened inviting him to kiss her again.

"You better get some sleep. You take the bedroom. I'll stay out here." He removed his arm. Her cue to proceed to the cottage bedroom—alone.

Her face heated with embarrassment "Uh, good night."

***

Webb Craig, his older brother, stood looking out of the cottage window. "The flight was smooth and quiet. The red eye is a good way to catch some sleep and be ready to go the next morning."

Jon nodded and surveyed him. His brown hair was shorter, but his eyes were clear and alert. Head high and broad shoulders back, he exuded confidence. It seemed marriage and his appointment as leader of the Rapid Advance Task Force agreed with him.

"Webb, is the family okay?"

"Doing good and Kate sends greetings too."

"Nice of the First Lady. I appreciate it—want a beer?"

"A cola, if have one."

He started to rise from the sofa, but Webb said, "Rest your leg."

When his brother returned with two cans, he set them on the coffee table and sat in a nearby club chair.

After small talk and hearing reports on the members of the Task Force team, Webb said, "Okay, what's on your mind?"

"Is it so obvious?"

"I'm your big brother, so, yeah."

"Shit, Webb, I don't understand how to handle what I'm feeling."

His brother nodded but didn't speak.

"Jon went to the kitchen counter, sat, and rubbed his neck. "I wouldn't admit this to anyone but you." He took a deep breath. "When Miranda was murdered, I died inside too. Nothing mattered. I took risks I didn't need to." He hesitated. "Maybe I was trying to assuage my guilt for being alive after I let her die. Or maybe I wanted to join her."

"It wasn't your fault. There was no way any of us could have known she was in danger." Webb joined him at the kitchen counter.

"Don't you think I've told myself the same thing? I wish I could believe it." He stood up ready to leave the room, but instead sat again. "I can't stop thinking about Skye."

"Did you tell her?"

"No. I'm not going to. I see her staring at me when she thinks I don't notice. She cares, but…"

"Miranda would want you to be happy, not stay alone."

He considered his brother's words. Did he tell the truth or would he try to help with a small lie?

Jon tried to picture Miranda's face. But she was fading and it was harder to bring her into focus. He groaned.

"Jon?"

"Webb, what can I offer Skye? You understand I'm not working and I might be losing my sight. My left eye went completely black for a moment yesterday. How can I return to the Task Force if…?"

"Whatever happens, you'll always have a place with the team—your eyes are getting worse?"

"The blurriness comes more often and lasts longer."

"What do the doctors say?"

"I need to take it easy and heal. If it continues, I'll receive a full workup with a specialist."

Webb scrubbed his hand over his face and frowned. "Discounting the eye problems, would you like to be with Skye?" As if to give Jon emotional space, he left the counter and gazed at a painting on the wall over the couch. Finally, he turned back. "Would you, Jon?"

"I'd like to take her to bed."

"Hell, there are a lot of women you can bed. I'm not asking about sex and you know it."

"Okay—yeah. She's brought me back to life, made me laugh for the first time since Miranda died." He paused and looked away from his brother's gaze. "I'm beginning to feel, to care again. Too bad I'm experiencing the flip side of those emotions as well, anxiety and fear for her well-being. If anything happened to her… I—I can't take the chance."

The door opened and Skye peeked into the cottage. "Am I interrupting something? I brought lunch, deviled egg sandwiches and homemade potato chips."

"Skye, come in and meet my brother Webb."

"Hi. Did you have a good flight?"

"Yeah, thanks."

Jon enjoyed her quick smile as she stared at his brother. She carried the tray of food to the kitchen counter. "I hope there is a sufficient amount."

She fidgeted as if nervous, gripping the tray tight.

"I'm sure there is." Webb smiled. "Join us?"

"Well, I…"

Jon caught her eye. Something was wrong. He saw it in her expression. Still, it seemed clear she didn't want to discuss anything with Webb in the room.

"Skye?" He asked a question by his expression, an unspoken sign of concern for her.

"It's nothing," she answered his silent query. "I told Mei I'd join her for lunch. We're going to discuss what to plant for the winter garden. I'll be off."

"Nice meeting you, Skye."

"You too." She left, closing the door behind her.

He and his brother ate quickly and sat on the sofa. Jon stretched out his injured leg and leaned back with a grunt.

"Still hurts?"

"It's more of an annoyance than anything else. I'm used to moving fast and this is an impediment. Damned annoying. I guess I'll never be a patient man."

"I don't think patience is in our DNA."

"Jon chuckled. "True. Did you find anything concerning the situation with Jenkins?"

"As far as the Russian newspaper you sent me, don't know why he kept the date." He hesitated. "I didn't find anything unusual about the issue unless an article or ad had been written in code." He ran his hand through his short hair. "We can check into that later, if we find an indication it would be probable but..." Anger twisted his brother's mouth from a pleasant countenance to a grim one.

"What? Webb, tell me."

"I don't like to mention this, but there's a reference to a Russian Oligarch in one of the articles. A person we've run into in a more personal way—Oleg Volkov."

Chapter 25

"**Mei, that was a wonderful salad**. Your tomatoes tasted amazing. So much flavor."

"Thank you. I have more than the family can eat. Remember to take some of them with you and I have a summer squash too."

"Great, thanks."

Her neighbor cleared the dishes while she carried the salad dressing and drinks glasses into the kitchen.

"That young man I saw hanging around the other day was back this morning."

"No."

"I'm afraid so. I went out to talk to him, but he ran off."

"Mei," She followed her to the living room. "he might be dangerous. I don't think Jon would want you to get close to him."

"Don't worry about me." The senior citizen peeked carefully out of the curtain on the front window.

"I do though. You might be injured because of me."

"You're kind, Skye. Tell Jon the guy is back. He'll want to know."

"I will."

"Is he still there?"

"Let me see." Skye glanced out of the window and then let the curtain fall back into place. "The tall guy in a hoodie leaning against the oak tree across the street?"

"Yes."

Skye shivered wondering if he broke into her place or worse, was the one who helped throw her boss out of his office's twelfth-story window.

"Want to follow him?"

"What?"

"Find out where he goes."

Shocked, Skye covered her mouth and stared at Mei. "Are you kidding?"

A slight smile met her shocked response. "No. We'll take my car. He won't recognize it."

How could this small, thin woman, who had to be in her sixties, be so bold? Skye trembled at the thought of tailing him, but Mei stood calm as if she had only asked if they should go shopping.

"Well?" Her neighbor walked to the entry hall table and picked up her handbag and turned toward the garage.

Skye hurried to catch up with her.

She entered the nondescript sedan, as the garage opened.

A silver SUV pulled up next to the oak tree across the way and the hooded figure jumped into the passenger seat as it sped away.

They followed the silver car at a discreet distance, but not too lose the auto.

What were they doing playing detective? She imagined Jon's angry words when he learned what they were doing. Assuming they returned unharmed. Perspiration ran down her neck, heat or fear?

Mei drove like a TV cop rapidly weaving in and out of the traffic. Skye wondered if she would be in more danger with the senior citizen's handling of the car or the man they were following.

Too close to the center line, vehicles going in the opposite direction swerved to make room for their auto. Still, no matter how fast the SUV went, Mei kept a constant distance between them. The neighbor leaned over the steering wheel, eyes on the road, her lips tight and her knuckles white.

Skye held her breath as they took a hairpin turn following the silver SUV as it rolled down a country lane and continued in to a shopping center. It slowed at the grocery store at one end of the mall.

The hooded man hopped out when the SUV stopped, but instead of parking the driver drove away as the guy entered the store.

Mei took a space in the lot when a wagon pulled out. She turned off the engine and waited, her eyes never leaving the entry door to the retail outlet.

Skye undid her seatbelt, and started to speak but changed her mind. She stayed silent and hoped he didn't go out the back door of the shop.

A few minutes later, Mei broke the silence, "There he is."

The guy carried a six-pack of beer, entered an old turquoise pickup truck, and drove out of the lot.

They followed a short distance behind him. Skye coughed as exhaust from the truck's engine spewed out of a rusty exhaust pipe.

"The old rattletrap needs a tune-up," Mei commented. She closed the windows and put on the air-conditioner. "Remember the license plate number."

"I got it." Skye wrote it into the memo pad of her phone and hoped in a short time she'd have a name to go with it.

Down a busy two-lane road, the truck slowed as if the driver searched for a particular home. He finally halted in front of a ranch house with a circular driveway. He turned off the engine and jogged to the front door, the six pack of beer in hand.

While he waited, he pushed off the hood and she snatched a good look at him. A vision of the thug standing in Andy's office on the day of his death flashed. She gagged and covered her mouth to prevent a scream.

He turned and watched as they drove by.

Shit. Did he recognize her?

"Skye, did you notice the house number?"

"No. I…I was so shocked to see the guy's face." She swallowed hard. "He came to my office the day my boss died."

Mei nodded. "The mailbox had one word written on it—Romano." Mei signaled her intention to make a left turn. "Could it be the home of Salvatore Romano, owner of The Wine Cave?"

Too upset to answer the question, Skye stared out the back window of the sedan. "You think he saw us? What if he follows?"

Her friend shrugged. "Don't worry. I brought my thirty-eight pistol in case he causes any trouble."

"Damn, Mei."

"It's okay. I have permission to carry a concealed weapon."

Skye opened her mouth to speak but nothing came out.

173

Who was this woman sitting next to her, the little lady who loved organic gardening and spending time with young grandchildren? The woman with a sweet disposition was a stranger to her.

"I'll remember the street name and the house number and you have the license plate to the truck, right? Skye."

"Uh—yeah."

"Okay, good. Let's go home. Jon will want to hear this information."

Would he be pissed she didn't tell him she left the farmhouse with Mei?

Chapter 26

"**You did what!**" Jon's angry voice echoed in the large country kitchen of the farmhouse. "Hell, Skye, are you crazy? I thought I made it clear you should tell me where you are at all times."

"Why? You're not my keeper."

"That's exactly what I am. You hired me—didn't what happened the other night when the hooded figure broke into your house tell you to be careful and not to go out alone?"

"I…" She paused because she'd done her best not to think about what had occurred the other night. She considered challenging him and saying she wasn't by herself. Mei was with her.

Fuming, she thought about yelling at him, but how childish would that be? "I'm not a baby who has to be told what I can do. Sometimes you are so madding."

He might be right, but it rubbed her the wrong way to be scolded by him. Even so, when she saw his startled expression, she laughed. "I'm sorry. I didn't mean to take my anger out on you." Her cheeks heated and she gazed downward.

"Jon, I understand you're trying to help, but sometimes you can be annoying."

He laughed. "You aren't the first to tell me that. My brother has often mentioned it."

"I didn't mean…"

"It's okay, Skye. The whole situation is stressful. Grab a soda and I'll tell you what I learned today. And you can fill me in on your—adventure." He smiled, but his expression soon became serious.

They sat on the couch. She moved away to be sure they wouldn't touch, even by accident.

"You go first." He stretched both legs out in front of him and leaned back against the leather sofa. "Hell. What were you and Mei thinking?"

"We found information, though I admit she scared the pants off of me with her driving. Uh—I mean." She stopped.

"I got it. I've driven with her." He laughed. "But you gave me a scary vision with the two of you racing after an SUV. You could have been in an accident. I can't believe you didn't tell first."

"You were with Webb and I didn't want to interrupt. Besides, Mei acted so fast, I didn't think. I…"

"Doesn't matter now, what did you find out?"

She gulped her cola and slumped into the soft padding of the couch. Without facing him she began, "The man in the hoodie was standing by the tree across the street, like he did before. A silver SUV stopped and picked him up."

In a quick but detailed description, Skye continued until she told her story. "We were lucky to get away. For a second, I thought the guy had recognized me and would follow us. Instead, he went into the ranch house and we drove away." She gasped for air and up looked up at him. "I was never so happy to see this house."

"Don't ever scare the hell out of me again."

"I wasn't aware it would make such a difference to you."

"It does!" Concern flashed across his face and then immediately disappeared.

"Oh." Did he care a bit about her? Or was he trying to keep a good reputation? How would it look if he was working to protect her and she was hurt?

"Webb can run the plates on the truck. It's easy for me to find out who owns the house."

"Did you know Mei has a handgun?"

"Yeah, a thirty-eight. She's a retired police officer. She worked in San Francisco for years, retiring at fifty, then she joined the U.S. government as a translator. She's fluent in Cantonese and Mandarin."

"Well, I'll be. She seems so gentle."

"She's a sweet lady—with the heart of a warrior."

"I believe that and she handles her car like a race car driver."

He laughed. "She's petite, but books shouldn't be judged by their covers."

"I guess."

He rubbed his neck and stretched. "Can you get into Andrew's office?"

"Tonight?"

"Yeah. From what I dug up, he was on a deadline and the end was coming up. We need to act soon."

She thought for a moment, wrinkling her forehead.

"The cleaners will be working in the building tonight—yeah, we can go in through the service entrance. Wait. What did you and your brother learn?"

"I'll tell you on the way to San Francisco."

***

Skye maneuvered the small sedan to the highway and drove south toward San Francisco.

"Jon, what did your brother tell you concerning my boss?"

Silence.

"Did you hear me?" She glanced at him and he opened his eyes.

She looked back at the freeway and pressed the gas pedal down. Why was he reluctant to answer?

He sat up straighter and cleared his throat. "Webb found a name in the Russian newspaper linked to a case he'd been involved in. There is no obvious connection to your boss, but odd Jenkins saved that particular issue of the paper," he mused. "Of course, it could mean nothing—only a coincidence."

"Jon, you don't believe in coincidences?"

"No, but I don't see how it has anything to do with what happened to your boss. Did he ever talk about Russia?"

"I don't remember him mentioning anything.

"Did he read or speak Russian?"

"Not as far as I understand. Of course, I don't know his heritage."

"I don't mean to grill you, Skye. Anyway, it's probably not important."

Even so, she wondered what was in Andy's background. While she worked for him, had he done anything out of concern for Russia?

"One other thing." He interrupted her thinking.

"Yeah."

"You remember I took bits of the blood splatter from Jenkins' office to be analyzed?"

"Sure, and I got his blood type from Ruth."

"Not Jenkins' blood, it belongs to someone else. There had to be another person in his office."

"But he never let anyone in his space. He met clients in the conference room."

"Maybe he didn't commit suicide."

She swerved the steering wheel and drove into the slow lane. "Are you saying you've never believed he was killed? Damn you."

"Whoa, Skye, watch the road."

"You never trusted me. All this time I..."

"Calm down. That's not what I meant. This is proof he wasn't alone in his private office. The police didn't act on your report because they believed nothing happened." He touched her hand, sending a jolt of heat through her.

"Don't."

"Be fair, Skye, they didn't look for evidence because they thought it wasn't necessary. The officers jumped to the obvious suicide conclusion as a way to quickly close the case. Many police departments are overwhelmed with open files. After all, Andrew's situation had no obvious indicators suggesting a suspicious death."

"But I told the investigators." She tried to manage her anger and control her rapid breathing.

"Hey," He reached over and adjusted the wheel because she accidentally veered into the fast lane. "Skye, be careful."

"I'm okay." She focused on the freeway. "Jon, I explained what happened. They wouldn't listen."

"You had no proof."

"But I..." She stopped. Annoying, but he told the truth. She'd been hysterical, and couldn't even give a good description of the men. "But with the blood test, we have proof someone murdered Andy."

"Not exactly. We can show a person, other than your boss, bled in his private office."

"But…"

"Unless we find documented proof someone threw him out of the window, his death will still be considered a suicide."

She gasped.

"Look, Skye, we collected the blood sample months after the incident. How many cleaners and others came into the office since his death? The authorities would say anyone could have cut or scratched themselves, drawing blood."

She groaned and then drove in silence. No point in trying to convince Jon to show the information to the police. As a government agent, he must be experienced in such matters.

***

The office building where Skye had worked for the last six years took on an eerie glow in the dead of night. Should they be there? Almost as if he understood her reluctance, Jon took her hand and led her around to the back of the building.

She noticed how well he managed with the medical boot, barely limping as he moved to the service entrance.

Though the door was closed, they found it unlocked. They entered and walked to the lobby, ignoring the man polishing the floor with a huge machine. He wore headphones and didn't appear to be aware of them.

In the elevator on the way up to the twelfth level, she began to tremble. "I can't stop shaking. I thought this time I'd be okay. To be honest, I never really believed I'd return to Andy's office suite again."

The elevator door opened smoothly to a place she'd once considered a home away from home. She froze.

Do this for Andy. Shoulders back, she moved into the office.

"We've looked over the outer lobby and conference room, but something you said earlier triggered a memory. You told me of a day you came to work early and found Jenkins in his office."

"It was weird. I found him on his knees behind his desk. A chunk of drywall lay on the carpet next to him. He quickly placed a vent cover over the hole in the wall and screwed it in place." She moved toward the back of the room and pointed. "Here."

"Did he say anything?"

"He said remember this if anything ever happens to me." She swallowed a sob, sat in a chair and stared out of the window. "This is where he lost his life."

"Anything else?"

"How can you be so hard? He died in front of me."

"I'm trying to make sure nothing happens to you. Skye, help by answering me."

"I laughed at him and said nothing was going to happen and Andy said, 'From your mouth to God's ears.'"

With his pocket knife, Jon unscrewed the register cover.

"It's fake. Just a hole in the wall." Skye knelt and scooped up everything in the hiding place. She carried it to Andrew's desk and sat in his chair and spread the papers out before her.

Jon picked up a small piece of notepaper. "It looks

like this is the password for the Cayman Island bank account." He handed it to her.

"The date is my mother's birthday! Why would Andy use my mom's? It should have been Ruth's mom."

"Because you'd never forget your mother's birthday."

"Why would I need the account information?"

"Skye, you know the answer. I don't think you want to admit it. Jenkins wanted you, not his wife."

"No. I never gave him any reason to think I was interested in a relationship with him. Never!"

Jon stared. "You didn't need to convince me. Regardless of your feelings, the old man had a fantasy—you apparently. He put you on his accounts to prove the issue."

"No way."

"Appears he dreamed of the two of you living in the Grand Cayman Island together, sun, surf, sex and money."

"That's disgusting. He was like another dad to me." She dropped the note and walked to the window. "He never even so as much as put a kiss on my cheek."

Jon came to her and wrapped her in his arms. "I believe you."

***

"Thank you." She relaxed a little. "Jon, I just…"

"Skye." He caressed her cheek with the back of his hand. "I understand." He paused. "Let's find out what else he hid."

"All right." She sighed.

They took the documents from the office, and in the silence of the late night, sat in the conference room looking through the paperwork.

"I'm staring at the secrets of a man I thought I knew. How did a sweet middle-aged man, who appeared to have nothing to conceal, in fact, be someone completely different and I didn't realize?" She swallowed hard. "It turns my stomach when I think what this information would do to Ruth if she ever found out."

"It's possible she may have to be questioned."

"No. Jon, it would break her heart. She spent thirty years of her life loving him and now that he's gone, she must never grasp who he…" She covered her mouth, unable to say more.

"I can't promise, but I'll do what's possible to keep this on a need-to-know basis."

"Thanks."

A few minutes later Jon cleared his throat. "Skye, Salvatore Romano presented himself as the owner of The Wine Cave, but guess who holds the paper on the place?"

"I don't have a clue."

"You remember I mentioned my brother found the name of a Russian oligarch in the newspaper Jenkins gave to you?"

"Yeah." Skye glanced at him. "But what does that mean?"

"According to this," he waved a letter, "the Russian holds a short-term loan on Romano's business and the note comes due in a matter of days."

"And Andrew took Mr. Romano's funds and sent them to the Cayman Islands," she completed his statement.

"Looks like."

"Andy's dead."

"And who has control of the account now?"

"You mean me." A shiver ran down her spine.

"Yeah, Skye, and how many other clients did he steal from and take their funds off-shore?"

Shocked at the notion, she sat open-mouthed but silent. What could she say and what should she do now? She picked up another report. "Dear God," she gasped. "Jon, I just found airline and hotel reservations for the Grand Cayman Island. Both are in Andrew's name and mine. I swear he didn't tell me about them. This is the first time I've seen the bookings."

***

In his office at The Wine Cave, Salvatore Romano gazed at the blackness of his Sonoma vineyards. At three in the morning, all seemed bleak. Soon the orange harvest moon would shine on the rolling fields lighting everything with a yellow hue. The golden land he loved, now mocked him for his stupidity and greed. He groaned and shook the memories of future plans from his head. Would the winery and the surrounding land, still be his by the time of the hunter's moon rose?

Now, the weather was too hot and dry for his new vines to survive much longer. Even if the days had been perfect, the cost of water during this drought was becoming unbearable. If he had his precious savings… Under his breath, he cursed Andrew Jenkins. "Stronzo!" The asshole deserved to die.

"Merda!" Salvatore spit. His mama always said his temper would be the ruin of him. Throwing Jenkins out of the window was not part of his strategy, at least not until he had recouped the funds. However, when the man stone-walled him and refused to return anything,

Sal's temper flared. When Andrew told him there was nothing he could do about it, everything had gone terribly wrong. And the girl, of all the bad luck, had entered the private office in time to see him.

He gulped the rest of his private reserve wine and stumbled toward the sideboard, to replenish his crystal goblet.

Maybe he could talk to Ms. Turner, and plead his case until she realized her boss had stolen his money.

In the dark, he banged his knee and nearly fell to the floor. *Hell.* What was he doing? Blotto now, the last thing he needed was more alcohol. He threw the goblet across the room. It hit a handmade pottery lamp on the side table and they both crashed to the hardwood floor, shattering.

Jenkins' secretary, Skye Turner, must have what he needed. So, no more kid gloves, it was time to get her cooperation or know the reason why.

Chapter 27

"Jon, I'm going to the police." Skye stood from Andrew Jenkins' desk and searched for her bag. "I can use my cell phone."

"And tell them what?"

"I…"

"If the money is in the Cayman Islands, the case would be out of the local police's jurisdiction. After you reported Andrew's murder and got no attention, why do you think they'd be interested in a farfetched recounting of a possible theft?"

"Someone needs to understand."

"Look, Skye, I commend your desire to do the right thing." He took a deep breath and moved closer. "But at this point, your protection is the most important thing. The other matters can wait. Do you honestly believe even if you gave the money back, there wouldn't be a consequence to you?"

"If I gave the funds to the police, I'd be safe. Wouldn't I?"

He turned away, letting the question hang in the air.

His silence was a response. *Damn.* Would she ever be secure again?

"Let's gather this paperwork and get out of here."

He scooped up everything and stashed it in his backpack. "It'll be dawn soon, better if no one sees us."

"Jon, what about the cameras?"

"The cleaning crews should be finished by now. We'll take care of any surveillance on the way out."

***

On Highway 101 going north, the glare of the headlights coming at the car blinded Jon. He groaned and covered his eyes against the flashes of the brightness.

"You all right?"

"Yeah, just tired."

It was almost true. His body ached for sleep, but his vision was getting worse. How long could he deny the truth? His brother had told him to go to a specialist. The thought of the news the doctor might deliver held him back. He was trained to fight in battle, facing a bayonet, rifle or even a rocket-propelled grenade, but how did he fight this?

Until he heard the words, "You're going blind," he could pretend life would return to normal. Only his leg needed to complete the healing process. Soon, he'd be back at work. Maybe then he could let Skye understand how he felt.

Keep fooling yourself. How far would lying to himself take him?

If he was out of commission, who would protect Skye? The authorities didn't appear to be interested. His problem could wait until she was safe.

"Hey," she yelled and slammed on the brakes of the sedan.

His seatbelt tightened, sending him against the back of the seat and headrest. "Skye, you okay?" He opened his eyes, but everything remained dark. *Shit*. He shut them again.

"A damn truck suddenly stopped for no reason—you all right?"

"Good—all good." He blinked, shook his head and peeked out at a colorless blur. With a silent moan, he considered the isolation of day-to-day living if his sight never returned.

***

Hope makes a poor dinner but a good breakfast, to paraphrase Francis Bacon, Jon supposed as he woke on the leather couch in the cottage. The sun shone through the cracks in the window shades. His vision had returned clear as he ever. The messy room looked beautiful. He wanted to shout yahoo but feared he'd wake Skye sleeping in the bedroom.

"Thank God." He sat back and enjoyed the view of the dirty dishes on the kitchen counter.

Later, he took off the plastic medical boot and rotated his ankle. With a cringe, he worked through the discomfort and remembered the doctor's words, "It will hurt, but ignore the pain and do the work. You'll grow stronger. If you don't, you'll never be your old self again."

Damned if it wasn't true. In the last few days, the muscles responded and the pain lessened. Soon, he hoped to throw away the boot and walk freely—even run.

"Hi."

Skye's husky voice caused him to smile. "Hi, yourself. Sleep well?"

"Yeah, I did." She smoothed the blue plaid pajamas he'd lent her.

She grinned and he was tempted to comment on her sexy appearance but thought better of it.

She yawned, pushed her long hair out of her face and sat so close to him that he smelled her floral shampoo.

"It's a beautiful day. I want to work in the garden and pretend the last few months never happened."

He reached for her. She leaned against him and let her head rest on his chest. What would it be like to have her in his life every day and realize after work she'd be waiting for him?

She turned to look up at him and he kissed her. With a sigh, she ran her hands through his blond hair.

He traced her mouth with his fingertips, then roamed her body, to follow her curves while he trailed kisses on her neck. For the first time, he realized she wore no bra. Her nipples peaked as he caressed them and his need grew.

"Jon, I've needed this for so long," she moaned, found his mouth and teased him with her tongue.

Desire raged in him, but he closed his eyes in opposition to the need to take her.

"No, Skye."

"Why not? You want me. And I ..."

"It wouldn't be fair to you."

"But..."

"Right now, our lives are so complicated, better not to add to the intensity of the situation." He avoided a direct answer. "Skye, I like you, but..."

"That's another way of saying you're not interested in me. Okay—I understand." She held out her hand.

He stared at her. "What are you doing?"

"Shake and I'll remember to keep things on a

professional footing. Isn't that what businessmen do?"

"I'll never think of you as a male." He gazed at her pert breasts pushing against the cotton fabric of the PJs she wore. "I only want to be sure you stay safe, Skye. And I have to deal my own issues."

"Issues?"

"Work in the garden and I'll let my brother know about the information we found last night. He may have a few ideas to help you out."

"But…Whatever." Her eyes flashed and her full mouth tightened. She stormed out of the cottage, slamming the door behind her.

Damn, she's gorgeous when she's angry.

***

Salvatore awoke with a raging headache. Though he didn't recall doing so, he'd made his way to the suite last night and flopped on the king bed.

Fully clothed, he still wore his handmade Italian leather loafers. With a groan, he sat up and tried to swallow. *Shit.* Not bothering to find a glass, he grabbed the metal carafe of water on the nightstand and drank until it was empty. He choked, coughed and spit slid down his chin.

You better get your act together or…

His ass was in a ringer. Unless he got hold of his cash, he'd soon be homeless. The Russian oligarch, Igor was happy to offer the loan. He'd be doubly pleased to toss him out and take the property.

Hell. Hate for Jenkins filled Sal, if the man was in the room, he would kill him again.

Was Skye Turner an innocent pawn or did she and Jenkins plan to spend the money together?

It was all hers now and she'd never need to eke out a

living as a secretary again.

No way she'd let it go of the assets. He sure as hell wouldn't. If he wanted his funds, he needed to intimidate her, and put everything she loved in jeopardy.

He stumbled out of bed and dialed. "Kid, I need you. Get your rear here, ASAP."

***

Skye ran down the path from the cottage and was halfway to the farmhouse before she realized she was still wearing Jon's pajamas. Would it be a good idea to go back and get her things in the bedroom of the old adobe?

Tears began to slide from her eyes and she rubbed them away and groaned at the thought of seeing him again.

Embarrassed for making overtures to him and then demanding he shake her hand... Her cheeks burned. Still, he wanted to kiss her. They both wanted it, but he'd mentioned his issues. What? Maybe if he shared them...

Get real. M*ind your own business.*

If she did something stupid again, it might signal the end of his participation in this investigation.

Skye entered the house through the unlocked backdoor. The realization of how foolish it had been to not secure the door before leaving struck her. As a routine, she always locked the windows and front door but had a habit of leaving the back entrance unsecured in the safe neighborhood.

Times have changed. She groaned. Her world had spun out of control and even here in her new home, she wasn't safe. All because Andrew Jenkins was a dishonest man. For the first time in her life, she hated someone.

An hour later, after a long tub bath, Skye sat on the living room couch wearing her favorite worn jeans and a blue T-shirt. The rest of the paper correspondence Andrew left for her sat in a box near her bare feet.

Why he'd chosen to keep paper files was a mystery, but here they were in black and white. She returned one file and reached for another.

The more she learned about her boss, the more reasons she found to detest the man. How could she have believed him to be a kind sincere gentleman—a man of integrity?

His files were filled with blackmail information about individuals who were his clients. How was he able to amass a group of men with such dubious histories? Whatever the answer, they appeared to have trusted him.

Perhaps that was his strength. He seemed to be a trustworthy man. The guy they could rely on to keep their secrets and protect their back.

In the silence of the old farmhouse, she realized the dynamite information she held in her hands. The idea men would kill to get it back struck like a punch to the gut. The image of Andy struggling to save himself just before he was shoved out the window of his penthouse office played in her mind.

With a sudden chill running down her back, she realized as long as she had these files, her risk would continue to be extreme.

Andrew had carefully documented each client's wrongdoing. He'd left her the reports without a warning to be aware of the hazards involved.

Hidden in plain sight in a box of old correspondence, at first glance, the files appeared to be of no importance. They sat buried under the piles of other useless letters. She thought Jon had the important material.

Only an extremely patient person, or someone who had nothing to do on a miserable day, like her, would take the time to wade through the myriad of minutia to find these.

What should she do now? Though the police hadn't been helpful up to this point, would it be something to show them? *Damn.* She wanted to ask Jon but...

She pulled out the next letter and read it. A Russian name jumped out at her, Igor Volkov. It meant nothing to her. However, there was a similar name in the foreign newspaper taken to be translated.

Again, she wanted to talk to Jon—but not today. Her embarrassment was too strong to entertain the thought of contacting him again.

She stood and stretched. Where should she hide the files? Under the bed? Back in the closet? She shook her head. As Andy had done, it must be in plain sight but somewhat unusual.

She entered the kitchen and scanned the room, then opened the fridge. She emptied the vegetable drawers with carrots, cucumbers, and assorted greens. After putting the papers in freezer bags, she stored the letters in the drawers, covered them with the vegetables, and closed the refrigerator door.

She sighed and grabbed an apple to munch on.

The doorbell rang.

Jon—no, he wouldn't use the bell.

No one had used it since she'd moved in. All the

neighbors knocked.

From the window over the sink, she glanced at a middle-aged woman dressed in jeans and a chambray cotton shit. The lady looked harmless, even familiar, though she couldn't remember where she'd seen her.

When she peeked at the stranger through the sidelight, the stranger smiled at her.

Still cautious, Skye opened the door slowly.

"Skye Turner?"

"Yes?"

Chapter 28

"**Hi. I'm Kate.** I stopped by to see Mr. Lancaster, but he's not home. I wondered…"

"He's not?" Skye glanced outside. His car was gone. However, a huge white SUV was parked in front of the house. A man wearing dark sunglasses sat in the driver's seat.

"Could I come in for a moment?"

"Oh, of course." She stood back and let the woman enter.

"I've always liked this old house, but you've added pretty to the décor."

"Thank you. You've been here before?"

"A couple of times. Whenever I'm in the area."

Skye shook her head, suspicious of every stranger. "How do you know Jon?"

"May I sit down?"

The woman didn't appear dangerous. "Uh—sure." She backed up and almost tripped over the box of letters still in front of the couch. She quickly slid the paperwork under the end table and motioned to Kate. "Sit. Have we met?" Skye stared at the woman as she settled on the sofa.

"I don't think so."

"You look so familiar. I was sure... I just don't remember where."

"I'm Kathryn Nielsen. Kate to my friends."

"No shit!" The words slipped out before Skye thought better of them and embarrassment burned her cheeks. "You're the First Lady. OMG."

Kate smiled. "The Lancaster's have been my friends for some time."

"Well, I'll be...May I offer you something—to drink?" What was the First Lady doing in her home? Jon knew Kate? Was her friend? It showed how little she understood the man.

"Skye?" Kate waved at her.

"Oh, I'm sorry. What did you say?"

"Any tea?"

"Yeah, green tea or lemon herb?" God, she was acting like a star-struck kid seeing a movie or rock star, completely tongue-tied.

"Lemon sounds refreshing."

"Great. I'll be right back." She entered the kitchen and froze in place. She glanced at her torn jeans and faded T-shirt. Of all the days to wear her worst clothes.

With the tray of tea and almond cookies, she went into the living room. What should she say to the First Lady? Why was Kate here? Something had to be transpiring. As a renter on the property, did she deserve to find out?

Kate put her at ease with small talk. Soon they were talking about gardening and she told Kate the dream of starting a vineyard. The woman shared the fact she was looking for a house in the Bay Area and Jon's sister-in-law was helping her search for one.

"Jon likes you." Kate surprised her.

Skye coughed and cleared her throat. "He's a nice man. I'm happy to live in this house. It's so hard to find anything to rent for a reasonable price in Sonoma. I'm a student, so my budget's tight."

Kate nodded and sipped her tea. "I mean he *likes* you."

Skye choked and took another sip of her drink. "He does?" How would the first lady know? Did she guess how she felt about him? "How can you…"

"He's an employee, though I'd like to think we are friends and he mentioned you. He didn't need to say much. It was in his voice when he said your name."

"Well, I'll be. "I *like* him too. I've never responded to anyone the way I do to him. I care and worry about him. Kate, today I kissed him and made a fool of myself." She hesitated. "I understand he lost his wife in a brutal way—I should have waited for him to make the move."

She was talking too much, but there was something about Kate. Skye felt her secrets would be safe. "I hope you won't tell Jon. I don't understand why I'm saying all this. Guess I needed someone to talk to. I'm sorry."

"I'm glad to realize he has someone who feels affection for him. In the last two years, life hasn't been easy."

They sat in silence drinking the tea until Skye finally asked, "Kate, if you don't mind my asking, what does he do for work—exactly?"

The First Lady frowned. "He spends much of his time in Northern Europe," she said evading the answer to the question. "Of course, as a Norwegian speaker, the Government sends him there. Part of our contingent to monitor the Russian border."

"He speaks Norwegian?"

"Along with French and German. In that part of the world, his ability to ski is an asset, too."

"I had no idea." She bit into a cookie and the crumbs landed in her lap. She brushed them away and swallowed. "Once, I asked if he skied. He said he did."

"He was on the U.S. Olympic downhill ski team."

"No way! He never told me. Only said he hoped to ski again when his leg healed."

"He wouldn't say anything—too modest. Skiing's been an important part of his life." She took a sip of tea. "This is not the first broken bone received in the line of duty. Something I hate to recall, but such is the job." Kate picked up a cookie but returned it to the plate without taking a bite.

"Will he go back to Europe when he returns to work?"

"I couldn't say. He and Webb will make the decision."

Kate finished the tea and set the cup and saucer on the coffee table. "Skye, Jon's leg will heal. It's his eyes that worry me."

"His eyes?"

"Oh, I hope I didn't speak out of turn. Since he cares for you, I thought maybe he'd shared…"

"No, but I sensed something was wrong. I wanted to ask but... He's helped me so much. What can I do?"

"I brought the name of a doctor. One of the best in the nation. I didn't want to put it in a text or phone call—mine are monitored and this is a private matter. If you could give it to him, I'd be grateful."

"Sure." She took the small envelope. "Kate, thanks for telling me." On an impulse, Skye hugged the First

Lady, then jumped back. "I shouldn't have done that."

"Don't worry." Kate smiled. "I better go. Please tell Jon I stopped by to say hello."

Sky waved goodbye to Kate, as the man jumped out of the SUV to open the door for her. The Secret service?

An hour later, Jon still hadn't returned. With his eyes, should he be driving?

Skye peered out of the front window in time to see Mei and her grandchildren wave and drive away.

Alone in the neighborhood, a sense of abandonment overwhelmed her.

***

The kid slammed the phone down onto the nightstand. "Get your ass over here!" he mimicked Salvatore, then grunted. Time to jettison the relationship with the asshole.

He threw back the sheet and sat up. What time was it? Too damned early, whatever the hour. He wandered into the kitchen and grabbed a mug of cold stale coffee, then carried it to the bathroom.

Dressed in his usual jeans, T-shirt and dark hoodie, Terry Nowland slammed the door of his basement apartment and jogged to his wreck of a truck.

The clunker wouldn't look too bad once he completed the paint job. But for now, the grey primed fenders stuck out against the original turquoise paint of the vehicle.

The lock on the driver's side struck, so, he entered the passenger's side and crawled to the driver's seat and tried to start the engine. At first it didn't turn over. He wanted to stomp on the pedal but instead tried the key once more. The old engine sputtered to life.

Reggi Allder

The gas gauge was broken, so to be sure he didn't run out of fuel, he decided to stop for a few gallons on the way to Salvatore's place.

He pulled out the last of his cash, a crumbled twenty-dollar bill from his jean pocket. "Shit." That left him five bucks and some change to buy a breakfast burrito and coffee on the way.

Terry entered The Wine Cave's private quarters for the first time, and a maid opened the door and ushered him into Sal's inner sanctum. Romano must be desperate if he let him into his domain. The suite was decorated in California swank, nothing too good for the vineyard owner. All fine to Terry, aka the kid. His price just went up.

Dressed in monogrammed white silk pajamas and black velvet slippers, Salvatore sat at a glass dining table laden with food.

Even though Terry's stomach burned from eating the spicy burrito and black coffee, the aroma of the food caused him to salivate.

His employer glanced up from his bone china plate. "About time, kid." He pushed his plate away. "Come into the den."

So much for the idea he might be offered sustenance.

"Here's the deal, I need Skye Turner. She has information that is rightfully mine." Romano plopped down on his chair behind an ornate desk and put his feet up. "Since you were not able to find the file at her house, there is no way she is going to return it unless we give her motivation."

"Like what? Money? You don't need me for that."

"If I had all the money in the world, I wouldn't give

200

a dime to the bitch. Not after what she and Jenkins did to me."

Surprised by the vehemence of the words, Terry remained silent and waited for his boss to calm down

Sitting on a small chair near the desk, he glanced at the red-faced man. Slowly, Romano's color returned to normal.

"If you want me to hurt the woman, it will cost you," Terry offered.

"I want her in good condition, at least while she holds the data I need."

"I don't get it."

"Healthy, but under my control. After I have what I want, she can disappear."

"Won't her people wonder…"

"I've taken care of things. There will be a trail to Belize." He shrugged. "Let them search."

Terry scratched his head and stared at his boss again. "Before I do anything, I need a down payment and an agreement on the full price for the deal."

Salvatore grunted but nodded his agreement. "Name your fee."

Astonished by the quick acquiescence, he grinned and doubled the number.

"You need to grab Turner. Don't screw up."

"And bring her where?"

"I've arranged a spot for her in one of the unused caves on the property." He stood and stretched. "It would be best if you took her at night under the cover of darkness."

From a locked drawer in a cabinet against the wall, Sal counted out more money than he'd ever seen in cash and handed it to him. "Here, kid. Let me know where you want the rest deposited."

A few minutes later, Terry shivered as he followed Sal deep into a dark, musty, and dank cave in the mountain. Unused wooden barrels lined the rock walls and a single light bulb hung from the ceiling.

"She can scream all she wants, but no one will hear. The girl is not leaving until I have what I need."

Terry shuddered at the thought of being locked in the cold dark cave.

The sooner he took Skye Turner and this job was complete, the better.

Chapter 29

The Russian oligarch, Igor Volkov, should not be in California. It wasn't in his original plan.

Salvatore Romano had guaranteed a high rate of return on his money when he suggested Volkov use Andrew Jenkins as his American financial advisor.

Now because of Romano, Jenkins was dead. Salvatore needed to learn a lesson. Igor would meet him in person. He would have his money back or receive the keys to Salvatore's winery.

Driving north on Highway 101, he frowned as the dry ugly California hills rushed by. Called the golden hills by the citizens of the state, he preferred the green of the mountains near his home. He closed the window of the imported German sedan and put the air conditioner on high, and then swore under his breath.

Get your anger under control. No man was at his best when livid. Certainly, Sal had learned that when he tossed Jenkins out of the twelfth-floor window. Igor wouldn't make the same mistake with Romano, but he would still take the man for everything had.

Damn, he didn't want the man's winery. But if it took that threat to secure the funds entrusted to Romano…

Still, something unexpected had come out of the fiasco. Igor had found Jon Lancaster, the younger son of the man who killed his father. He swallowed the sweet taste of possible revenge.

He might take care of two problems at the same time. Recoup his funds and kill a U.S. Government Rapid Advance Task Force member wanted by his family for years.

He smiled and turned down the air conditioner. His heartbeat slowed and his breathing returned to normal as his anger retreated.

***

In the bedroom of the farmhouse, Skye dressed in a favorite outfit, a sleeveless, V-neck, chambray cotton dress belted at the waist, then flowing to her knees. She stepped into her silver leather sandals and wiped tears from her eyes, applied lipstick and flicked her shampooed hair back.

It was her birthday. With all the problems in her life, she'd forgotten until she received a card in the mail. "We'll be out of town, but have a good day, Love, Mom and Dad. P.S. Buy something nice for yourself." A hundred-dollar check was tucked neatly into the card.

She tossed the card onto the coffee table. *Have a good day—fat chance. The day was over.*

Night had arrived, but Jon had not returned. He probably hated her and was searching for a way out of his offer to help.

She received a "Happy Birthday" text from her best friend, who was still in Japan for another year of teaching. Damn, she missed her friend.

Exasperation filled her as she sniffed and scrubbed tears from her cheeks with the palm of her hand. *Stop feeling sorry for yourself. Move on.* Jon is never going to care for you. Not in the way you do for him. She was being selfish. He had problems too.

With Jon helping her, she'd been able to pretend all would work out and soon everything would be fine.

Maybe she might ignore the Jenkins' bank accounts and the fact he had put her name on them. If the funds stayed untouched in a Cayman Island bank, what was the harm?

She groaned, closed her eyes and rubbed her forehead. Men were after her and no matter the denial, she couldn't change the past or alter what the guys wanted from her. Before they found her, the funds in the account must be dealt with, but how?

Don't think about it anymore tonight.

With a bowl of popcorn sitting next to her, she gorged herself on the carbos and started to stream a favorite movie, one about saving the world. No romance, only people blowing up everything in sight, releasing her need to do the same.

Was that a knock on the door or only another

explosion in the movie? She paused the film and went to look out through the sidelight.

"We need to talk." Jon stood back from the door and stared at her. What should she do? *Are you up to dealing with him?*

"Skye."

"Jon, I don't think I want…"

"Just open the door."

The expression on his face was hard to decipher, but she wondered if he wanted to apologize. Unlikely, but she would never find out if she didn't talk to him.

She relented and he walked in. Strong, tall, self-assured, his piercing blue eyes scanned her.

***

"Skye, you've been crying." Delicate, pale and trembling, she blinked back a tear. "It's my birthday. I'm twenty-five today. I forgot until a card from my parents came in the mail." She caught a tear with the back of her hand. "Don't mind me. I'm being silly."

She started to turn from him when he touched her hand and brought her to him. He brushed another tear from her face.

"Happy Birthday," his voice was husky, showing emotion he couldn't hide. Damn, no matter how hard he tried to ignore his love when he was near her, he failed.

"Thank you, Jon."

Still holding her hand, he coaxed her to him and wrapped her in his arms. The aroma of her floral shampoo wafted to him and he breathed in deeply. "Are you okay?"

"Yeah."

"You sure?" He pushed her hair back from her face, then bent to kiss her cheek, tasting the salt left from her tears. He pulled back. "Skye, I want to kiss your lips. Not shake your hand."

"I was stupid this morning."

"No, Skye, it was me. I acted like a fool."

She sighed when he pressed his lips on hers. Hunger roared in him. The need to take her hard and fast pushed against his desire to demonstrate his concern for her. Her moan of pleasure as his tongue played with hers, almost undid his self-control.

Her full breast pressed against him as he tightened his grip, his rapid-fire breathing increasing as she ran her fingers through is hair.

Finally, she pulled away. "I can't breathe. My heart's pounding so fast. Feel." She took his hand to her heart. "Your kiss is overwhelming. I've never experienced anything like it."

His heart was racing too and a sensation unfamiliar to him went through him like fire more intense than anything he'd ever felt with Miranda.

How much should he tell Skye about his emotions? Realizing she had as much as necessary to handle, he kept his love for her to himself. Later, if and when both their lives were restored to normal and the time seemed right…

They walked to the couch and sat down. He put his arm around her and she rested her head against his shoulder. Together they watched the movie world being saved as they shared cold popcorn and hot kisses.

***

In the kitchen of the farmhouse, Jon sat at the table. Early in the morning, Skye slept. He forced his mind from the sweet recollection of her touch as she welcomed his attention. He'd used all his self-control not to bed her. He wouldn't, not when she was vulnerable and needy. His job was to keep her safe and he wouldn't fail like he had with Miranda. Even if he didn't survive, Skye would.

Time to concentrate on the new data found in the box in the living room. He rubbed his forehead and poured over the letters.

With a shake of his head, his eyes came back into focus, and he read the dispatch again. Damning evidence concerning Jenkins' connection to the Russian oligarch, Igor Volkov, why hadn't Andrew secured this under lock and key? Instead, he'd had his wife, Ruth, deliver this and the other paperwork to Skye.

A chill ran through Jon. A foreign government was hatching a scheme to bring Russian rubles into the U.S. and launder them by investing in the Jenkins Company. According to the communication, the funds were to be used later in real estate investments in California, New York, and Washington D.C.

What were the nefarious plans? With Jon's experience concerning the oligarch's family, something was in the works to damage the U.S. What?

When should he share this material with his brother? Until he figured out the plan, would Webb, as leader of the Rapid Advance Task Force, be interested?

Was Volkov in the States now, or were the transactions accomplished online?

Too many questions without answers.

Damn. He'd hoped never to hear the existence of Volkov again. He pushed back his dish of half-eaten eggs and toast. Nausea turned his stomach at the thought of his dead wife and child, harmed because of his work.

Any idea he and Skye might have a chance together vanished. Not as long as any possibility she would be tangled in his family's intrigue existed. *Shit.* Had she already found herself involved—no matter how innocently?

From the box on the floor, he reached for another stack of papers and set them on the table, but didn't read them. Though he wished it wasn't true, his brother needed to understand what he'd discovered.

Webb had recently gone through a trauma and wanted time to recoup. The last thing desired was a reminder of the danger he'd survived. Jon grunted. The return of the Volkov family overcame his brother's wishes.

Jon ran his hand over his chin and grabbed another

letter. His eyes blurred. He blinked and read it again. Igor's strategy was to start a super pack with the misleading name Americans for America.

The recently laundered capital would send money to politicians willing to support the Kremlin, giving the communist another chance to control the U.S. Government from within.

It surprised him so many men running for office were willing to look the other way and not ask the right questions when tempted with dearly needed funds to defeat their opposition. Were they that naïve? Perhaps see no evil, speak no evil was their motto. Or could be the desire for power overrode their ethics and their belief in U.S. constitutional law. Perhaps the men had no ethics, no moral compass.

Though Jon believed money could be the root of all evil, too many people regarded the rich as morally superior because of the wealth they had accrued. Some politicians would never check into Igor's background, instead, they'd rely on his wealth as an indicator of his purity.

Jon had searched for reasons to explain why Salvatore Romano killed Andrew Jenkins, but never thought the hunt would lead to a Russian oligarch and danger to the U.S.

Hell. Decisions must be made soon.

Chapter 30

Skye entered the kitchen and found Jon, fully dressed in a white polo shirt and blue jeans, sitting at the table staring at an envelope in his hand.

"Morning." She bent down to kiss his cheek.

"Skye, I didn't hear you come in."

She smiled, but it wasn't returned. The warmth she'd enjoyed last night had disappeared.

"I made coffee. Grab a mug." He put the envelope back in the box.

"Okay."

"We need to talk." His voice was harsh and she didn't like the foreboding emotion running through her. What now? How could things be any worse?

With a mug of dark brown liquid, she sat next to him and reached for the sugar bowl. A full teaspoon of sweetness plopped into her cup and she stirred, careful not to spill any coffee. After a restless night, she needed the energy to handle a day that appeared to be destined to test her stamina.

Jon squeezed her hand for a second before letting releasing it. "Did you realize you have a bank card for the Cayman Island account?"

"Do I?"

"Your name is on it. I found it in a business envelope in the pile of paperwork."

"No way." Again, she wondered why Andrew hadn't told her. Not that it mattered at this point. "Does that mean I can check the account balance? I mean the deposit account might be empty."

"This Cayman Island bank has links to an American bank. It's possible you might be able to check with the local branch office of the U.S. bank and retrieve the information."

"Would it be that easy?" Nothing else had been, but maybe they were in line for a break.

"Have breakfast and we'll go find out."

"When I know the balance, then what?"

"You're asking a complicated question. Let's take one step at a time. If the balance is small, possibly you would be able to drop the whole thing, but…"

"If there isn't much money that would explain why Andy never told me about it."

"I wouldn't count on the idea of little or no funds."

She took a drink and choked as the hot coffee went down the wrong way.

"You okay?" Jon stood and gently patted her back.

She coughed, nodded, and wiped her chin. "Yeah, I'm fine. It was hotter than I expected."

Heat rose in her. Not only because of the warm drink, but Jon's touch caused a fire to flow in her veins and sent a flush to her cheeks.

Their eyes caught and he leaned toward her. "Skye."

She held her breath, waiting for his kiss.

His eyes scanned her as if he wanted to memorize every feature. His face was so close, but she resisted running her fingertips over his lips to coax them to link with hers. Heart pounding, breathing quickened, without realizing what she was doing, her tongue ran over her bottom lip.

His expression softened. He caressed her cheek with the back of his hand, as he learned nearer.

"Eat something, Skye. I'd like to leave in twenty minutes."

Stunned, she was unable to speak.

He left the room without glancing at her again.

Disappointed, she slumped into a chair.

***

When he heard Skye enter her bedroom and slam the door, he returned and called Kate on the secure phone she'd given him. The president and his wife were on vacation in the area, rare for them to take time off. He hated to interrupt the couple. Still, Kate must be alerted to this new information on the Russian. She would pass it to the president.

As he learned more, the rest of the Rapid Advance Task Force would be notified.

He could use a good accountant. One name came to mind, Juan Garcia. Had he returned to California? Not only a buddy and Task Force member but one of the brightest minds on the team. Accounting was his expertise. No one loved digging into numbers more than Juan and understanding hidden accounts, fun and games for him. Jon would text him.

After Jon spoke with the First Lady, he sent a message to Webb, "Bro, we need to talk. M."

Using Miranda's initial would let Webb realize this

was Task Force business.

His phone whistled with an incoming text containing one word, "Noon."

The old-fashioned regulator clock on the wall stated the time as ten-fifteen. *Shit.* There wasn't time to go to the city, retrieve the banking info, and be back by noon to meet Webb.

Skye would be frustrated, but there wasn't any other way to do both meetings efficiently.

The team needed this report, but it had to be delivered in person. A hard and fast rule that kept them alive and the team safe, no emails, no clouds, nothing important in a text.

Suddenly tired, the weight of his past connection with the Volkov family dragged him down. He limped to the kitchen counter and poured more coffee.

After sitting so long, his leg muscles twitched and he almost fell, recovering in time but spilling the hot liquid. With a curse, he wondered how much longer he'd be saddled with the medical boot limiting both his speed and balance.

Tempted to remove the damn thing, he sat clumsily and drank what was left in the mug. *Don't do anything stupid. Skye needs you.*

"Jon, what's wrong?"

Skye entered dressed in a navy business suit, with her brown hair pulled back in a silver clasp.

"Be careful, I spilled my coffee."

"No worries." She grabbed a paper towel and gracefully wiped the spot on the floor.

He admired the curve of her rear as she did the deed, she truly was beautiful, maybe not in the skinny, plastic, Hollywood sense, but in a Renoir style. A female you could hold tight and feel your arms were filled with a real woman.

"I thought I'd try to be businesslike. Since we're going to the bank and all." She tossed the paper towel into the compost. "I haven't worn this since Andrew…" She sniffed and turned from him.

"You look nice." He scanned her. I've never seen you so…"

"Like an adult, not a student?"

"I wasn't going to say so, but yeah. Still, you always look good to me."

"Thanks." She grinned appearing pleased by his statement.

"Unfortunately, there's been a change in plans. Webb will be here at noon. You and I will have to wait until later this afternoon before we can leave for the bank. I wouldn't do this if I had a choice."

Her smile disappeared. "Okay." She paused as disappointment registered on her pretty face. "I realize you have other obligations."

"It's complicated, but I do. When you mentioned Igor Volkov, the situation changed."

"How?"

He scrubbed his chin with his open hand as a headache began to pound over his left eye. "The man's family and mine have a long history." How much should he tell her?

"Jon."

"My wife and son were killed by Igor's older brother."

She gasped. "Oh, God. I'm so sorry. I…"

"Yeah."

Only the tick of the regulator clock broke the silence.

His voice deep with intensity, Jon finally said, "It's imperative, I alert my brother and his Task Force. Igor might be in the Bay Area."

Chapter 31

"Jon, you're as handsome as ever."

"Kate, you're still good a liar." He grinned.

"Thank you." She laughed and gave him a quick hug before entering his cottage.

"There's tea waiting for you on the counter. I even have milk."

"I'm impressed."

"Webb should be here any minute."

"Good."

"Too bad I had to interrupt your vacation."

"No problem. We were in Sonoma for the afternoon. Not too big a drive. Let me grab the drinks." The First Lady moved to the kitchen island and carried a tray with a teapot, mugs, and a creamer. She set everything on the coffee table and sat in a nearby club chair.

Small talk came easy to them and they fell into discussions of the houses she and her husband were considering, wines of the local vineyards, and, of course, the dry Northern California weather. No mention of his medical condition or when he might return to work.

At the stroke of noon, Webb knocked on the door

and entered. "Hi, all. Kate, nice you could make it."

He too was given a hug. "Tea, Webb?" She smiled.

"Thanks, brings back living in the UK. Sometimes I miss the place. This is a coffee-drinking nation and I've had my share, still…" He sat on the couch, leaned back, and sipped from his mug.

Silence filled the room.

"I'll take over as mother." Jon grinned and poured milk into First Lady's empty cup then added more warm tea.

With the niceties expressed, the meeting started for real.

"Didn't want to interrupt your day, guys, but I've linked Andrew Jenkins, Salvatore Romano and Igor Volkov. My skin is crawling."

He returned to his chair and straightened out his booted leg. "I nearly choked when I saw Volkov was one of Jenkins' clients. I'm no forensic accountant, but the man had LLCs linked to foreign banks used to launder money. It appears Igor allowed Skye's boss to manage his funds."

"Now Jenkins is dead," Kate stated. "And it seems he left all his files and accounts to Skye Turner."

"So, she's involved in his nasty business," Webb spoke and it wasn't a question.

"No," Jon responded too sharply.

"Then why leave everything to her? And how does Romano come into this?"

"Can't say for sure. If Juan is back and you don't need him for a while, I believe he might unravel some of the mystery and help us understand what exactly was the goal of these limited liability companies—besides hiding the truth from the tax man."

"Webb, how do you feel about lending Juan for a couple of days?" Kate took the tray back to the kitchen counter.

"Fine with me. Of course, Juan would have the last word. Still, I can ask him."

Jon sat forward and wished he'd taken something for the headache that had returned. "From my vantage point, it appears Salvatore was swindled by Jenkins and is looking to get his money back now the man is dead. If this paperwork is true, Romano's deeply in debt and might lose his property if he doesn't cough up cold cash to cover his debt—soon."

He rubbed his forehead to release the tension. "My real concern is why a Russian oligarch is involved."

"Not just any oligarch," Kate added.

"No, a very specific one." He cringed, remembering the loss of his family.

"How is Ms. Turner involved?" his brother asked.

"When her boss died, and I believe it was murder, she became his heir."

"Not Jenkins' wife?"

"Don't stare at me like that, Webb."

"It's only…"

"Yeah, got it. You don't trust Skye."

"Bro, you have to admit the whole situation has a rotten odor."

"Hey, we'll check her out," Kate interrupted, "but Skye came across as a sincere young woman, without a hidden agenda. As you realize, I've become skilled at nailing phonies who try to hang around the president."

"Okay. Let's check out the questionable files." Webb changed the subject.

***

Skye glanced out of the window. A white SUV and a British sports car were parked in front of the house. A man sat at the wheel of the white vehicle as he had when the First Lady had visited.

She must be in the cottage with Jon. How long would she and his brother stay?

She kicked off her heels and slumped onto the sofa.

No gardening, not in her business suit. Did she have time to change and still be ready if the meeting ended quickly?

Thumbing through the latest issue of Gardening World took about ten minutes, her mind unwilling to focus on the articles that normally would have interested her. She tossed it on the side table and stood up.

The bank account was in her name. Why not go check on the account while Jon was busy?

***

Terry drove toward San Francisco. Anger still burned his gut after he met with Salvatore. Damn, the man. It hadn't been enough that he'd agreed to do the job get the girl and take her to the cave. But the shithead, Romano, told him how to do it and not only that he'd called him kid.

After working for the guy for over a year, Sal hadn't bothered the learn his name.

Terry's knuckles on the steering wheel whitened as his grip tightened. It wasn't as if nasty jobs were new to him. No boy scout, that didn't mean he didn't have feelings or want respect.

Why else go to classes at the university if not for the desire for respect and the need to change his life?

But nowhere else could he be paid this kind of money, He had to suck it up and take the guff from Romano.

Skye would be delivered but his way. Build her trust and it would make it easier for both of them. No point in terrifying the woman and having to hurt her before necessary.

***

The bank in San Francisco was near Andy's office. Guess that shouldn't be a surprise, he was always one to choose convenience.

An impressive building near the heart of the financial district, it loomed over the street and cast a wide shadow that dared anyone with a small account to think before they entered.

Why were her hands cold? As an accounting student she shouldn't be intimidated, but somehow, this was different.

She paused, adjusted her shoulder bag and glanced at her image in the impressive glass door, before entering the white marble palace. The entry echoed at the sound of her heels and imposing Doric columns appeared to hold up a grand ceiling.

She shivered. Why did corporations put on the air-conditioner on cool days? Perhaps it encouraged visitors not to linger on the premises.

She buttoned her suit jacket and asked the guard at the information desk where to go.

Asked for ID, when she presented her bank card, he stood at attention. She almost thought he might salute her.

"Follow me, please." The fortyish male, in extremely good condition, led the way.

They entered a door marked VIP Lounge and she

was introduced to an efficient woman clothed in an obviously expensive wool suit. Designer label, if Skye had a guess. She suddenly felt shabby in her well-worn business attire.

Offered a variety of refreshments, she declined and was told someone would be with her, ASAP. She sat in a glove leather chair so welcoming she feared she might doze off before the promised banker could arrive.

"Miss Turner?"

"Yes."

"Mr. Garner." A gentleman of the old school, he bowed slightly rather than offering his hand. "How may we help you." He gave her his card, *William Garner, VP General Affairs*, whatever that meant.

She smiled when he used "we" as the representative of the company. Seemed a lot of fuss to bring out this important bank officer, so she might collect the balance of Andy's account. *Your account now.*

They entered his impressive domain and she took a seat facing his enormous carved wooden desk.

Seeming to be in charge of sales, she listened to him regale her with all the products she might avail herself to from this company.

She was about to suggest it was time to leave when he handed her a letter with the list of the assets in her name.

If she'd been standing, she'd have stumbled into a chair. The balance of the interest checking account jumped out at her—seven figures. A long line of money market accounts, investment accounts and LLCs finished the report.

"I hope this is satisfactory. Of course, if you wish to

make changes, we can do that for you, or you may deal directly with the Cayman Island Bank."

"Yes," she squeaked out the response. "I—my accountant will contact you if necessary." She hesitated. "For now, I'd like to make a withdrawal." Her hand shook when she wrote the number down and gave it to him.

Heat was burning her cheeks, but if the man noticed, he never let on. "Where would you like me to direct this, Ms. Turner?"

"I'll take eight thousand dollars cash and send the rest here."

With more cash than she'd ever had in her life, she felt there was a sign on her back that said, "Rob me."

She shook her head. *Don't be ridiculous.*

She paused in front of the bank and breathed in deeply. The cool breeze was welcome.

"Hey, is that you, Skye?"

She glanced in the direction of the male voice calling her name. She'd seen him at college and then at The Wine Cave, working as a waiter. Now, he was here in front of the bank in San Francisco, what the hell?

Chapter 32

"Are you following me?" Skye stared at the man smiling at her.

A puzzled expression changed his smile to something she couldn't try to define.

"I might ask you the same thing." He grinned. "I work here in the financial district."

"I thought you worked at The Wine Cave." Was the situation with Andrew making her paranoid? This guy seemed nice.

"I do—part-time, but I picked up a couple of lunch shifts down the street. The business crowds give pretty good tips if they drink a lot."

"Oh."

"Skye, I was about to grab a coffee— join me."

"I'm on my way back to Sonoma," For a second, she struggled to remember his name. "Terry."

"Hey, a quick coffee. I don't often see a familiar face in the city."

"It's getting late."

"You don't like me?"

"Oh, it's not..."

"Then let's go. I'll have you on the road before the commute traffic starts."

His friendly manner put her at ease. Maybe it was okay to do something normal like talk to a guy about nothing important—just shoot the breeze.

"Yeah, all right."

"I saw a coffee bar around the corner."

Jazz played quietly over a hidden speaker and the cozy room was full of men in business suits and ties and women with shopping bags on the floor near their heeled feet.

"How about the table over there." Terry pointed to a table for two in the corner of the room away from the cashier.

She shrugged, followed him, and sat facing the front of the building. He slid his chair so he was next to her but not too close.

"I'll get the drinks. Skye, what's it going to be?"

"Just decaf with cream,"

"Can't talk you into a latte or something sweet to go with the coffee?"

"No, thanks."

While he went to order, she checked her phone, two o'clock and no text from Jon. He and his brother must still be busy.

"Working at Romano's fancy bistro is okay," Terry said between bites of the banana bread he ate, a large steaming drink near his plate. "Hard to live on one or two shifts a week. Wish there were seven Saturdays in a week." He laughed. "The restaurant is jumping on the weekends. I'd pull down the big bucks if all days were like Saturday."

"Really." She sipped the strong decaf.

"Yep. The other nights are a lot slower. I mean, I'm at work but might as well not be for the number of tips

I receive."

"I never thought about how important they are." She smiled and encouraged him to continue to speak about himself. He appeared to enjoy the topic and it relieved her from thinking about her life, not that she'd be willing to share with him.

An open, friendly, regular guy, he bore no relationship to the handsome but brooding Jon Lancaster. Terry wasn't nearly as handsome or commanding or as overwhelming. Right now, that was exactly what she needed. No tension, no desire.

They shared their need to finish the next semester at the university and talked about the professors they'd both had.

"Terry, I better take off," she finally said, surprised at her reluctance to leave.

"So soon?"

"The traffic is building. I don't want to but..." She stood from the table.

"Okay, but do me a favor."

"If I can."

A crowded table of men laughed and the music seemed to grow louder.

He leaned closer and whispered, "Have dinner with me tomorrow."

What would Jon think? Why care? He had no interest in a real connection with her. He wasn't over his wife. Skye sure couldn't blame Jon for his deep love for Miranda, but there was no reason to believe he'd ever be ready for a new relationship with her.

"Skye, dinner?

"Uh…"

"You choose the place, Chinese, Italian, Tex-Mex."

"I guess."

"Outstanding. Give me your address and I'll pick you up at six tomorrow."

***

Terry noticed the sway of Skye's hips as she walked out of the coffee shop, a nice person. He hadn't laughed and enjoyed talking with a girl for a long time. Why would anyone want to hurt her? What had she done to Salvatore to want her under his control and in the damp, musty cave? He winced at the thought.

"Are you using the chair?" a man in a grey business asked.

"No." He got up and walked out of the building. Better text Sal and let him understand the girl would be delivered tomorrow night.

***

On the drive home, Skye second-guessed her agreement to go out with the guy she hardly knew. A mistake? She sighed. The fact Andrew left her in a mess didn't mean her whole life had to be run by it. It was time she took charge and started to live by her own rules.

What about the money? The cash in her purse was easy. She'd pay herself the two weeks' salary Andy owed her and send the rest to his wife, Ruth. And the other accounts?

Her car entered the Golden Gate Bridge when the smartphone chirped—a text from Jon. With nowhere to pull over, she wondered what he had to say.

Chapter 33

Salvatore paced the vineyard near his restaurant. Late afternoon and still he'd heard nothing from The Kid, except another promise to deliver. So far, Terry had brought him squat, nada.

If the kid failed this time…he kicked a dirt clod, sending it flying.

One of the field hands stared but only said, "Good afternoon, señor."

Without bothering to respond, Sal continued his walk in the vineyard, breathing in the aroma of vines and damp soil, watered by the elaborate sprinkling system he'd had installed.

Igor would be here in a short while. Sal planned to wine and dine him in the private dining room, plying him with his best vintage Cabernet taken from the private reserve.

The longer he could put off telling the man he didn't have the funds, the better.

Housekeeping had prepared a room for the Russian and if the man wanted to be entertained, he had arranged a choice of ladies willing to divert him at least for the evening.

Romano faced the waning light. Nevertheless, the

California sun warmed him as nothing else could, even as it lowered on the horizon. He wiped his brow and turned toward the restaurant. At the edge of the road next to the vineyard, he shook the dirt from his shoes.

"Romano."

Igor Volkov, stood tall and fierce next to a black limo.

"Igor." Sal forced a smile and extended his hand, giving him a strong handshake. *The shit-head is early.*

"Salvatore."

"How is it going?" He threw his arm around Volkov's shoulder and walked toward the entrance of The Wine Cave.

The limo driver maneuvered the stretch vehicle to follow them.

Damn. Sal realized it was destined to be one hell of a long night.

***

Jon checked his cell phone, then glanced out of the living room window in the farmhouse.

Skye hadn't answered his text. Fear and anger began to rage in him. They'd had a conversation about her never leaving alone. She'd agreed not to, but the house was empty. She was nowhere to be seen and no message had been left for him. What if he left to search for her and she returned to find him gone?

Damn, didn't she realize danger was everywhere?

He slumped onto the sofa and rubbed his forehead. His eyes ached and he closed them. *Skye, stay safe.*

The day had brought him nothing but annoyance. First, he had been compelled to remember the night of Miranda's death, all because of Igor Volkov's link to Andrew Jenkins.

An image of his wife sent a sharp pang in his chest. Every time he tried to move on with his life the Oligarch's family name interrupted him. When would it stop? *Not until you or Igor is dead.*

He took a breath to slow his thundering heart.

Though not as well defined, a vision appeared in front of him. "Miranda?"

He shook his head. Was he asleep?

"Jon, you have to let me go. I'm in limbo as long as you won't accept my death.

"What are you saying?" He struggled to wake up.

"Please, Jon, I can't move on until you do."

"I can't—I love you."

"I loved you too, but I'm on a different level. You must realize there is nothing more you can do for me.

"No."

"Please, Jon."

"Miranda don't ask me. I …"

"Sweetheart, believe me, it wasn't your fault." She smiled.

How could she? "Mandy, you can't be serious."

"I'm in a good place—or will be if you'll let me."

"But… Don't go."

"Jonny, I'll be waiting for you when the time comes, but not for many years. You'll be a very old man."

He stared as she appeared to rise in the air.

"Be happy."

"Don't leave." He begged as her vision began to fade.

"Remember, be happy." She blew him a kiss and disappeared.

No matter how hard he tried, Miranda didn't return. For the first time since her death, he sobbed.

***

Skye drove the old compact into the driveway and turned off the engine. The gas tank was nearly empty, still, she didn't take the time to fill it when Jon might be waiting for her.

Instead of exiting the car, she sat staring out of the windshield at the dark house. This afternoon she'd been sure there was time in the day to be back by dinner and before Jon noticed the betrayal of the promise not to go without him. But she hadn't factored in meeting Terry for coffee or getting trapped in the commute traffic accident.

With a sigh, she exited the car and walked to the front door.

"Where the hell have you been!" Jon growled when she entered.

"You scared me. What are you doing here in the dark?"

"Waiting for you. Why didn't you answer my text?"

"I... You don't have the right to question me. You're not my father." She dropped her bag on the entry table and walked into the living room.

"No, I'm not. I've done things your father couldn't even imagine. That's why I'm able to defend you."

"Yeah? Well, I don't have to tell you anything." His attitude angered her and she fought back, speaking before good sense stopped her. "What if I don't need or want your help?"

He moved toward her, his fierce expression sending a shiver through her. "That's a foolish statement."

"So you say," she shot back. For the first time in days, she'd experienced a normal afternoon, enjoying coffee with a friend and now Jon had spoiled it by cross-questioning her. "You have no right to yell at me—I want to be alone."

He blinked. "Really? Do you think that's a smart idea? What happened the last time you'd stayed by yourself in this house?" He glared at her his intense blue eyes narrowing.

"Jon, I think you should go. It's been a long day and I'm not up to arguing with you."

"Skye, I worry about your safety." His angry expression softened as he reached for her and took her in his arms. "Don't you understand being in control of Andrew's accounts puts you in danger?"

His warm breath caressed her cheek. He brushed her hair from her face. "I can't help you if I don't know where you are. What would I do if something happened and I could have stopped it?"

"I thought I'd be back before you realized I was gone."

"Yeah, okay. But Skye, help me protect you."

He kissed her cheek and she leaned closer wanting more. She touched his face and let her fingers roam the plains of his strong jawline. "I'm sorry. I should've talked to you before I took off."

She stood on tiptoes, pulled him nearer, and kissed him as the heat of desire flooded her. He cared what happened to her.

Appearing surprised, he tensed, then opened his mouth to hers. Their tongues met in a dance to nature's music. Her staccato breathing increased as he explored the contours of her back, following her curves lower and coxing her to him. Soon they moved in unison, their breaths matching.

His smartphone rang.

"I have to take this." He pulled away from her, leaving her breathless and hungry for him.

Suddenly serious and almost standing at attention, he said, "Roger that."

"I have to go."

"I thought…"

"You misunderstand. I want you to come with me."

"Now?" She released the silver clip that was no longer able to control her long mane. She smoothed her hair where Jon had run his hands. "Where are we going?"

His penetrating gaze sent heat flowing in her again.

"Kate just asked us to join them for a late dinner."

"Oh. How do I dress for dinner with the First Lady?"

Chapter 34

Jon shrugged. "I don't know anything about women's clothes. Kate's staying with her husband at a retreat in Sonoma, not far from here. The hotel is California casual, so—can you be ready in fifteen minutes?"

"Sure."

After a quick shower, she wondered what would be appropriate to wear to meet Kate and the President of the United States for a late supper.

The blue chambray dress she wore on her birthday slipped on easily. But instead of choosing the silver sandals, she found navy flats and a matching belt with a silver buckle.

A chill of nerves ran through her as she drove toward the hotel where Kate was staying.

Handsome in dark slacks, a grey T-shirt and a charcoal sports jacket, Jon sat next to her and smiled when she glanced at him.

The five-star hotel was located about seventy miles north of San Francisco in the middle of Sonoma County's wine country. The private lane appeared to go for miles before the huge beige mansion appeared.

A man, in casual attire, opened the car door for her.

"Welcome to the Hacienda."

"Thank you."

Jon took her arm and walked through the entrance door.

California elegance greeted her in the wide-open lobby, casually decorated with flagstone floors, mission furniture, and wrought iron chandeliers. Huge clay pots planted with indigenous flowers and native grasses helped with the indoor, outdoor ambiance so popular in the golden state. Vintage oil paintings of landscapes hung on the adobe walls, their gold frames shining like mother lode gold dug from the foothills by the forty-niners.

A cool breeze from the perfectly temperature-controlled air conditioner relaxed her.

At the desk, a man dressed in a crisp white shirt, with a name tag that read Robert B, smiled.

When he saw Jon, the clerk nodded. "You're expected, sir."

"Thanks, Bob. I know the way."

A golden retriever ran up to Jon, wagging his tail.

"Hi Skipper, old boy. Have you been a good dog?" He bent down and rubbed the animal's ear. "I don't have time for a walk now, I'll catch you later." He patted the dog's head and Skipper seemed to understand because he went back to his bed near the front desk.

"Not your first time here," Skye stated.

"We've been here often."

Who was we, his wife, family, associates? She didn't want to mention sad memories, so she didn't ask.

A sign pointing toward the dining room hung on the wall.

"This way, Skye." He took her arm and led her down a long hall, away from the dining room.

As they walked, she scanned the high-end shops carrying international designer labels she recognized from fashion magazines.

A woman, casually, but expensively dressed, entered one of the last shops and was greeted with a smile and called by her name.

At a single elevator, Jon pressed the button. A screen emerged, he pressed his thumb on it and punched in a code.

"Hey, where are we going? I thought we were going to dinner."

"We are."

"Up in the penthouse?"

"Not exactly."

The elevator door opened to a large carpeted lift with obvious cameras on display. A uniformed guard with a weapon, who had to be seven feet tall, stood at the ready.

"Sir, miss." The soldier stepped back and let them enter.

Skye startled when instead of going up, the elevator car moved down. Two, or three stories?

She wanted to ask exactly where they were going, but the officer was staring at her, so she held her tongue. Anxiety raged in her. She'd agreed to go to dinner with the First Lady and that was unnerving. But Jon's request was turning into something else completely. His shoulders were at ease, his body language appeared relaxed. While her heart pounded and claustrophobia threatened.

Finally, the elevator stopped and the doors opened

to a room filled with electronic equipment. People milled around computer monitors and spoke to each other in quiet voices.

Who were these people? She scanned the area for a clue but discovered nothing helpful. Any thought of eating dinner fled. "Jon, what is this place?"

He leaned near and whispered, "I'll explain later. Don't worry. It'll become clear—soon."

She stopped. "You tell me now or I'm not going any further." She crossed her arm and glared at him.

"Skye, not here."

"Then I'm out of here." Could she make good her threat to leave with the officer standing guard?

"I mean it. I'm not staying."

She must have yelled because everyone stared at her. Heat crept into her cheeks and the sense of being trapped swamped her.

"Of course, all this is strange to you." Kate stood in a doorway and smiled. "We have a private world down here." Dressed in sneakers, blue cotton pants and a long plaid shirt, the First Lady took her hand. "Let me show you around."

They went further into the chamber.

"Skye, you're looking at a communication center. We are able to remain in contact with and monitor the rest of the government—the world for that matter. I'd tell you more, but I'm afraid that's code word information."

"What's that?"

"Top secret," Jon answered. "You'd need the proper security clearance to know."

"Oh."

"I'm pleased you came to visit on such short notice.

Shall we go to dinner?" Kate walked briskly down the hall and stopped at a door flanked by two uniformed officers.

One saluted and opened the door for them. When they entered, the man Skye had seen standing by Kate's SUV was there—Secret Service, no doubt.

Kate smiled at him and in a deep voice he said, "Ma'am."

They followed Kate into a state-of-the-art kitchen with a round oak table and chairs in the middle of the room and set for dinner.

"I didn't expect anything like this," Skye reacted before she could think. She surveyed the six-burner range with a built-in grill. "That's an amazing stove."

"Isn't? They brought in here just for me. I don't often get a chance to cook anymore. I hope you like Irish stew." She stirred a pot.

"I do. May I help you?"

"I'm fine. Sit." Kate pointed to the table—anyplace."

The table was big, able to seat eight or more. She slumped into the nearest chair, while Jon went to the sub-zero stainless fridge took out a quart of milk and poured a glass. He held the carton up to her.

"No thanks." Surprised how he made himself at home in the First Lady's domain.

"The chefs at this hotel are fabulous," Kate interrupted her thought. "They are all Cordon Bleu trained and I've had excellent meals. But when my hubby and I are here, I like to cook for him. I don't usually get have a chance these days."

"This kitchen is certainly beautifully outfitted."

"I like it."

Webb, Jon's older brother, joined them and he and Jon spoke together while she and Kate talked about food and recipes.

Jon brought homemade brown bread and butter to the table and they sat to eat.

Though the small talk continued, she had the sense they weren't there to enjoy the First Lady's cooking.

"I hope I'm not too late." A tall, well-built man with greying hair entered the kitchen.

"Of course not." Kate jumped up from the table and rushed kiss on the cheek. "Sit down. You know everyone but Skye Turner. This is my husband."

Skye stumbled to her feet. "Mr. President."

"Call me Robert." He smiled and it was even more charming in person than on TV.

"Jon, Webb." He nodded to each one and sat across the table from Skye.

Kate served him a large bowl of stew and sat next to him.

"Thanks, for making my favorite, babe."

Kate grinned.

The conversation resumed and to Skye's relief they didn't force her to join the repartee. Still, she offered a comment here and there when appropriate.

After dinner, fresh fruit and various cheeses were served with tea and decaf.

Soon afterward, Robert stood. "Nice meeting you, Ms. Turner."

"You too Mr. Pres—Robert."

"Shall we go?" the President asked Jon and Webb.

Jon took her hand, "I'll be back as soon as I can."

Chapter 35

After the men left, Kate said, "I'll clean up and we can go to the den and be more comfortable.

"Let me help."

"I'll wash. You dry. Skye, don't look so surprised. I like doing everyday chores."

"It's only that I thought as the lady in the White House..."

"Oh, I have lots of help now, but I didn't grow up that way." She paused as though remembering. "As the oldest of a horde of kids, I've done my share of washing up. My poor mother spent all her energy nursing and cooking for her brood. Clean up was my area of expertise." She laughed. "Back then, having servants was a dream."

She tossed a kitchen towel to her and Skye caught it in the air with one hand. "Thanks."

When the dishes were finished, Kate showed her to a cozy room with over-stuffed sofas and a tall wing-back chair. She'd bet it was the president's choice. Several wide-screen TVs hung at one end of the room and filled bookshelves lined the other.

Kate must have seen her staring at the books because she said, "Robert's an avid reader. I've tried to convince him to try an e-reader, but he likes paper and the idea of turning the pages."

A faux fireplace flanked by a rocker and the high wingback chair sat across from the sofas.

"The wing chair is Robert's. He has one just like in the White House."

"Really?" A little bit of trivia she would never be able to share with anyone. "Looks comfy."

"Take a seat." The First Lady sat in the rocker and slowly moved back and forth.

She dropped to the sofa and crossed her legs. "It's lovely here."

"We enjoy being here in Sonoma, one of the places where we have time together, discounting tonight's meeting." She shrugged. "These things happen."

"I guess you have to get used to meetings and interruptions."

"Anyone married to a high-placed government worker has to understand what they're getting into." She sighed. "Webb's wife would most likely wish to have him with her tonight. They're expecting and she's dealing with morning sickness that seems to last the whole day."

"I wonder why they call it morning sickness?"

Kate laughed. "Good question."

They moved to different topics with ease and Skye relaxed and wished she could be friends with this warm, plain-spoken woman who appeared to welcome her input, but given the situation she didn't hold out much hope once Kate returned to the White House.

"How long do these meetings usually last, Kate?"

"It's hard to say. Some have lasted most of the night."

"You're kidding?"

"Afraid not. Don't look so startled. It won't be that long tonight."

"Oh, good—I mean I enjoy your company." Heat rose in her cheeks.

"Take it easy, Skye. All too often, I've wished the meeting would end too but…"

She stood from the rocking chair and walked to a shelf lined with photos. "Have you seen this?"

Kate handed it to her, a photo of two kids dressed in school uniforms, stared at her, one with blonde hair and the other with dark brown. Both the boys had blue eyes and she instinctively knew the blonde was Jon.

"Did you know them back then?"

"No, but Robert did. Their stepfather, Harold Lancaster, is an advisor to the president."

"I wonder how old they were."

Kate looked closer. "I'd say early teens. They grew up in the UK you know, until their father died. Later, their mother married Harold and moved to the States.

"Oh, I didn't realize." She paused. "They were cute kids."

"And handsome men, no?"

"And handsome men, yes." Skye grinned.

They walked slowly to the other end of the shelf stopping to view various photos of Robert and officials in his administration. She guessed personal wedding pictures would be in the couple's residence at the White House.

"Shall we sit down again? I can ring for tea or sweets."

"Oh, I'm fine unless you want."

"I'm good."

When they were seated, Kate said, "I've been called a snoop." She smiled. "I hope you don't mind my saying so, but if you care about Jon, you need to understand what life with him would be like."

"I…"

"Skye, I wanted you here to see what dating him would mean."

"I've, we haven't…"

"Long nights alone, sudden meetings at all hours of the day and night, secrets kept from you, unexplained missions, dangerous ones."

"I…he hasn't asked me on a date. He's helping me find out what happened to my boss."

"But you care for him."

A question? It sounded like a statement and she couldn't deny the truth. Kate wouldn't believe her if she tried.

"Yeah, more than I meant to." She hesitated. "I don't think I'm ready for—I mean this is overwhelming. I'm just a student trying to get through the mess I find myself in. Now this."

"If you're not ready. Please, for Jon's sake, don't encourage him."

Silent, Skye didn't know what to say.

"You've seen his scared chest and broken bone."

"Yeah."

"He got that at work, still, the real injury is his loss when his wife and child were killed—let's just say it concerned his work and he's felt at fault—it wasn't."

She stopped as if wondering how much to share. "This is only between us."

"Of course, Kate." She leaned forward.

"Skye, I was really worried about him after they

243

died and he was hurt. Jon was like the walking dead. He's tough, no doubt about that, but don't let him fool you, he's been wounded, body and soul."

Kate hesitated. Was she waiting for her to speak?

"For a while, I didn't think it was possible, but Skye, you've brought me hope for his recovery."

"I don't know what to say."

"When he's near you, he smiles—laughs. Something he hasn't done since the terrible events that hurt him and took his family. I feared it might never happen."

"Whoa, I like him, but..." She rubbed her head. This whole evening was becoming too much to digest. She needed an aspirin.

Kate smiled. "I didn't mean to swamp you with my concerns. I'm afraid I'm a mom at heart and all the people around the president are my kids. Especially Jon and Webb, they are my guys figuratively if not literally. Just remember if you cannot accept Jon's dangerous work, walk away now, before he's hurt again. I won't see him harmed once more. If you can deal with it, I'd welcome you."

"Uh, I'll think about what you said and Kate, I do care…"

"Am I interrupting?" Jon peeked into the den.

Chapter 36

Salvatore paced back and forth in the private kitchen of The Wine Cave. The aroma wafting in the room waking his taste buds. He took a deep breath. No one cooked like his executive chef. A damn shame to waste the man's culinary talents on the Russian oligarch, Igor Volkov.

Igor was late and hadn't bothered to call with a new later time or to beg off.

"Do your best to keep the food warm but not overcooked." He forced a smile and bowed slightly to his head chef. It was never a good idea to antagonize a man of the cook's delicate temperament. Chefs of his standing could be snatched up in a second by owners of many of the five-star restaurants in the country.

"Louis, you're the best. The man we're entertaining should kiss your ass for the opportunity to eat your beef Wellington." He paused. "Igor's only a serf, but a rich one. An oxymoron, I realize, but such is the state of today's affairs. We all must cater to the filthy rich never mind how they got that way."

"Louis wiped his right hand on his apron and extended it. "He will not be disappointed. The meal will be well above his social station."

"Good man." Sal shook his hand. "If all goes well, we will both be rewarded. He smiled and left reassured at least one thing this evening would go well.

Now to find an appropriate bottle of wine. A good California vintage, but not too a fine year. Why waste a premium beverage on a palate that wouldn't recognize the difference between mediocre and outstanding?

He entered his private dining room as the housekeeping staff scurried from it. White linen tablecloths and napkins in place, his personal crystal stem wear set as if a king were going to dine. "No flowers," he shouted. "Get these the hell out of here. It's not a date."

"Sorry, sir. I... It won't happen again." A plump woman, in a white uniform and a hair net, grabbed the vase and held it to her full breast. He liked big-breasted women. If circumstances were different, he might get to know her better. He grunted. "See that it doesn't and tell the staff or they may be looking for a different job."

"Yes, sir."

He slammed the door as she left, nearly hitting her in the rear as she exited.

Where the hell was the kid? Did he have Skye Turner with him? He sat and surveyed the vineyard from the huge glass window. He loved this view of his domain.

Next week, he was to be voted into an exclusive club of entrepreneurs, movers and shakers on the cutting edge of the wine business.

His winning premier wine and the careful public relations campaign were paying off after years of planning. Still, if anyone got wind of the fact his finances were not as stable as presented…

He could ring Skye's neck. His fingers tingled at the thought. First, he needed the information only she could supply. Without her, he'd never see his assets. He had to keep that in mind. *Better not blow it like you did last time. If you hadn't killed Jenkins, none of this would be happening.*

His alarm buzzed. Time to get ready for a dinner meeting with Igor Volkov, damn the Russian oligarch. Still, if he could fill him with drink and good food, maybe the man would mellow and give him a little more time to return his funds.

***

There was a different man in the elevator when she and Jon entered for the trip up to the ground floor and the lobby of the hotel. He greeted Jon warmly with a slap on the back.

"Hey, Jon, like the footwear."

"Yeah, the latest boot. You ought to try it."

They laughed and then the man nodded to her. "Miss."

Another man entered the elevator and the rest of the ride was done in silence.

When they entered the lobby, Skipper ran up to Jon wagging his tail. "Hello, boy."

The golden retriever nudged his hand.

"Jon, you did promise him a walk." She glanced at his booted leg. "Uh, I meant if you are up to it. I don't mind."

"Is that what you want, Skipper?"

"Jon, he understands. He's heading for the door." She laughed.

"Well, guess we can't disappoint him." He grinned and took her arm.

The dog appeared to recognize the trails and choose the way. Perhaps sensing Jon's slower ability to move with this leg brace, the animal elected a slow pace, occasionally jogging ahead, then stopping to wait for them to catch up before going off again. At the top of a small hill, a wooden bench was stationed to give a panoramic view of the vineyards and the mountains off in the distance.

Skye sat to allow Jon to rest. He might not need it, but she understood he would never ask even if he did.

The setting sun sent a glow over the golden hills turning them to a warm orange. Soon the harvest moon would rise. "It's beautiful here. Peaceful."

"It's a favorite location of mine. Skipper and I have walked here many times. Haven't we old boy?"

"So that's how he knew where to go."

Skipper wagged his tail, then lay down next to Jon. He rubbed the dog's ear.

"I hope Kate didn't bore you."

"Of course not. She showed me a photo of you when you were a kid in the UK."

"No way." He laughed. "I shouldn't have left you alone with her. She is libel to tell all my shortcomings."

"She talked like you were one of her own."

"As you probably know, Kate was my boss in the Rapid Advance Team. She retired after she became First Lady."

"Even so, you all became close friends?"

"All for one and one for all as Robin Hood used to say." He laughed, but his voice had a melancholy tinge to it.

She wanted to comfort him and mention what she'd learned tonight. Instead, she reached for his hand and held it, surprised, when he didn't pull away.

"Skye, my meeting had information concerning you and Andrew Jenkins."

***

Igor belched and rubbed his flat stomach. "A little greasy, but tolerable." He wiped his mouth with the white linen napkin and threw it on the table.

Salvatore glared at the ignorant man. *Greasy.* The peon wouldn't know decent food because he'd grown up eating slop. He reached for the bottle of red wine and poured it into Igor's, once again, empty glass.

"Da. At least your wine is good."

Russian fool. Sal had chosen wisely when he decided to give a lesser grade of wine to Volkov.

"Don't think you can get me drunk. I've drunk more liquor—vodka, than you will ever imagine." Igor rubbed his forehead. "It's hot in here."

After Sal filled Igor's glass he sat down and forced a casual posture. If the man noticed he wasn't drinking, the man said nothing.

No matter how much he consumed, the Russian retained his demeanor, no slurred words or sleepy eyes.

"Romano, I understand what you're doing, but you will talk about my money. Your head is clear and your glass is empty, so no excuses. Da?" He pulled a cigar from a case in his pocket and lit it with a gold lighter. Then sent a puff of smoke in Sal's direction. "No more games."

***

As far as Skye could tell, they were the only people on the path. She leaned back on the bench in the tranquil setting of the Sonoma hotel grounds and sighed.

Lights twinkled in the far-off valley and a line of car lights made their way to and from the hotel. Though the night was warm, she sat frozen.

"I understand this is all strange to you, Skye. I think that's why Kate wanted you to come here, for you to see how we live. Honestly, to find out if it scared you off."

She stared at the view, not wanting to understand what he said. This whole situation was frightening her and why not? Any normal person would be terrified, with guards, hidden rooms, and secrets.

"None of this seems real." She hesitated. "Jon, did

you ever have the feeling you were living in an alternate universe? A surreal world where nothing is as it appears?"

Before he could answer, she continued, "A few months ago, I believed life was simple, go to school, obtain a job and do my work. When I was growing up, my mom had a couple of lines from a poem she liked to quote, 'God's in his heaven—all is right with the world.' I believed that, but..." She sighed. "Now I realize there is no truth to the poem. Things most people will never observe or consider are going on under the surface."

"What can I say? It's necessary."

"Maybe, but I don't want...You might as well tell me what you and your brother found—not that I want to grasp it."

"All right, but remember I'm the messenger, not the person who did any of this."

"Okay."

"Webb had his forensic accountants look into the files you gave us. We expected Jenkins would be mixed up with crooks. Why else would he need so many limited liability companies, except to hide the deals and illegal transactions? Andrew was deeply involved in money laundering and payoffs and worked for some truly shady characters."

"No way."

"Afraid so. As you remember, he gave you a Russian newspaper, and the name of Igor Volkov, an oligarch, was in the paper and also the files."

"Why would he do that?"

"A heads up?"

"I can't accept that Andrew had no integrity."

Skipper must have sensed her distress because he came to her and put his head in her lap. "Thank you, boy." She petted his head and he wagged his tail. "You're a good dog."

She glanced at Jon. His expression turned grim. "You've discovered something else."

"Yeah. We were looking for how Salvatore Romano was involved with your boss, but the Russian oligarch's name kept coming up in the documents. Your boss was linked with both of them. They may have been his major source of income."

"How?"

"For a percentage, he invested their money. They trusted him, though that belief was misplaced." Jon stood and stretched. "Before any of this happened, Webb and I discovered Igor Volkov's father was a spy in what used to be called the KGB, now the FSB."

He swallowed and cleared his throat. Moisture glistened in his eyes when he spoke again, Volkov's older brother killed my wife and child."

"No," she gasped.

"So, you can imagine what I felt when I saw his family name in the Jenkins' files."

"Dear God. Did Igor have anything to do with it?"

"I don't think so, but…"

The bleakness in his voice tore at her. She wanted to hold him and say she cared. Instead, she asked, "Are you saying this man is a murderer too?"

"I don't know, but Jenkins held the guy's assets and your boss is dead." He faltered. "If I'm right, Volkov wants his funds returned with a profit and won't stop until he achieves his goal. His resources are in your name."

"But I…" She shivered.

"Jenkins was smart. I'll give him that. He built a complicated link of business companies to hide the real owners of illegitimate businesses, including real estate enterprises."

"But why? He made a respectable living being an honest accountant?"

"Seems not. We don't appreciate his circumstance or his debt level. For some men, money is how they calculate their value as a person. The more money, the better person they think they are. So, they never have an adequate amount." Jon shrugged. "Skye, the important part for you is that you're named as a partner. As I said before, the right of survivorship was written into his business contracts and his will. Now you must decide what to do with the resources in your name."

"Give it back." She swallowed hard. "It's not mine. I don't want the money."

"Not a good idea."

"Why?" She frowned. "Let Salvatore and the Russian fight over it, as long as they leave me alone."

"Where did the money come from? Does it all belong to them? Would you be cheating someone who legally invested with Jenkins?"

"Dammit, Jon, how do I know?" She jumped up and walked to the edge of the path and stared at the vineyards below. "I don't want to find out. I just want my old life back. I wish I'd never seen any of you."

"Hey, you're upset—but we'll figure it out."

"I'm tired of the whole business. This afternoon I had coffee with a friend." She stared at him. But Jon didn't indicate his feelings.

"We talked and I laughed. Do you know how long since I laughed? I used to do it all the time, but since Andrew was killed and I met you…"

"Skye." He put his arm around her and gently held to him, then bent toward her.

She pushed him away. "Stop. Leave me alone. You're all involved and I'm not ready to—I don't want help. I just want to go home and be left alone."

Chapter 37

The atmosphere in the car chilled Skye. Jon hadn't spoken since they left the Sonoma hotel. So, she drove in silence, already regretting her angry words.

Traffic moved quickly and she was grateful. The sooner they returned to the house and cottage, the better. Could she continue to live in the house after tonight? It might be time to pack and move in with a friend until she could work out better accommodations. No, the only friend who might let her share a place was teaching in Japan until next year. Maybe a motel...

She glanced at Jon's stoic expression. Hurt had radiated from his expressive blue eyes when she told him she didn't want his help. She wasn't ready to deal with what was going on in her life let alone the way he lived.

This evening had capped off the last few months of tension. It had tested her resolve, her courage and found her wanting. Maybe not exactly a coward, she was only a normal person wanting an average existence.

Jon's quiet strength and confidence were admirable and she wouldn't deny she wanted him. Muscled and tan with blue eyes that radiated kindness and seemed to see into her soul, she'd imagined him touching her, loving her until ecstasy flowed within her.

However, she was near the breaking point. Even if her problems were solved, tonight, Kate had given her an ultimatum, if you can't live the way we do, leave.

***

Skye parked and got out. Jon followed and turned to her. As he stared, her cheeks heated and she shifted under his scrutiny. Their eyes caught. Frozen in place, she waited for him to speak.

His eyes were shielded and his mouth formed a thin line. Was he hoping she would speak first?

Should she apologize? For what—telling the truth? At this point, she was overwhelmed and...

He stepped toward her, his blue eyes flashing an emotion she wasn't sure she wanted to decipher.

She leaned forward, wanting him to hold her. "Jon, I..." She resisted the need to touch him and run her hands through his hair. Without her volition, she reached for a lock that fell onto his forehead and pushed it in place.

He blinked and his strong biceps flexed, but otherwise he didn't move.

The request to be held in arms sat on the tip of her tongue. Before she spoke, Kate's words stopped her. *Just remember if you can't accept Jon's dangerous work, walk away now before he's hurt. Skye, I won't see him harmed again.*

"Good night, Jon." She turned to leave.

"Skye, I... I should stay with you. It's not safe."

She faced him and blushed under his intense gaze. Did he notice the longing in her eyes? "No, Jon. I'll lock the doors."

"Be sure you do and Skye, don't do anything foolish."

She entered the house, slammed the door and locked it. Did she regret her decision to refuse his request to stay with her?

Too tired to analyze her feelings, she glanced at Jon through the sidelight as he walked toward the cottage. Was it anger or sadness showing in his body language?

Why did guilt slash her? She'd kept her part of the original bargain to help him while he recovered from his injuries. To receive lower rent on the front house, meals were made on time and the cottage was cleaned.

The mistake was asking Jon for help. He had given more time than promised and discovered facts she would never have imagined. Perhaps too much information caused her to rethink her relationships and the ability to recognize the truth in people. It was apparent her trust came too easily, but until she met Andrew Jenkins there'd never been a reason to question people's motives. Today, second-guessing a person's statements was now first nature.

She sighed and walked toward the bedroom shedding her clothes as she went. Sleep, if she found it, would make the problems go away, at least for a few hours.

Jon was stronger now and didn't require as much help around the place. Nevertheless, the agreement to make meals ahead of time and freeze them would be continued—if he let her stay.

They didn't need to see each other socially. Once more, she was reminded it was a mistake to involve him in her situation. However, she'd been confused and he'd understood what to do. How could she have known a Pandora's box would be opened by their investigation?

Of course, today she understood Jon was a man of tremendous appeal but with more baggage than she was able to contemplate. If she had, she would never have fallen in love with him, but now it was too late.

The memory of his touch sent longing spiraling within her. "Jon," she whispered, "what am I going to do without you?"

***

Jon sat in the bedroom of the cottage and from a closed-circuit camera, watched the images of the farmhouse. Skye would be pissed if she realized he'd placed cameras in the various rooms of the house. He doubted she would have undressed on the way to the bedroom, wearing only her underwear by the time she got there.

The bedroom was covered too. Still, to allow her some privacy, he'd left the walk-in closet and the adjoining bathroom without cameras.

He felt like a voyeur, but if she was to remain protected, the monitoring was necessary. He wanted to tell her but understood she would never allow him to place them in the home.

Skye was able to manage on her own—not likely. He smiled remembering how they'd met. A Louisville slugger ready to strike him, she demanded his driver's license or else.

If he were honest with himself, even back then he'd been attracted to her. So different from Miranda's sophistication, but with an earthy sex appeal that radiated from her warm smile, big eyes and full breasts. However, her expression had left the impression she would clobber him with the bat if he didn't comply with her demands to prove who he was. He grinned.

He might have taken her with one move but didn't want to hurt her. Funny, that is exactly what he'd managed to do, upset her deeply.

"Shit."

He picked up his secure cell and dialed his brother, Webb. After receiving clearance, he dialed a member of the Rapid Advance Task Force team.

"Hey, Marty, I have a favor to ask."

***

Sleep had been elusive last night. With little reason to get up and still in her underwear, Skye threw off her covers. Propped up on two king size pillows, she read a novel she'd been promising to finish for months.

After a quick shower, she worked in the back garden, a futile effort as she would be moving out soon. Even so, she couldn't resist preparing the soil for future renters so they might plant a winter crop. Somehow, it calmed her and prevented her from thinking about the current situation.

At two in the afternoon, she looked out of the kitchen window of the farmhouse. The hot sun beat down on the land, another hot dry fall. Would the rains ever come?

With scrambled eggs and coffee waiting at the table, she sat and forced a bite down her dry throat.

Jon, where are you?

She hadn't seen him all day and missed talking with him. Even after her angry words last night, she hoped he might come and at least say hello.

You told him you didn't want his help. After that, what did you expect? Get over him. Was that possible?

Did she want to?

With a moan, she pushed the uneaten plate of eggs away.

***

Terry checked the parked car on the street in front of his place. Every object he might need tonight was stowed neatly in an easily accessible bag in the back seat of the rented auto.

He didn't like the idea of grabbing Skye—not any of it. She was about his age but somehow acted younger. A nice kid, she made him laugh and feel like he belonged with the college crowd and not the outcast he was.

What was her upbringing like? Not the same as his. As he grew, all too often, he was forced to do others' bidding to survive.

Skye probably had parents who protected her. The kind of girl who never went without a meal or wondered where she was going to live. Her parents only let her see right and wrong, black and white. The straight and narrow for her. There were no gray areas in her life. Was that why her smile was so sweet and naïve?

He relaxed his stranglehold on the steering wheel of the sedan and glanced at his smartphone. There was plenty time to get ready and still arrive at the eatery with Skye as Romano directed.

Do this for Salvatore and you'll have money to set yourself up for life, no more worry about where your next job is coming from.

Did that make what he was about to do okay? Better not to think about it.

He went into his home to shower and dress as the

college student Skye expected. Following directions, in a while, he'd be on her doorstep as planned. He grinned thinking of the payment that would soon be his.

Chapter 38

Jon stood in the modern, neutrally decorated beige and gray waiting room of the ophthalmologist's office. Skye had given him the name of the doctor the First Lady gave to her.

Kate had promised the doctor was the best in his field. He had to have confidence that she was correct. His eyes were getting worse, so putting off visiting a specialist could no longer be an option.

The excuse he that couldn't take the time away from Skye and her problems was now mute. If he lost his sight, it would be hard to help her or anyone.

Even though Skye had said she didn't want help, he'd finish the assignment. He never quit anything once he started.

Marty would take over while he was at the doctor's office, but he would soon be back on the job.

"Mr. Lancaster, the doctor will see you now." A middle-aged woman, dressed in white slacks and a blue smock, called his name.

With some trepidation, he followed her into an examination room.

***

Skye ignored the knock on the farmhouse door.

However, whoever was there didn't want to take no for an answer. The knocking continued.

Finally, curiosity got to her and she glanced out of the sidelight next to the front door.

Though small, a clear sense of self radiated from the petite woman staring at her. Slim but with a strong stance, she gave an air of confidence not presented by most people.

"Skye Turner?"

"Yeah."

"Hi, I'm Marty. Jon sent me. I think he mentioned I'd be here today."

In blue jeans and a maroon sweatshirt, Marty smiled.

Jon hadn't said anything about someone coming. She gripped the baseball bat behind her, out of sight. Should she let the woman into the house?

She and Jon hadn't exactly been on speaking terms last night. Maybe he would have told her if she had given him a chance. "I'm not in the mood to talk to anyone. Go away."

"I can't."

"Where's Jon?"

"Let me in and I'll tell you. I'd rather not discuss this out here in front with the neighbors nearby."

When she didn't do as asked, Marty groaned, reached into her backpack, and pulled out her ID. She held it up so Skye could view a card. It read Rapid Advance Task Force team member and Skye saw a U.S. Government logo but wasn't able to learn Marty's last name before the woman put the ID away.

"We all right, now? Will you let me in?"

She didn't want the woman meddling in her life.

Still, if Jon cared enough to go to the trouble of asking her to stop by... She released the lock and stood back to let Marty enter.

"Where's your car?"

"I parked down the street. No reason to let anyone who drives by understand where I'm visiting."

Whoa, careful, Skye had to admit.

"Jon had an appointment with an eye specialist. Kate got the name of a doctor for him. I thought you knew."

"Sort of—just didn't realize it was today."

Without waiting to be asked, Marty sat on the couch. "Got something to drink, diet cola, juice, whatever? I'm thirsty."

"Want apple or orange juice?"

"Orange is fine. Might as well get vitamin C while I quench my thirst."

"I'll be right back."

She returned with two glasses of juice and sat in a chair next to the sofa.

"Nice place you have. So huge. I'm used to small city apartments."

"You're not from here."

"No, we travel a lot, the team and I. Jon didn't tell you?" She shrugged. "I'm visiting. We go way back."

Was she his lover? How stupid of her to think he was alone. It had been years since he lost his wife, why not have a girlfriend? She could feel her face heat with embarrassment. Did Marty notice?

She gazed at the woman, and a new emotion she'd never experienced ran through her—jealously. A dislike for the female who was here to help, all she could think about was Marty and Jon together.

"Skye. Skye, What's wrong?"

"Nothing. I just zoned out for a second."

"Listen, if you need to do any shopping, I'll go with you or any place you want to go."

"What does Jon mean to you?" A non sequitur but Marty would understand.

Still, she must have surprised her because Marty stopped with her glass of juice halfway to her mouth. "What are you saying?"

"I think you know."

"Hey, we work together. We're on the same team."

Silence.

"When Jon was hurt on the last assignment, I was given the job of guarding his hospital room."

"You don't look like a guard." Too beautiful and petite.

"Right. One of the reasons I was chosen, but I'm well trained."

"Yeah?"

"Spending days together in the private room, I'll admit we got to know each other incredibly well. I like him. He's a great guy. You won't find many as good as he is."

"You care for him."

"Of course."

Skye slumped in the chair. Jon and Marty had a thing going. She should have understood a guy as kind, handsome, and strong as Jon would have a partner.

"I'm going to take a shower. Do whatever you want."

"Skye, I think you…"

She slammed the bedroom door on Marty's words.

***

Oh, dear God, what a fool I made of myself. Stress had to be taking a toll on her. Skye stared at her red face in the bathroom mirror. She acted like an idiot to a stranger who had come to help. What must Marty think?

Damned hot today. She threw cold water on her face and dried it with a towel. She'd already taken a bath, but at least she had an excuse to stay away from Marty and wouldn't need to make happy talk with her. How could she face her again?

Get yourself together. Stop letting the situation control you. She needed to manage the horrible situation she was living in.

She sat on the cool tile floor in a lotus position and forced her breathing to slow. *Relax. Everything has a solution.* With her eyes closed, she let her heart rate steady. *Clear your mind.*

***

"Skye, are you okay? It's been over an hour."

She stood and went into the bedroom. "Marty, I'm fine. I must have dozed off."

"Okay. I'm here if you need anything."

In the walk-in closet, Skye searched for an outfit. What to choose when she hadn't decided where and what she was about to do?

Dinner with Terry was on the agenda for tonight. A nice idea when she made the arrangements, but now— not so much.

Since Andrew's death, too many moments were spent deliberating how to deal with the mess he put her in. Before the murder, her life plan had been simple, but afterward, her idea of what was important had changed.

At this moment, Marty was distracting her. Skye wanted time to be on her own and think.

She dressed in navy cotton pants, a baby blue tank top, and a matching cotton sweatshirt, then stored the house key and her wallet in a pocket.

If she went out the front to her car, Marty would ask where she was going and probably insist on leaving with her. It was better to slip out unseen—no questions asked and no answers demanded. Later, after decisions were made, she could explain why she left.

She exited the house through the bedroom's backdoor and jogged in the field behind the house to a bus stop. She took a bus heading south toward San Rafael.

Chapter 39

"**Jon,** I had no idea Skye would do a runner. You should've warned me—I let you down."

"No, Marty, I let you down." He took a deep breath to hold back an expletive. "I thought she understood. Skye promised not to go anywhere alone. Damn, she knows she's in danger. What was she thinking?"

"That's the thing. I don't know if she was alone. She went out the back. I didn't see her go. She could have met someone.

"Shit."

"Jon I…"

"Marty, it's just…" He shrugged. "Never mind. She's a grown woman and I have no hold on her. She can do whatever she wants." Did he mean it? Hell no. She was a fool, but he was a bigger one because he'd believed she would stay. After all, she'd promised not to go off by herself.

He'd never show the emotion, but he was worried sick.

***

At the Terra Linda stop, Skye got the bus off and walked toward the civic center and the nearby duck pond.

She sat on a bench a few feet from the fountain and listened to the joyful sounds of kids playing on the lawn while mothers laid out blankets and picnic baskets on the green. With her eyes closed she enjoyed the sounds and pretended she had no worries. Life was easy and her choices were many.

Later, the park cleared as the dinner hour approached. She should go back. Daydreaming was over. If she was able to catch a bus soon, she would be home by seven o'clock.

It would be too late to see Terry and tell him she decided not to go out with him but… She'd never stood up anyone before and would have called him but had no number. She didn't even remember his last name, another stupid mistake. With a sigh, she headed toward the bus stop.

***

"Hi, Jon. I didn't expect you to be here," Skye smiled as she entered the farmhouse.

"Where the hell have you been? You were supposed to stay here. We agreed and you promised.

"Well, hello to you too."

"You should know better. There are men who want to hurt you. Your denial is dangerous. Remember what they did to your boss."

"Jon, I…"

"Skye, I get it. You don't want to believe you're at risk." He hesitated and ran his hands through his hair. His blue eyes flashed. "I'm a trained agent able to protect myself in most circumstances and still in the last assignment, I was damned near killed.

"These people play for keeps." He stopped as a grim expression clouded his handsome features. He moved toward her. "You scared the hell out of me. I imagined your death. I understand you don't want my help, and don't need my advice, but I can't just stand by and let something happen to you. I…"

"Shut up, Jon—I love you."

"What?"

"I love you."

"Skye."

"I don't expect you to love me back. I'm sorry I scared you. I never wanted to cause trouble for anyone, but I had to get away. I needed to be alone to think. And I…

"Skye, you shut up. I love you too."

She stared as he came nearer and wrapped his arms around her. "Just don't ever frighten me like that again." Before she was able to answer, his kiss took her open mouth and with a sigh, she leaned into him.

"Dear God, Skye, I never thought I could love again, then I met you." He paused "You captured my heart."

He caressed her cheek and sent clusters of kisses to the nape of her neck before claiming her mouth once again. This time his tongue danced with hers while she ran her hands through his hair and moved with the rhythm of his undulating hips rubbing against her.

The sound of her erratic breathing pounded in her ears as her heartbeat increased. The need to touch his need flared. She found his rear and compelled him to come closer.

"Oh, sorry. I'm interrupting."

Skye glanced up at Marty standing in the front doorway. Skye jumped back from Jon and straightened her shirt, feeling her cheeks burn with embarrassment.

"Come in, Marty." Skye waved to her. "I apologize for running out on you today. I shouldn't have." How much did Marty understand about Jon's feelings for her?

"All's well that ends well and stuff." Marty grinned. "It's my turn to say sorry, but Webb's in the cottage. He wants to talk to you guys."

"We'll be right there," Jon answered.

"Okay, I've done my good deed. So, I'll take off. See you around, Skye."

"Thanks, Marty. The next we meet it will be in better circumstances."

"From your mouth to God's ears."

Skye ran to Marty and hugged her. "I really mean thanks. You guarded Jon too."

The petite woman nodded and whispered, "Take care of him. He's a good man."

***

Jon took Skye's hand as they walked toward the cottage. "Don't upset me again. Let me watch your back. Deal?"

"For as long as you want, Jon."

He didn't say more, it was sufficient she was safe and with him. Something he'd thought wouldn't happen.

She smiled and squeezed his hand. "Jon, I never dared dream you would care."

He stopped and hugged her. "I do, more than I can express."

She kissed his cheek. "I wish we were alone,"
she spoke into his ear.

"Soon," he promised returning her kiss. He glanced

up to see Webb staring and looking puzzled.

"You okay?" Webb called from the cottage door.

"Yep, all good." Jon moved quickly toward the cottage, still holding Skye's hand.

"Hey, I grabbed some Chinese takeout for dinner. Hope you're hungry." His brother stood back to let them enter the cottage.

"I'm starving," Jon said as they entered.

"Glad to hear it, bro. It's been worrying you haven't shown any interest in food. You used to eat me out of house and home."

"I think you put away your share." Jon laughed. How much time had passed since he'd had an appetite? Longer than he wanted to remember.

He glanced at Skye. Uncertainly shown in her eyes. He wanted to hold her and tell her everything would work out. They had to because she'd brought him back to life. For the first time in years, he wanted to live, to be with her. Something he'd never considered possible, until now.

"You okay, Skye?" Webb smiled.

"Fine, thanks."

Jon wondered what his brother thought when he saw them kiss. Would he be pleased or concerned he was making a mistake in getting involved with a woman linked, no matter how innocently, with the crook Jenkins and the oligarch Volkov, a man whose father killed their father?

He shook off the anger growing at Igor Volkov, not the hour to consider the Russian. "Let's eat."

He went to the counter and served a plate of rice and one of the vegetables. He added prawns to the plate and handed it to Skye. "Sit."

"Wow, Jon, I don't think I can finish so much food." She took a seat at the counter and stared at the mound of veggies and rice.

He laughed at her shocked expression. "Eat as much as you want." He took the seat next to her. "I'll finish the rest. I can't remember such an appetite."

A fire raged in him, a desire to experience Skye's love and share his with her, and demonstrate how much she meant to him. He would never be able to put it into words, but when they made love, she might understand.

They all talked about innocuous subjects as they dined. Jon had the impression Webb was being careful not to distress Skye by mentioning anything that concerned what he learned about the funds she now controlled.

After dinner, they drank green tea around the coffee table and opened fortune cookies. Jon smiled and said, "A new love will enter your life."

Skye blushed and read hers out loud too, "You will soon meet with good luck." She whispered, "I already did, you, Jon."

Webb broke his cookie but stuffed the fortune in his pocket.

"Aren't you going to find out what it says?" Skye asked.

"No, I can't top the ones you and Jon found. I'll just enjoy my cookie."

They sat quietly eating dessert and drinking tea, almost as though each wanted to avoid the reason for the meeting.

Finally, Skye spoke, "Webb, what did you find out about Mr. Jenkins and his accounts?"

"You want to talk about it now?" Jon moved closer

to her on the sofa. "We might start this tomorrow."

"The sooner I solve this, the quicker it will be over."

Her voice cracked, but her expression told him she meant what she said.

"Whatever you want, Skye." He admired her strength. "If you're sure."

"I am."

Webb got up and brought in a folder with some of the paperwork she had given him.

"As you know, Jenkins dealt with some shady characters. The team's accountants and I discovered he had deep-seated ties with Igor Volkov. I think Jon may have mentioned the man." He continued without waiting for confirmation from her. "It appears the Russian oligarch is here in the Bay Area."

Jon sat up. "Are you sure, Webb?"

"Afraid so."

"Damn, Webb, this information is more disturbing than Salvatore's. He's a difficult enough problem."

Jon breathed in deeply. "What does Igor Volkov want from Skye?" A chill ran down his back. "Does he understand she now controls Jenkins' accounts?" If so, the danger to Skye had increased.

"We can't be sure what he knows. But he must be here to shake up Salvatore Romano. The paper trail appears to show a connection with Romano and Volkov. Seems Igor loaned money to Salvatore so he could buy the winery and the surrounding acreage. They were also entangled in other enterprises."

Jon rubbed his chin. He didn't like what he was hearing. Still, he wouldn't say he was surprised. Oligarchs often controlled millions of Russian rubles.

Their assignment was to launder them into U.S. dollars.

He glanced at Skye as she slumped onto the sofa, a scared expression marring her beautiful features. Gone was the joy he'd seen in her eyes. He wanted to bring back the smile he'd seen earlier. No point in trying, she wouldn't be okay until this mess was over.

She was much too quiet for his liking, but what could she add to the conversation? Probably out of her depth, all she might do was hold on while her world spun out of control. He would do his best to keep her safe, as long as she cooperated. Was he a fool to think that after today she'd keep her word and not take off like she did this afternoon?

"My idea," Webb interrupted Jon's thoughts, "have the forensic accountants, on the Rapid Advance Team, go through these files and the bank account in the Cayman Islands, to follow the money."

"Skye would have to give permission. Hire you guys, so to speak." Jon touched her shoulder. "Skye, are you listening? You all right with the scheme?"

"What would I need to do? Give you the rights to be my accountants?"

"We would require you to give us permission, in writing, to access your accounts. Once we take a peek," Webb paused. "we'll be able to unravel what Jenkins did and how exactly he got the funds and from whom. Afterward, you can tell us what to do next."

She signed and leaned against Jon as if to absorb courage from him. "I'm frightened I'll make the wrong decision." She hesitated. "Go for it. I'll sign whatever you want. I just hope it's not a mistake."

Chapter 40

Skye waited in the cottage while Jon walked his brother to his car. With the leftover takeout food put away, she did the dishes and returned to the living room.

Through the open living room window, she gazed out at the clear night and let a cool breeze caress her.

The brothers stood near Webb's auto, chatting for a few minutes. With a quick wave, Webb entered his vehicle and drove out of sight.

She sighed with relief. A weight had been lifted from her shoulders. The forensic accountants, under the watchful eye of Jon's brother, would see that she had the information needed. It was obvious the money and investments didn't belong to her. Once the accountants knew where they came from, a discernable path would emerge and she'd understand what to do with the funds under her supervision.

Sitting on the sofa, she leaned back and closed her eyes. Jon loved her. Had he really said that? A shiver of longing ran through her. She touched her lips remembering the kiss they'd shared and imagined his touch in her more private places.

Jon entered the cottage. "Tired?"

"Relaxed." She smiled.

"I'm glad—I think you made the right choice. I trust Webb. There isn't a man with more integrity. Of course, he is my brother." A serious expression spread across his handsome face. "Even if he wasn't, I'd still recommend him."

She stood and walked to his waiting arms. "Jon, I'm comfortable with my decision. I only wish I had some way to thank you for helping me." She reached for his face and traced his mouth with her finger, then stood on her tiptoes to run her hands through his thick blond hair.

With an amused stare, he remained still, scanning her with his intense blue eyes.

"Aren't you going to kiss me, Jon?"

He stroked her cheek as his kiss landed gently on her lips. He pulled away. "Your sweetness takes my breath, but also lights a fire in me."

"I need you, Jon."

"Stay with me tonight."

Breathless, she was barely able to answer, "Yes."

He scooped her up into his arms and she snuggled nearer. Resting her head on his shoulder, she listened to his staccato heartbeat.

He carried her toward the cottage bedroom. "Skye, you make me feel alive," he whispered.

"Jon, you're the most alive person I've ever met." A shiver of desire ran down her spine.

Gently, he set her on the bed.

A single night light broke the dimness and allowed her to admire him as he undressed. His body flexed as his desire for her grew.

"Jon, you're beautiful, inside and out."

He grinned. "Have you ever made love with a man wearing a medical boot?"

"No." She laughed. "I can't wait." She started to unbutton her shirt.

"Let me." With ease, he released her from the constraints of her clothing and joined her on the queen bed.

"I'm all yours." She reached for him and sighed when his weight pressed against her.

She closed her eyes and he shared the love he had flowing within him, making them one.

In the middle of the night, she reached for him and once again received the gift he offered.

Breathing hard but sated, she fell asleep in his arms.

***

She awoke and smiled when she found Jon sleeping beside her.

The small red light of the alarm system blinked in the corner of the bedroom. He had remembered to set it. Last night, all she had thought about was being with him. But he had started the alarm to protect her.

"Morning." She kissed his bare chest.

He stretched. "Hey, come here." He lifted her on top of him. "I need more of your sweetness."

She sighed, closed her eyes and let him take her to heights she didn't realize existed.

***

Hours later, Jon got out of bed. "Join me in the shower?" He held out his hand.

"What about your medical boot?"

"I take it off to bathe." He grinned. "I might need to lean on you."

"Anytime." Her heart boomed as she stood, letting

the cotton sheet drop from her body.

She ran her hand over his muscled contours. Heat surged within her when she kissed him.

He coaxed her mouth open and she let his tongue caress hers, his kiss tender but firm. With her hand on his heart, she was surprised at how fast it was beating. Her breathing turned ragged as he deepened his kiss.

His need increased as he led her to the bathroom. She watched while he released the medical boot. Then balancing on one foot, he opened the shower door and turned on the water. "Ready?"

"More than you know."

***

After the shower, they sat in the kitchen. Skye set out a pitcher with orange juice and was about to ask if he wanted oatmeal or eggs when he spoke. "You understand what happened to my wife."

She was startled at the unexpected subject. "Yeah." She remembered Miranda had been murdered a few years earlier.

"We were young when we married. She was eighteen and I was twenty. I was attracted to her incredible beauty. I don't know what she saw in me, but still... He shrugged. But too often my job took me away from our social life, still, she never complained." Moisture filled his eyes. "Miranda was a good person who would never hurt anyone."

Skye wanted to say something, but what words would lessen his pain? "I'm so sorry."

"Yeah." He stared at her, a grim expression on his face. "So am I." He hesitated. "She didn't deserve to die the way she did. They were after me and she paid the price." He sipped his drink and swallowed hard.

"Webb told me I had no way to find out what the Volkov family had planned—I should have realized, should've stopped them, should…"

Skye began to shake with undefined emotion. "You didn't hurt her, Jon. Evil men did."

"Oh God, Skye, don't ever leave me."

"Never—I love you."

He seized her hand and she felt his life's spark flow to her.

"Skye, I'd give my life before I let anything happen to you."

***

"The girl was supposed to be in your hands by now." Igor spit and lit another cigar.

Salvatore glared at the Russian. What should he say? Terry had let him down again.

"Igor, don't smoke in my office." To appear relaxed, Salvatore forced his tense body to sit at his desk chair and put his feet on the polished wood top.

"Volkov, you will get your money as soon as I have mine. Not a moment before."

Terry walked into the room as if he didn't have a care in the world. Sal wanted to strangle him. Instead, he walked over and shook his hand. "Here's the man who can secure the girl for us." He slapped the kid on the back.

Terry coughed and froze appearing stunned.

"Well, kid."

"Yeah, sure, that's what I wanted to say. I know where she is and I'll have Skye this afternoon."

"What's your name kid?" Igor sat up and glared.

"Terry Nowland—uh, sir." His eyes opened wide and his fear was obvious.

"You like money, Terry?"

"Yeah. Who doesn't?"

"My time is limited in your country. So, I'm willing to sweeten your income, if you can deliver the woman by noon today."

"Noon? I'd like the money, but I might need a little more…"

"On time or nothing. Got it?"

"How much?"

"Shall we say an extra ten K?"

Rubbing his chin and wiping his mouth as a starving man might after drooling, upon seeing a scrumptious meal, Terry nodded. "Okay." He started to sit down.

"What the are you waiting for? Out. Grab Skye Turner." Sal perched on the edge of his desk. "Get the hell out of here!"

Upon his exit, Terry slammed the door.

Romano groaned. What was he going to do with Igor Volkov to keep him diverted until they had the secrets she alone could provide? He turned to Igor and realized the jerk was still smoking his stogie.

Shit.

"Romano, if I don't have what I need by this afternoon, I will expect the deed to this place."

Sal flinched. No way was he going to let Igor put his grubby hand on what belonged to him. Still, he held his tongue.

Igor walked to and glanced out of the window as if he were surveying his new property.

Over my dead body, Igor. He flexed his fists. If Terry didn't come through, he'd break the kid's neck and retrieve the bitch himself.

Chapter 41

With a deep breath, Skye sat on the lounge chair on the back patio of the cottage and smiled. Perhaps, with Jon and his brother's help, there was a way out of her dilemma despite everything that had happened.

Jon was talking to Webb right now, making plans for the accountants to set a timetable to figure out the financial records mentioned in the file folders she gave them. Research might take a while, but at least it had started.

The warm harvest sun beat down on the landscape. For days, the land she loved had been ignored because other problems had swamped her. A sense of forbidding had colored her world with a grayness preventing any positive thought or awareness of the matters she cared about. Today, the world appeared brighter, and the road to a solution clearer. She found she was humming a favorite tune.

The cell phone rang. "Hello."

Mei, her next-door neighbor, invited her to brunch, so they might finish the plan for the winter garden they wanted to share.

Could her life return to normal, at least long enough for a meal with a friend? What would Jon think? Mei was a retired police officer after all. She'd seen the woman's thirty-eight caliber weapon.

If Skye went into Mei's home by way of the back door, no one would know she was there. She had argued to convince Jon it was okay.

***

Skye entered Mei's house through the back door.

"Come on in, Skye," Mei called and hugged her when she entered the home. "Shall we eat?"

In the dining area, a feast had been laid out. Her friend motioned to a chair. "Sit. Help yourself to the food."

"I love your homemade egg rolls." Skye bit into the crisp outer shell and wiped the crumbs from her chin. "Yum."

"Thanks. I hope the Szechuan vegetables are not too spicy. I made them milder than usual."

"They're perfect. Your food always awakens a huge appetite in me—Jon will be here in a few minutes. I know he's going to enjoy them."

Mei grinned but changed the subject and talked about the winter garden. She had saved organic seed from last year's crop and had started seedlings.

Because the weather was so warm last season, they agreed to try a few unexpected veggies.

"With global warming, I think they'll do okay, assuming this winter is like last year," Skye added.

"If water is available."

"True."

"Skye, if you don't mind, this year I'll leave much of the digging to you. I twisted my back the other day, lifting my grandkids. They are too big, but they still want granny to pick them up."

"No worries, I'm happy to. How old are the kids?"

"My granddaughter is six and my grandson is a big four." Mei grinned and stretched. "I think I'll tell them they are too grown up."

Her friend walked to the window of the dining area and pulled back the curtain. "My daughter and the kids will be here in a minute to pick up the food I made for them. They don't have time to eat with us because the children are on the way to swim lessons. Oh, they're here." She rushed to the living room door, unlocked it and the kids burst into the room.

Skye smiled when she was introduced. They said a polite "hello" and then hugged Mei, their mutual love obvious.

With excitement, the kids competed to tell their grandmother about news from their school and their music programs.

Mei watched the kids as they carried two bags of food to the car. Then she waved to her daughter waiting in the sedan.

"After swim class, they'll be hungry and lunch will be ready," Mie said, appearing pleased.

"Your grandkids are adorable. How great they live nearby." She hesitated. "I didn't know my grandparents."

With lunch finished, tea was served.

She wondered when Jon would arrive. He must have heard her thinking because she received his text. "Is everything okay?"

"Yep." She added a thumbs-up emoji.

"Be there in ten minutes."

"Jon will be here soon."

"Plenty of food for him." Mei adjusted her shirt and

for the first time, Skye noticed she had a shoulder holster with her thirty-eight at hand.

"Mei, someone's at the front door. It's Terry." She turned the handle.

"Skye, don't."

The door flew open as Mei reached it.

Terry grabbed the woman and stabbed her with a hypodermic.

"No!" Skye yelled.

Mei's eyes widened and she crumbled to the floor. Her eyes remained open, but she didn't move.

"What did you do? Terry, are you crazy?"

He kicked the front door closed and seized Skye holding her to him. She squirmed and tried to go to her friend.

"Stop." He slapped her hard across the face. "Scream and I'll shoot her."

"What did you give her?" She hit him and he tightened his grip on her arm.

"Hey, she's not dead. Cooperate and she'll be fine. I don't need her—where's the old lady's car?"

"I'm not going with you."

He lifted her chin and stared at her. "I saw the cute kids. It would be a shame to leave them without a grandmother. You want the old bitch to live or die?"

"You wouldn't…"

Before she finished the sentence, he withdrew a pistol from his waistband and fired. Mei jerked as she took a hit in the shoulder.

A muffled cry choked Skye's throat.

"In the car—now."

With one last glance at her friend, she noticed blood dripping from the shoulder wound. *I'm so sorry.*

She gasped for air as Terry dragged her to the garage. He pushed her forward. "You drive."

***

In the cottage, Jon hung up his secure phone. The call with Webb took longer than he'd thought. Still, Skye would be gratified with this new info. So, he didn't believe she'd be upset at his tardiness.

He added notes to Andrew Jenkins' file and closed the tablet. The forensic accountants found Andrew kept two account books, one with local clients doing honest business and another with those running questionable enterprises.

It didn't take long to realize Andrew made a sufficient living on his local clients. Most people would consider their earnings above average and might count themselves lucky. Not Jenkins, his greed caused greater desires.

The off-the-book accounts allowed him to live like a millionaire, even if the money was dirty.

Apparently, he'd imagined he could steal from his shady customers without consequences. Andrew might have gotten away with it if Salvatore Romano hadn't lost his temper and tossed the guy out of the twelve-story office window.

More investigation would be needed to learn the details of Jenkins' thefts and the names of those he hurt. However, Webb discovered a trust fund for Ruth, Andrew's wife. The man was smart enough to take the money from his legal accounts for her. Ruth would receive a moderate income for life. Skye would be delighted. He understood she worried about her friend trying to make a viable living when the woman had spent thirty-plus years as a homemaker.

He rubbed his chin, better shave, and changed into decent clothes before joining Skye and Mei for brunch.

Minutes later, he locked the cottage and carefully walked toward Mei's house, minding to avoid the dug-up backyard. Maybe when his leg recovered, he'd put a stone pathway leading to her back door, it must be hard for Mei to deal with the backyard as well.

He stopped to admire the work Mei and Skye just started for the winter garden. He couldn't imagine Miranda digging in the land and getting her hands soiled. Miranda and Skye were different, but both held a special place in his heart.

He passed his neighbor's garage and was surprised to discover the garage open and her compact gone.

With a frown, he knocked, then entered the house through the kitchen.

"Hi, it's Jon. Are you here?"

Something fell in the living room with a loud crash.

"Mei?"

No answer.

"Skye, Mie?"

The dining room appeared empty, but he noticed a place had been set for him at the table. Odd the food lay on the other plates half eaten with no one there.

Someone groaned in the living room. He ran toward the sound.

"Mei! What happened?"

He knelt beside his neighbor. She blinked but didn't answer. Blood oozed from her delicate shoulder.

Shit.

To stem the bleeding, he grabbed clean napkins from the dining table and pressed them against her wound. With his other hand, he dialed 911.

His respirations increased as he stated the reason for the call. He did his best to explain the urgency of the problem and the need for medical care, ASAP.

A hypo was on the floor near Mei. *Damn. What had the intruder given her? Had Skye been given an injection too?*

With a sharp intake of breath, he ignored the rapid thump of his heart and kept the pressure on Mei's wound.

"Where's Skye?"

His neighbor grimaced and closed her eyes but she managed to say, "Taken. She called him Terry."

He was about to ask another question when a siren drew his attention. "Help will be here soon."

"Jon, he took my car."

"Okay, good to know."

"You go! Get the bastard!" She moaned. "Skye needs you."

Mei was right. And if he stayed, he'd be forced to answer questions from the police.

"Jon, leave."

It was important not to move Mei, so he grabbed a designer pillow from the couch, took the throw from an easy chair, and did his best to make her comfortable. When he removed his hand, she managed to put hers on the napkins covering the gash.

"Mei, my friend, I'm sorry you were hurt. I'll come back as soon as I can."

She took a small breath. "Just find Skye."

Chapter 42

It was unfortunate Terry had seen the car key hanging in plain sight near the kitchen door. He'd grabbed it, forced Skye into the driver seat of the compact, and slammed the door. In the passenger's seat, he pushed the key into the ignition. "Drive, and don't think of doing anything stupid."

At the first turn of the ignition, the engine roared to life. Should she stall and wait for Jon to arrive? The nozzle of Terry's firearm poking her in the ribs changed that thought.

"Turn left and drive toward the hills."

Where did the street go? She'd never been there. As far as she knew there was nothing in the area.

"Do it!"

Minutes later, she clutched the steering wheel of Mei's vehicle and searched the unknown neighborhood. No traffic. They appeared to be the lone traveler on the two-lane thoroughfare. On the back road of the county, they sped away from civilization.

"Where are we headed?"

"Drive."

"Where?"

"Keep going."

The small two-lane road meandered thru the uninhabited, rural and hilly scenery. She might run the car off the road, but with no other vehicles in the area, there'd be no help. He might shoot her and leave the body in a ditch. How long before someone would find her?

A chill ran through her and her hands began to shake.

She glanced at Terry. His stoic features were devoid of emotion. She had the sense any plea for mercy would fall on deaf ears.

The images of Mei bleeding on the floor of her home, flashed before her eyes. She gasped. Was her dear friend still alive?

"Why are you doing this? Terry, I thought you were my friend."

"Shut up."

Was he bought and paid for by the people who killed Andrew Jenkins?

"Terry, is this about money?'

"None of your business."

"You shot Mei for money. She never did anything to you." Her voice became shrill. *Don't lose it.* "Terry please, this isn't you. You're a nice guy."

"What the hell do you know? You didn't even show up for our date."

Oh shit. Could this be about being stood up? Or was her life in danger because of the money Jenkins left her? Whatever, Terry was crazy. She glanced at him and the car swerved.

"Watch the road. You want to kill us?"

He didn't want to die, but how did he plan on treating her? She scanned the road for an escape route.

Nothing but empty rolling hills stared back at her.

***

Jon nearly fell as he tried to run to the cottage. *Slow down. Breaking your leg again isn't going to help Skye.* He stood, leaned forward with his hands on his knees and forced a slow breath.

Mei said the man's name was Terry. The image of the server, working in The Cave's dining room, came to mind. Skye had talked to him and he'd appeared normal enough. She'd called him a friend.

He rubbed his chin in thought, was this the same guy?

In the cottage, he grabbed his wallet, the secure phone, given to him by the First Lady, and the rental car key fob. He grabbed his nine-millimeter weapon, and shoulder holster.

Damn, the battery was dead. He hit the steering wheel of his rental car with his fist. What did he expect? He hadn't driven the car for almost three weeks.

Skye's subcompact was parked in the driveway. He raced to the farmhouse to get the car key.

After some adjustment of the driver's seat, he managed to sit down, grateful the medical boot was on his left leg and the car was an automatic. He started the engine and drove toward Romano's restaurant.

First fear and then hot rage built in him. His hands were clammy as he clung to the wheel. His breathing tightened in his chest and his heart stumbled.

It couldn't happen again. The thought of losing Skye as he had lost Miranda… He wouldn't think about it, couldn't—never mind he already had.

The view of the road blurred. *No, dear God, don't*

take my vision. Not now. With a trembling hand, he rubbed the moisture from his eyes. He pulled the car to a sudden halt, threw the transmission into park and rested his forehead on the steering wheel.

The ophthalmologist's word echoed in his ears, *No stress. Take it easy, rest. We'll schedule surgery as long as you promise, no work, no mixing it up with the bad guys.* The doctor had smiled, appearing to be pleased with his joke, little did he understand the work Jon did.

He blinked several times and shook his head once. His eyes began to clear.

"Thank you." He glanced upward and whispered into the empty car.

His hot rage turned into cold determination as he forced the compact to speed toward The Wine Cave with the hope Skye would be there.

At the freeway turnoff, he pulled over and texted Webb. *STAT* and then the address.

An almost immediate reply came back. *B there ASAP.*

No reason to explain what was happening to his brother. STAT in the text was all the explanation Webb needed. The problem: how far away was his brother and how long would it take for him to arrive?

The entrance to the parking lot of The Wine Cave was blocked and a sign read: *Closed for a private party.* But Mei's car was in plain sight in the lot. Bold but stupid, Terry must have assumed he wasn't followed because he didn't bother to hide the vehicle. Was Skye there as well as the car?

To case the restaurant and grounds, Jon slowly drove by the place and parked on a dirt lane past the main entrance and out of sight.

Only one way to find out if Skye was being held there. He stared at the slope he would need to hike to gain access to the back of the building.

He was tempted to take off the medical boot but thought better of it.

After the exertion of the climb in the hot climate, sweat dripped from his forehead and he breathed rapidly. It was damned annoying to be in his weakened condition. But what had he expected after the beating he took and the length of time it was taking to recoup from the broken bones?

He scanned the property. There was little movement, except the ducks floating in a pond outside the bay windows of what he thought was the dining room.

At the backyard of the building, movement caught his eye—Skye. She pulled her arm free from the man twisting it and ran, screaming.

The guy tackled her bringing her down hard. She kicked him, but he dragged her toward the back hallway.

Salvatore stood in the doorway, "Tut, tut, Terry. That's no way to treat a guest," he said mockingly. "Ms. Turner, I apologize for Mr. Nowland's rough treatment."

Sol, helped her stand and even from a distance, Jon saw fear in her expression and something else—anger and determination.

She wouldn't easily go along with whatever they planned for her.

He cursed thinking of what they might do to her. He leaned against an oak tree, checked his weapon, and hoped there'd be no reason to use it, but…

After the group went inside, he quickly started down the hill. His medical boot caught on a tree root and he tumbled to the bottom, stopping with a grunt on the blacktop parking lot. *Shit.* He blinked as his eyes blurred, then cleared. With a deep breath, he continued around the edge of the building.

Through an open window, he could see Skye sitting at a table facing the window, her back to the entrance door. She was surrounded by Terry, Salvatore and another man, young, big and intense.

The men's voices sounded reasonable at first, then more demanding, shouting at her.

A look of terror spread across her pretty face.

Jon reached the building and relief surged when the back door opened to an empty hallway.

Skye's voice came from a room on the left. He listened making a mental map of where the men were standing in relationship to the door and her.

He touched his shoulder holster. If he went into the room like a cowboy with his gun blazing, Skye would be hurt. Though a need to take action raged, he wouldn't put her in more danger than she was already. He breathed deeply and waited for an opportunity when the odds would be more in his favor.

With his ear to the door, he focused and strained to hear any movement in the room.

Skye spoke rapidly as if running to save her life. Her tension was clear to anyone who knew her.

In limbo, and unable to come to her aid without causing more risk, he was in a kind of time-warp, at least until someone in the room made a move.

He admired her cool for not letting on she

understood the full realization of the situation. However, how long could she pull off the ploy?

***

Skye stared at the men surrounding the table. She stopped on Salvatore's furious expression, his face reddening as he demanded what he believed was his.

Shock struck like a bolt of lightning as she realized he was the man she'd seen in the twelfth-story office where Andrew Jenkins was killed.

She hadn't recognized him the last time she was here. Perhaps because she'd blanked out that horrible day as protection from her fears or because he wasn't a blond now. Instead, black hair hung over his ears. Today, comprehension flashed when she saw the familiar rage in Sal's eyes.

Her hands trembled. *Stay calm.* She put her hands under the table in the hope he wouldn't notice the shaking.

Her mind whirled. How could she stall long enough for help to arrive? There would be help, right?

"You know, Sal, I love this restaurant. It's so tastefully decorated and all. What a lovely setting, overlooking vineyards." She forced a smile. "I can only imagine how wonderful the food must be. I mean, I read you hired a chef from the UK, an award winner." Amazed she kept the quiver out of her voice she continued, "Putting a fireplace in the dining room was such a cozy idea. Even in the heat of California and it burns real wood." She noted the pile of oak stacked near the hearth and now understood the woodpile outside the back entry. "And your wonderful grapes, how incredible your wine must taste. I'd be happy to sample a bottle."

"What is this babble? Enough!" Sal shouted. "Ms. Turner, you realize why you're here."

She blinked and gave what she hoped was a look of innocence. "You didn't need to be so harsh. Why not just ask me to visit you, Mr. Romano?"

Salvatore Romano glared and slammed a legal-looking paper on the table pen. "Sign!"

Chapter 43

In The Wine Cave's dining room, Skye read the paperwork that would sign over all the holdings from her to Salvatore Romano.

When she touched the pen, the men standing around the table appeared to hold their breath.

Left-handed, she picked up the pen in her right hand and held it near the signature line. If the signature didn't match her usual one would that stop them from taking the funds? She set the pen down again. *I'll be damned before I give anything to the man who murdered my boss—Jon where are you?*

The larger, unknown man, fisted his hands and stepped toward her.

If she wrote her name, it would be her death warrant. *Dear God, what should I do?*

"You might as well sign. You're not leaving until you do."

"Mr. Romano, what will happen to me after I do?"

"Why we'll take you home, of course. Or anywhere you want to go."

Terry looked surprised at Sal's words.

When pigs fly. To cover her nervousness, she smiled again. "Really?" If the men had their way, she would never leave the place alive.

"An adequate amount of talk," the stranger said in a gruff voice. "Miss, do what you are told."

A Russian accent? Could this be the man whose family murdered Jon's wife? No longer able to control her trembling, her whole body shook.

"I won't sign."

The large man's cold eyes fixed on her trembling hands, then he turned to Sal. "The little lady desires time to contemplate how dire her situation is."

"Kid, take Ms. Turner to the old cave we have prepared for her." Romano smiled.

Terry yanked her out of the chair and pushed her toward the door.

With the hope he could be talked out of doing what he planned or maybe somehow find a way out, she didn't resist.

Her optimism plummeted when he pulled a handgun from his jacket. "Move." His expression challenged her to try something as though he wanted to shoot her.

"Open the door." He poked her in the ribs with the barrel of the weapon.

Outside the sun blinded her and she stumbled over a log that must have rolled from the woodpile near the backdoor.

When she bent down to shift the log, Jon hit Terry hard and knocked the revolver from his hand.

Stunned, she swallowed a scream, not wanting to let anyone in the building realize Jon had arrived.

The kid grunted but managed to kick Jon in his wounded leg. He staggered but stayed upright.

The men exchanged blows.

Jon took several hits to his head.

She wrapped her hand around the log, waiting for the opportunity to strike Terry.

"Run, Skye." He slugged Terry.

She froze.

"Get out of here," Jon growled.

The backdoor opened and she jumped behind it.

"Halt!" The foreigner who'd been in the dining room stood in the doorway.

She peeked at him but his focus appeared to be on the men.

"What the hell is going on?" he asked, but without waiting for an answer, raised his weapon and fired.

Was Jon shot?

She slammed the log against the stranger's gun hand. He yelled and the smell of wine and garlic assaulted her. The pistol fell and fired when it hit the ground. The bullet went awry, missing Jon. Terry grabbed his abdomen and slumped to the ground blood spurting from his wound.

The firearm landed near her feet and she rushed to retrieve it. The man shouted an expletive, before knocking her out of the way. Unable to stop her fall, she crumbled to the ground.

Jon kicked the man with his uninjured leg, then sent a right cross to the guy's jaw that sent his head back with a snap. He grunted, fell, and tried to rise, but unable to, he lay immobile.

"Skye!" Jon hobbled toward her and reached for her hand. Concern was displayed in his blue eyes, he hugged her and then pulled from her embrace. "Take the keys. Your car is over the hill, parked on the dirt road. Leave now, I'll take care of this mess."

"What about you?"

He checked the carotid artery on the men lying still on the blacktop. He shook his head. "They're done for—go." His expression hardened. "Hell— just leave."

"Ms. Turner is not going anywhere." Salvatore Romano smiled as he joined them. With a grin on his distorted face, Sal fired his weapon.

Jon spun out of the way. Still, the bullet grazed his shoulder, and a red line of blood ran down his arm.

She cried out as alarm rose in her.

Before Sal fired again, Jon pulled his handgun and took him out with one bullet between his eyes.

With a stunned look on his face, Romano's legs dropped out from under him. His eyes open and unblinking, he didn't move again.

The terror she'd controlled, now overwhelmed her, and she couldn't stop screaming. She wanted to, tried to. Her shrieks became sobs when Jon wrapped his strong arms around her.

"Honey, are you hurt?"

"No, I'm okay." She sniffed. "But I—I"

"It's going to be all right." He pushed her hair from her face and dried the tears that ran down her cheeks.

In his embrace, she believed there was hope.

"Skye, I've got this. Go home and lock the door. I'll send Marty to stay with you until I return."

"Jon you're bleeding. Oh my God, he shot you."

"Nothing to worry about. Please, for my sake, take off."

She hesitated, unsure.

A hawk squawked and circled overhead as if waiting for the male carcasses that lay in the area.

"Please. I'll see you soon"

"She's not leaving."

***

Jon's sight blurred and he blinked to bring the person who spoke into focus. Igor Volkov smiled at him.

The pain in Jon's shoulder paled in comparison to the agony surging as he stared at the man whose family killed his wife.

He forced Skye behind him. "This doesn't concern you, Volkov." He couldn't keep the vile from his voice.

"No? I must differ with you, Jon Lancaster."

"Wait," Skye interrupted. "If you're Igor, who's he?" She pointed to the stranger dead on the ground.

"Some poor slob who worked as a bouncer here," Igor sneered, disdain in his voice. "Now the property belongs to me, I will make sure better men are chosen."

"She's not signing anything over to you." Jon touched the nine-millimeter strapped near his ribs.

"Mr. Romano is dead. I inherit." Igor glared at him, a grin forming on his thin lips. He bowed toward Skye. "I only need Ms. Turner's signature. This is not your fight, Lancaster."

Jon watched the man sneer and recognized the bulge of a shoulder holster on the left side of Igor's expensive silk sports coat.

Volkov set his feet slightly apart in the stance of a man ready to exchange fire. "Hand over the girl."

Skye grabbed his arm, "Jon, no."

Over my dead body.

He blinked and narrowed his eyes to maintain focus on Volkov. With a grunt, he shook free from her grip, then wrapped his hand around his weapon.

The sun glared on the polished handgun Igor drew

from his holster. Jon saw the bullet hit the ground before he heard it. He shoved Skye out of the way and fired from a prone position on the blacktop. He rolled away from her, bullets popping around him as he did.

Dust flew in his eyes, blinding him, but he aimed at the sound of the footsteps running from the building toward him. He fired twice and shook his head to bring back his vision. Igor dropped in front of him, the gun still in his hand, an angry expression on his death mask.

"Jon!" Skye ran to him and helped him up. "When you fell, I thought he'd killed you!"

He winced when she touched his wounded shoulder.

"I'm sorry. I hurt you." She wiped the moisture from her eyes.

"Honey, you didn't hurt me. You brought me back to life. Without you, I'd have no reason to go on." He gently kissed her. "Let's move out of here."

"I love you, Jon."

"Skye, you'll always have my heart."

She grasped his hand as they turned their back on the carnage.

"You better drive, Skye." He blinked and then focused to see where he was walking.

Slowly, they made their way toward her car and their new reality.

Epilogue

Two months later

Skye sighed and paced the farmhouse living room. Webb and the Rapid Advance Task Force had taken care of the situation at The Wine Cave. The forensic accounting team was still working out the details of Andrew Jenkins' accounts but had assured her results by the end of the month.

And she was pleased Mei had mended and held no resentment toward her.

Skye glanced at the time on her cellphone. Why was it taking so long for Jon to return?

At the sound of a car in the driveway, she rushed to the window.

No longer wearing a medical boot, Jon exited the car with ease. He stood tall and strong as he stretched, his muscled chest and broad shoulders straining against the white dress shirt he wore. His blue eyes flashed as he waved to her.

She rushed to the front door, threw it open, and hugged him. He surprised her when he picked her up in his arms and kissed her waiting lips.

Her breathing quickened and she ran her hand through his thick hair. Finally, she pulled away. "I love you."

"Skye, how can you? You haven't heard what the doctor had to say about my eyes?"

"Whatever the outcome, I'll love you. I thought you understood, for better or worse, in sickness and in health…."

He took her lips again, this time with more intensity.

Desire for him rose in her and she caught her breath. "Wait. What did the ophthalmologist say?"

"The retinal surgery was a success. He gave me a clean bill of health."

"Thank God."

"I adore you, Skye." He grinned, the look of love in his healthy eyes.

She smiled and kissed him again.

Read on for an excerpt from **Dangerous Web** and learn Webb's story. Copyright © by Reggi Allder

With Webb in the passenger seat, Emma drove the old sedan to their small West Coast bungalow and parked in the driveway. A memory of the first day she saw the home, with the for sale sign out on the front lawn, taunted her. Would he remember too? She didn't dare check to see if he appeared moved by the sight. What difference did it make now?

There was an almost imperceptible pause when he entered the place. Yet, his stoic expression didn't change as his hand raked through his thick dark hair. He scanned the room, pausing on the Danish furniture they'd picked out together. However, his deep brown eyes did not indicate his thoughts. He stood tall, strong, and in command and she couldn't help admiring him. *Damnit.*

"You know where everything is. I'm going to take a shower. It was a long hot drive."

She rushed to the master bedroom before he could answer. Why did she bring him to their home? Too many uncontrollable feelings were bubbling to the surface.

What would he think when he noticed his clothes were the way he'd left them? She'd kept telling herself it was time to throw them all out or donate the bunch to a needy cause. Somehow, she hadn't been able to do it.

Before long, he'd pick out some of his things from the dresser and maybe take items from the garage, then walk out. The marriage would be over. It couldn't come too soon. She'd been able to manage her emotions while they were at the cabin, but being near him in their house threw her off balance. Without equilibrium, her life had tilted out of control. She had to get her day-to-day life in balance, ASAP. Their relationship was dead and she'd carved out a new fulfilling existence. She had to hold on to the realization.

In the bathroom, she undressed and tossed her clothes into the hamper.

The spray of cool water lowered the temperature of her heated body, and the aroma of the coconut shampoo soothed her. She closed her eyes to enjoy the fact she was okay, and he'd be gone soon. When he left, everything would return to the "new" normal.

Out of the shower and wrapped in a pink bath sheet, she dried her hair with a hand towel.

"I don't mean to get into your private space, but I need a bandage. I'm bleeding again." Wearing only boxers, he came into the room appearing way too appealing even with the wound in his side.

"Shit." She held the bath towel tightly to her. "Uh, I think there are some in the plastic box under the sink."

"You don't have to protect yourself so carefully. It's not like I haven't seen you naked before."

She bent down as he came forward. Her line of sight was at his crotch. Involuntarily, she caught her breath and quickly searched for the first aid container.

"Here's some gauze and tape." She cleared her throat. "That should do."

Was it the steam from her recent shower or could he be making the room hotter?

"Thanks, Emmy. If you don't mind, I'll get cleaned up now."

She was barely able to grab the hairdryer when he dropped his boxers. She ran into the bedroom but heard him chuckle as she slammed the bathroom door.

***

He sauntered into the galley kitchen wearing the pale green polo shirt she'd bought him for Christmas the year before he'd disappeared and a pair of black jeans that fit too damned well.

"I made a couple of cheese sandwiches."

"Great. We can take them with us. Emma, go pack a bag."

"What do you mean? I'm not coming with you."

"You have to."

"Why?"

"It's not safe here. I can't secure the place, too many access points."

"I don't need protection in *my* own home," she said pointedly, not their house.

"Put a few things together. You've got five minutes."

She plopped into the nearest chair and crossed her arms. "I won't. If I were leaving, it would *not* be with you."

"Emma, we don't have time to argue."

"What can't you understand about I'm staying?"

She took the tray of food and the iced tea into the living room and set it on the coffee table. "Webb, be reasonable."

"Okay. I'm willing," he said, following her. "I'll listen." Nevertheless, his body language was tense and he didn't sit.

"You say I'm in jeopardy. Until you came back into my life, the only danger I had was the risk I'd miss a bus and be late for work or the possibility the grocery store would be out of crunchy peanut butter and I'd have to settle for creamy."

"Be serious, Emmy. I've explained the situation. I'm trying to protect you."

"Webb, you live in some weird scary world. I was miserable when you left me, but I was never in danger. I'm not in jeopardy now."

"Any strangers hanging around, things in the house gone missing, or out of position while you were at work?"

"No," she answered without taking time to think about his question. "Take the sandwiches, your clothes, and whatever you want, then get out."

He rubbed his forehead as if he had a headache. "Let me think."

"Okay, but it's not changing the situation. I'm going for a walk. Webb, don't be here when I get back."

She didn't hear what he shouted at her as she left the house because she wasn't listening. He didn't exist anymore, not to her. Two years ago, he wanted out and broke their marriage contract by abandoning her. He couldn't waltz back and tell her what to do, not now, not ever. He'd lost the right. He had tossed it in the garbage as if the vow was merely a lie of convenience.

But now, would Webb come after her?

*****

Books by Reggi Allder
Suspense

Dangerous Web
Dangerous Denial
Dangerous Money
Dangerous Moves

Shattered Rules

Contemporary
Sierra Creek Series

Her Country Heart
His Country Heart
Our Country Heart
My Country Heart

Historical

With Glowing Hearts

Coming Next

Dangerous Sisters